DARK WITCH

ENTANGLED FATES

THE CHILDREN OF THE GODS
BOOK EIGHTY-THREE

I. T. LUCAS

Published by Evening Star Press, LLC.

EveningStarPress.com

ISBN: 978-1-962067-39-3

JASMINE

J asmine pushed the pile of Fritos away from the edge of the table. "It's a shame that you ladies cannot stay longer and win back some of your losses." She collected her playing cards, reshuffled them a few times, and then returned them to their cardboard box.

As Lina translated what Jasmine had said into Russian, her two other poker buddies regarded her with mock animosity. Grabbing a handful of the winnings, Jasmine stuffed the chips into her mouth while mock-glaring back at the two and crunching loudly.

Lina was the only one of the three who was semi-fluent in English, but Jasmine had a feeling that the other two understood more than they were letting on.

Panya snorted and released a string of words in Russian that made the other two laugh.

"What did she say?" Jasmine asked Lina.

The girl's cheeks reddened, which happened often because her skin was so pale that it appeared almost translucent. "Panya said that if you keep eating your winnings, you are going to get thunder thighs, and it will serve you right for cheating."

Jasmine frowned. "I'm not cheating. I'm just good."

The two older women snorted derisively, and then Panya released another rapid-fire string of Russian words.

Lina translated, "She says that mind reading is cheating even if you are not doing it on purpose."

Panya must have gotten the idea that Jasmine could read minds from Amanda's visit to the lounge the other day.

Rumors about Jaz's uncanny streak of poker winnings had reached the neuroscientist who specialized in paranormal abilities. She had gotten curious and had come down to the staff lounge to test Jaz for telepathy and precognition.

The results had been unimpressive, and when Amanda had insisted on bringing others to test her further, the results remained underwhelming.

So, Jasmine might have fudged them just a little to avoid suspicion, but not by much. She really wasn't a telepath or a seer.

She was something else. She was a conduit for the divine spirit of the goddess.

Right.

It sounded good, but was it true?

Probably not.

Jasmine was just exceptionally good at reading people without having to peek into their minds.

"I'm not a mind reader. I'm a body language reader, and as much as the three of you try not to project what you are thinking, you still do."

After Lina translated into Russian, Panya retorted again, but this time her tone sounded more good-natured than derisive.

Lina translated. "She doesn't mind losing because it doesn't cost her anything. Even the potato chips are free. She says that playing with you teaches her how to guard her expressions and body language so that when she gets back home, she will win real money playing with her friends."

"I only play for fun." Jasmine cast Panya a mock glare. "Tell her to have mercy on her friends and not play for money. It will only bring her bad luck."

Under the table, Jasmine curled her thumb between her index and middle fingers, forming the *malocchio* sign to shield against negative energies and ill intentions.

Playing poker professionally could have made her rich, but after all the lectures she'd heard from her father about how it could get her in trouble with bad people or even killed, she only played for fun, or in this case, for Fritos and information.

Not that the Russians were particularly forthcoming. The bits and pieces she had collected so far were pitiful compared to what she could usually gather with nothing more than a few charming smiles and several carefully spaced questions.

As much as she was grateful to these people for rescuing her from the cartel and giving her a ride back home, she was dying of curiosity about them, and all the secrecy they insisted on was just ridiculous.

She was stuck in the crew quarters, not allowed to go to the upper decks, and no one was willing to tell her anything.

Panya waved a dismissive hand as she rose to her feet with Lina and Anya following her. "*Nevezeniye—eto yerunda*," she said before heading toward the door.

Lina translated, "She said that bad luck is nonsense."

"It's not," Jasmine murmured under her breath.

It was no use trying to convince the stubborn Russian that bad luck was very real. She would find out soon enough.

Jasmine munched on the last of her winnings, walked over to one of the plush couches in the corner, sat down, and stretched out her long legs.

With the kitchen staff leaving to start working on tonight's wedding dinner, the lounge was emptying, and the place that was usually bustling with activity and lively chatter was turning depressingly quiet.

Ever since Jasmine was brought on board, she'd been observing the same exodus happening every afternoon, but usually some of the staff remained because not everyone worked all three shifts.

Today, though, she'd heard rumors that someone very important was getting married, but no one would tell her who they were or even why they were important.

Well, since Lina and Marina were the only ones who spoke English, they were the only two she'd asked, and both had refused to answer, saying that it was classified information.

Whatever.

It didn't matter who was getting married. What bothered Jasmine was that with the staff gone, she was about to be the only one left in the lounge. The rescued women who occupied some of the cabins on this level only left their rooms to eat in the crew's dining room and never visited the lounge, but even if some of them decided to brave it, they only spoke Spanish, and she didn't.

The truth was that Jasmine hated being alone, and she hated being stuck in places with no windows, but the staff quarters and facilities were all below the water line, and she was not allowed to venture to the upper decks where the Perfect Match Virtual Studios management mingled with the distinguished guests, who were all former users of the service who had found true love in a Perfect Match adventure and were getting married on this super-secretive, exclusive cruise. Not that she knew any of that for a fact, but she had gathered enough tidbits of information to deduce that.

The other thing that Jasmine hated was sleeping alone in her tiny, windowless cabin, but it didn't seem like she would be able to find anyone to share it with for the last three nights of the cruise. The number of male staff members was pitifully small, and they were either too old, too young or in committed relationships.

Jasmine sighed, her fingers drumming an idle rhythm on her thigh. If only she could venture to the upper deck and mingle with the guests, she could perhaps find the handsome helicopter pilot whom she'd flirted with during the boat ride from Modana's yacht to the ship.

Edgar had been enchanted with her, and he seemed like a nice guy. The two guards who had collected her and the others were not bad looking either. In fact, she wouldn't have minded a tumble with any of them, but none had come down to see her, not even to say 'Hi, how are ya?'

Had she lost her touch?

Maybe they had been told to stay away from her?

It was ridiculous how tight-lipped everyone was about the whole Perfect Match thing. So what if the couples had met through the company's exclusive dating service?

If anything, it would make a fantastic PR opportunity.

Jasmine would love to become part of that PR effort, perhaps as the spokesperson in their commercials, or a character in one of their adventures. After all, they based their avatars on real people, or at least that was what she'd been led to believe.

Some sneered at the service and its users, but not her. It would be nice to have the computer find her the perfect guy. After the disastrous results of consulting her tarot cards on matters of the heart, Jasmine was much more inclined to trust artificial intelligence to find the perfect man for her.

The damn tarot had promised her a prince, and she'd foolishly believed they had meant Alberto, only for her so-called prince to turn into an ugly, wart-covered toad.

Jasmine's stomach churned at the memory of how easily she'd been fooled by the handsome, charismatic guy pretending to be an honest, well-to-do business-man. Alberto had swept her off her feet with lavish dinners, extravagant bouquets of flowers, and charming smiles. She'd been so sure that he was the prince the tarot cards had foretold, but instead of a happily-ever-after, she'd found herself snared in a nightmare.

Shaking off the painful recollections, Jasmine sat up and pulled out the worn velvet pouch nestled in her purse. Despite their disappointing guidance as of late, she cherished those tarot cards above all of her other possessions.

They had been her constant companions since she was a young girl, an unintended gift left behind by her mother.

Or intended, as she chose to believe.

Her mother had left the cards hidden inside a secret compartment in her jewelry box, which she must have known would go to Jasmine after her death.

With no one to instruct Jasmine on how to use them, they had initially been just a collection of pretty pictures, a reminder of the mother she'd lost, and a secret treasure hidden from her father. But when Jaz got old enough to be allowed access to the internet, she'd found all the instructions she needed.

Over the years, Jasmine had come to rely on the cards' guidance, finding comfort in their cryptic messages and, more often than not, finding out that they had been right. But sometimes, she had done so to her detriment.

Well, only once.

They had never steered her wrong before leading her to that scumbag Alberto. May his dark soul rot in hell.

Glancing around to ensure that she was truly alone, Jasmine pulled the deck out of the velvet pouch and began to shuffle. A smile spread over her face as the familiar motions relaxed her better than meditation, yoga, or just about anything else.

Well, save for sex. But that wasn't in the cards until she got off the ship.

Jasmine snorted. Not in the cards—now that was funny.

She closed her eyes, focusing her energy on the question that had been plaguing her since she was brought on board.

Was her prince on this ship?

Was that why the cards had led her to Alberto, so she could end up here where her prince awaited?

With a deep breath, she laid out the first card, The Six of Cups. The image of two children exchanging gifts stared back at her, a symbol of innocence, nostalgia, and the promise of a new beginning. Jasmine's heart skipped a beat. That card hadn't popped up before. Could this mean that her prince was someone from her past? Perhaps it was a guy that she'd met in school and hadn't noticed back then but who had admired her from afar? And who was also secretly a prince?

Jasmine chuckled. Talk about romantic fantasies. She sounded like a character from one of her period romance novels. She'd never really thought that the cards were promising her an actual prince. They must have meant a prince of a man, and she would be more than happy with that.

The next card was The Lovers. The naked figures of Adam and Eve were intertwined beneath the watchful eye of an angel, the image relaying a profound connection and a union blessed by the divine. After pulling that one, she knew what the final card would be even before laying it down, the same way she knew when she was about to get a winning hand.

And there it was—The Knight of Cups, a dashing figure astride a white horse, holding out a golden chalice as if in offering. The embodiment of romance, chivalry, and the arrival of a suitor. And behind him, rising from the horizon like a beacon, was a castle.

Her prince.

The first few times the same sequence had unfolded, Jasmine had been so excited that her hands had trembled, but now, it seemed more like a curse than a blessing.

It was nothing, a fluke, a cruel joke that some malicious spirit was playing on her.

Her father had warned her against relying on the cards, and at the time she thought he was being superstitious, but maybe he'd been right. After all, cartomancy had only been her introduction to the occult. Since then, she had delved into more serious stuff, but she still had a lot to learn about being a proper witch.

The devil's playground, her father called anything he considered witchcraft, but he was wrong. Hellish or divine, it all depended on the practitioner.

2

KIAN

Kian left Margo's cabin and headed toward the elevators, intending to finally have a long overdue chat with Jasmine.

When she'd been brought to the ship, he hadn't paid her much attention because he hadn't deemed it necessary. After all, the woman had just been someone whom Margo had befriended, a magnet for trouble who had gotten Margo entangled with the cartel. But since day one, people around him had been talking about Jasmine as if she was someone special, and that included Syssi and Amanda, whose opinions he valued.

According to his wife and sister, Jasmine had an uncanny ability to read the most minute changes in expression and body language, which allowed her to excel at poker. She'd won against Amanda, who was an excellent player herself. That and her likability led them to believe that Jasmine might be a Dormant.

Given the way the Fates worked, Kian had no problem believing that she had found her way to the ship with their guidance, but the skeptic in him was still very much to the fore, and before he accepted the supernatural explanation, he needed to make sure that Margo's befriending Jasmine in Cabo had indeed been a coincidence, and that the woman wasn't a plant.

Stopping by the elevator, he considered for a moment calling Anandur and Brundar to accompany him. Protocol demanded that they be with him in all meetings outside the village, but since the ship was under his control, it was like an extension of the village, and therefore he didn't need bodyguards to be with him when he visited the woman.

Not that he would have needed protection from the human under any circumstances, but he had vowed to follow his mother's rule in that regard, and even though he used every available loophole to avoid dragging the brothers everywhere with him, he never disregarded it completely unless he had no choice.

Besides, the two were enjoying themselves at Onegus's bachelor party, and Anandur was most likely drunk by now. Not that it would make the Guardian any less effective. Anandur was lethal even when inebriated, but Kian was loath to pull either of the brothers away from the festivities.

As he pressed the button to summon the elevator, it occurred to him that he didn't know where to look for her. He knew where the clinic was located, but other than that, he wasn't familiar with the crew quarters, which was where she was staying.

Kian could call the security office to ask, but it was a little embarrassing to admit that he didn't know his way around his own ship. Syssi would know where Jasmine could be found, but she was in the pool with Allegra and he didn't want to disturb her, which left Amanda.

His sister was at Cassandra's bachelorette party, but that shouldn't prevent her from answering him unless the party was so loud and boisterous that she didn't notice it.

His phone rang a moment after he'd sent her the text.

"Why do you want to know where to find Jasmine?" Amanda asked without much preamble.

"I'm intrigued. Isn't that reason enough?"

She chuckled. "It is. I'll come with you."

Kian frowned, glancing at his watch once more. "Are you sure? I don't want to pull you away from Cassandra's celebration. It would be rude for you to leave in the middle of the party."

Amanda laughed, the sound light and breezy. "Don't worry about that. Cassandra is indulging in a bubble bath, and her mother and sister have everything under control. Geraldine and Darlene are getting ready to attack Cassandra's hair, and Eva has her bag of tricks with her, although I doubt Cassandra will let her touch her face. The female is gorgeous, and she knows how to use makeup to her advantage. She doesn't need Eva's help."

Kian stifled the urge to roll his eyes. "I'll take your word for it."

Amanda laughed again. "Too much information?"

"You could say so. Makeup is not my field of expertise."

"I get it. Where are you now?"

"Outside the elevators on Margo and Frankie's deck."

"What are you doing there?"

He'd just finished updating Margo about the successful evacuation of her parents and her brother and his fiancée from their homes, but Amanda wasn't aware of the latest crisis, and he didn't want to tell her about it while waiting for the elevator.

"I'll tell you on the way to the crew quarters. Meet me next to the staircase on the promenade deck."

"See you in a few," Amanda said before ending the call.

As Kian made his way to their designated meeting spot, his thoughts drifted back to Margo. He hoped that her transition symptoms were not a false alarm and that she was indeed turning immortal. He also hoped that no Doomers would show up at her parents' and brother's houses so her family could return to their homes.

Right now, they were on their way to the clan's mountain cabin with Turner's team to keep watch over them.

Kian didn't like that the cabin's location had to be compromised for Margo's family and that there was no one there to thrall away the memory of where it was from all the humans involved, but he'd had to come up with a location on the spot, and the cabin was his go-to safe house.

Lost in his musings, Kian didn't notice Amanda approaching him until he heard the clicking of her high heels on the marble floor. She looked fantastic in an elegant cocktail dress reminiscent of the fifties. If he wasn't mistaken, Audrey Hepburn had worn something similar in one of her iconic films.

"You look distracted." She leaned toward him and kissed his cheek. "Everything okay?"

Kian started down the stairs, which were thankfully deserted. "Margo may be transitioning, and we had a close call with her family." He proceeded to tell Amanda about Carlos Modana showing up with two Doomers at his brother's mansion and then the two talking about Margo. "We got her family out and installed cameras to monitor both houses. I hope no one shows up so they can return home, and we don't need to relocate them permanently."

"What a mess." Amanda sighed. "It's like the Fates are constantly throwing challenges at us. Couldn't they have given us a break during this ten-day cruise?"

"My thoughts exactly, but then we have been gifted two new Dormants during this vacation, so perhaps it could be called a good trade. Maybe three if Jasmine proves to be one as well."

"True." Amanda slowed down her pace and stopped on the landing. "But Frankie and Margo are mated to gods, and they are not part of our clan. I don't see why we all had to suffer so the gods would get a boon."

Kian turned to his sister. "I don't know, but I'm sure the Fates had a good reason."

Amanda smiled. "What a transformation you have gone through. My jaded, skeptical brother has faith now."

"I do, and I don't. It depends on my mood on any given day." He continued down the stairs.

Amanda followed. "And what is it today?"

"That still remains to be seen."

JASMINE

As Amanda entered the lounge with a man who could only be described as a god, Jasmine got a little lightheaded.

Was that what swooning meant? She'd always wondered about that word when it appeared in the historical romances she favored.

His features were chiseled, his eyes a piercing blue, and his presence seemed to fill the room with tangible energy.

"Jasmine, this is my brother Kian," Amanda said. "Kian, this is Jasmine."

Jasmine pushed to her feet, but her knees refused to lock, and her heart fluttered in her chest. Could this be him? The prince the tarot cards had promised, the one who would sweep her off her feet?

Except, unlike most men, Kian seemed indifferent to her charms. His gaze was cool and reserved, and as he inclined his head in greeting, there was no spark of interest and no flicker of attraction in his eyes.

Confused and a little hurt, Jasmine tried to mask her disappointment.

She really should stop relying on the damn tarot. They had either lost their potency, or all their prior successes had been flukes.

As if reading her mind, Amanda smiled knowingly. "Kian is Syssi's husband. They have the most adorable little girl named Allegra." She opened her purse and pulled out her phone. "I have to show you her picture."

Jasmine felt like knocking on her own head to check if anything was loose in there. She'd been so stupefied by Kian's looks that she'd forgotten that Amanda had introduced Syssi as her sister-in-law.

Then again, Amanda could have more than one brother, right?

"Here is the little princess." Amanda thrust the screen in front of Jasmine's face.

"Absolutely adorable." Jaz smiled at Amanda, silently thanking her for the reprieve she'd given her by showing her the picture. She then turned her smile on Kian. "She is a mixture of you and your wife." She pushed aside the foolish notions of princes and destiny.

"But I'm sure that you didn't come down here to show me pictures of your daughter."

"I did not. Let's sit down." Kian waved a hand toward the couch and then lowered himself to a sitting position with more grace than a man his size should have been capable of. "As you know, Julio Modana was convinced by my associate to abandon his evil ways and embrace God."

She chuckled. "Kevin's hypnotic ability is mind-boggling."

"It is." Kian offered her a tight smile. "Julio's brother Carlos was obviously not happy about the one-eighty pivot his brother had made, and he paid him a visit. Fortunately, we'd planted listening devices around the estate, and we heard two of Carlos's goons talking about Margo and you. They even knew that Margo's family was under the impression that she was in the witness protection program."

Jasmine's eyes widened. "Why would they think that? Margo was supposed to board this ship, and her family knew her plans. They wouldn't have wondered where she was."

Kian looked at her as if she was dimwitted. "Margo was reported missing from her hotel room by her sister-in-law, and all of her things remained there. Her family was not informed of her finally being able to board the ship, and they also didn't know which ship she was supposed to board because we kept those details confidential on purpose." Kian turned to his sister with a smile tugging on his lips. "This time, you have to agree that my paranoia had merit."

Amanda winced. "I'm not sure that Mia kept the name of the ship from her friends. I just hope that Frankie and Margo didn't repeat it to their families."

Letting out a long-suffering sigh, Kian briefly closed his eyes. "I should never have agreed to allow Frankie and Margo on the ship. Evidently, I'm not paranoid enough."

Jasmine listened to the exchange, waiting for a break so she could ask what was going on. The level of secrecy Kian insisted on implied something more serious than protecting the identities of famous guests.

"Why was it important to keep the name of the ship a secret? Is something illegal going on here?"

Suddenly, Jaz remembered the poor women in the other cabins and wondered whether they really had been rescued from traffickers. What if they were being trafficked?

"Don't worry." Amanda leaned over and patted her thigh. "Our unfortunate entanglement with the cartel is all Margo's fault and has nothing to do with why we needed to keep the ship and its guests secret. We need to keep the paparazzi off our trail. You have no idea how resourceful they can be, how tenacious, and how low they are willing to stoop to get a story." She smiled. "But then, if Margo hadn't tried to help you, we would have never known that you were trafficked, and no one would have come to your rescue, so it's all good, right?"

"Now I feel guilty." Jasmine sighed. "If I hadn't gotten involved with Alberto, none of this would have happened. It's all my fault, not Margo's."

Kian lifted his hand. "Let's not play the blame game. Since the thugs mentioned you, we are concerned that they might go after your family as well as Margo's. They know how to locate Margo's family because her brother's fiancée filed a missing person's report, and they can find all the information they need by following her trail. We got her parents, brother, and future sister-in-law to a safe location. How easy will it be for them to locate your folks?"

"Why would they go after our families?" Jasmine asked. "What do they hope to gain by that?"

"Leverage," Kian said. "That's the cartel's mode of operation. They take hostages to pressure family members to give them what they want, whether it's money or information."

"I see." Jaz tucked a lock of hair behind her ear. "I'm not too worried about them finding my family. I use a stage name and I legally changed my last name years ago. My father and stepmother live in New Jersey, and we rarely see each other or even talk on the phone. If the cartel people check my records, they will see that most of my calls are to my agent, my acting coach, and my friends."

Jaz didn't have many friends, and she rarely talked with them on the phone, but it would have sounded pitiful if she'd only mentioned her agent and her coach.

"What about your brothers?" Kian asked. "Margo told me that you have two stepbrothers."

Jasmine snorted. "I see them once a year on Christmas at our parents' house, and we never call each other. There isn't much love lost between us."

"Good." Kian nodded. "I mean, not good that your relationship with your family is strained. It's good that we don't have to worry about it."

"Yeah." She winced. "Sometimes having an unhappy family is an advantage rather than a disadvantage."

"To quote Tolstoy's Anna Karenina," Amanda said, "all happy families are alike, but each unhappy family is unhappy in its own way."

4

KIAN

When Jasmine had explained her family situation, Kian couldn't shake the nagging suspicion that something was off about her story. She was hiding something, but then it could be just family drama that had nothing to do with him and the safety of his people.

He studied her carefully, noting the way she forced her eyes to stay focused on his, and smiled pleasantly when he knew that he was making her nervous.

Not that her reaction to him was surprising.

Kian made most people uncomfortable, even gods and immortals, and Jasmine was just a human female. She was beautiful, which no doubt contributed to her self-confidence, but she was also an actress, and she knew how to hide her tells remarkably well.

"It's a shame that you are not close to your parents." He offered her a smile. "Family is very important to me."

He cut a sidelong glance at Amanda. "Sometimes they drive me crazy, but most of the time, I'm grateful for having them in my life."

"Ooh, Kian." Amanda batted her eyelashes and put a hand over her heart. "That's as close as you've ever gotten to telling me that you love me."

He frowned. "Really? I must have told you that I love you hundreds of times."

"Maybe when I was little, but you stopped when I became a teenager."

"That's because you were a hellion."

Jasmine's eyes darted from him to Amanda and back. "What's the age difference between you? You don't look more than five years apart."

Amanda laughed. "Kian only looks young. His soul is at least two thousand years old."

He wanted to kick her leg to make sure she was more careful about what she was saying in front of Jasmine, but there was no way he could do that without Jasmine seeing.

"So, about these paranormal talents of yours," Kian said before Amanda had a chance to make another comment that she shouldn't. "My sister and my wife are very impressed by your ability to read people."

Jasmine shrugged, a coy smile playing on her lips. "What can I say? I've always been good at picking up on the little things. Body language and micro expressions are all there if you know what to look for. People call it a sixth sense or female intuition, but it's just good observational skills." She leaned forward. "I call it the 'staying quiet and letting others talk' skill."

"That's very astute. Did you learn it from your acting teachers?"

Jasmine nodded. "My coach's number one advice was to observe people. The more I learn and store in my mind, the more I have to draw on when I need to build a character."

"Interesting." Kian crossed his arms over his chest. "When did you discover that you could use your observational skills in poker?"

"It was a gradual process. I joined the drama club by the end of middle school, and I discovered poker when I was an adult, but I didn't have such well-developed observational skills back then. Not until I got professional coaching. So, I think that it was a self-feeding loop. Better acting meant more poker wins, and more poker wins made me a better actress." She leaned back to reach into her pocket and pulled out a deck of cards. "Would you like a demonstration?"

He arched a brow. "You want me to play poker with you?"

"Yeah, why not. Amanda can join us, right?"

Amanda glanced at her watch. "I don't have a lot of time, but I would like Kian to see you in your element."

Kian was not a great poker player. In fact, he tended to telegraph his emotions and had a hard time keeping them in check.

"I'm a very mediocre poker player," he admitted. "You two will have no problem beating me."

Jasmine grinned. "Good, then I should take advantage of your supposed lack of skill. If I win, you will let me onto the upper decks and allow me to attend the weddings."

Kian arched an eyebrow, amused by her audacity. Eva would have called it hutzpah, and she would have been right on the money.

Not many people would have dared to challenge him so directly.

"Did you really expect me to agree to that?" he asked.

Jasmine sighed dramatically, leaning back against the plush cushions. "It was worth a try." She fixed him with an assessing look, her head tilted to the side. "I hate being cooped up here with no windows to the outside, and I really don't understand why Margo gets to be up there while I have to stay down here." She pouted. "I will sign whatever NDA you want me to sign, and I will not breathe a word about the celebrities getting married on this cruise." She put a hand on her chest. "I swear it. I'm just dying of curiosity. I want to hobnob with the rich and famous and experience the glitz."

The woman didn't seem intimidated by him even in the slightest, which made Kian doubt her self-preservation instincts, but at the same time there was something refreshing about her irreverence and lack of fear, even if it was all an act.

Was she flirting with him? Or was she just using her charm to soften him up?

She was undeniably beautiful, and there was also a spark, a vibrancy to her that he found appealing in a completely nonsexual way.

Was that the affinity that Amanda had talked about?

Probably. It couldn't be anything else.

Kian was a happily mated male, bound heart and soul to Syssi, and the only thing he could feel for Jasmine was friendliness, which most likely stemmed from affinity.

Perhaps Jasmine was feeling that, too, but was misinterpreting it as attraction. If she were an immortal female, she would have sensed his bonded status immediately and never dared to approach him with even a hint of flirtation.

He waved at the deck in her hand. "Shuffle the cards, and let's play."

Jasmine shook her head. "We need something to wager, and I don't play for money."

That was strange. If she was as good as everyone was claiming, then she could make a killing playing poker professionally.

"Ever?" Kian asked.

"Ever. It's dangerous. I play for fun."

He supposed that it could turn dangerous if she played with the wrong kind of people. Criminal types were usually sore losers.

"That's smart. What do you usually wager with?"

"Chips, popcorn, crackers, grapes, etc."

"I'll get some chips." Amanda pushed to her feet and walked over to the vending machine.

While Jasmine shuffled the cards and Amanda collected bags of chips from the dispenser, Kian was tempted to delve into Jasmine's mind and search for a hidden agenda.

It would be so easy to reach out with his power, to slip past her mental defenses and pluck the truth from her consciousness. Except, it was against the rules to thrall a human without just cause, and curiosity didn't count.

5

AMANDA

"I win." Jasmine pumped her fist in the air and gathered her winnings, several flavors of Pringles Grab & Go packed in small individual containers.

Kian shook his head. "I'm positive that I wasn't telegraphing anything. How did you know that I had a crappy hand?"

Poor guy. He didn't even know how bad he was.

"You are a terrible poker player." Amanda patted Kian's knee. "You took one look at your cards, and your eyes narrowed like you wanted to shoot lasers at them and incinerate the useless hand, and the cloud over your head didn't clear as the game progressed, so Jasmine and I knew that you kept getting bad cards."

"I was narrowing my eyes not because I was angry at my cards but because I was looking at Jasmine and wondering if she had an amazing memory and incredible math skills. Usually, those are needed to be a good poker player."

Jasmine laughed. "I'm terrible at math. My memory is okay, but nothing special. It was just intuition and observation." She pushed to her feet. "If you'll excuse me, I need to visit the ladies' room." She glanced at Amanda. "Do you want to come with me?"

"No, thank you, darling." Amanda smiled. "I'll wait for you here. The truth is that I should be heading back to the party, but I want us to play one more game so Kian can win back the chips he lost."

Her brother waved a dismissive hand. "Contrary to what you think about me, I don't have to always win."

"I'll be right back." Jasmine rushed out of the lounge.

Kian cast Amanda a sidelong glance. "Did you have anything to do with her sudden need to visit the ladies' room?"

She shrugged and assumed an innocent expression. "I might have projected the suggestion to see if she picked it up."

"That was clever." Kian regarded his sister with appreciation. "Did you suspect that she was faking her underwhelming results with your tests?"

Amanda nodded. "She's unnaturally good with cards, so I suspected that she'd fudged the answers. Anyway, while she's gone, I wanted to suggest that you ask Edna to take a peek at Jasmine's psyche. Edna's talent is more akin to empathic reading than thralling, so it's totally within the rules."

"It is, but it's also not subtle. Jasmine will know that she's being probed."

"It's either that or thralling, which I don't mind doing if you are too squeamish about breaking the rules. You know that I don't believe in strict adherence to them, and since no one ever checks, I see no harm in taking a quick look. Jasmine wouldn't even feel it."

He tilted his head. "Why is this so important to you? Do you suspect that something about her is not as it seems?"

"Not really." Amanda sighed. "She's hiding things, but that's not an indication of anything malicious. We all have things we hide, old pains that we don't want others to see, shame, and guilt. But I want Jasmine to mingle with our eligible bachelors, and I know that you won't let her onto the upper decks without making sure she's harmless. So, we need Edna to take a peek, or I can do that and break the rules for a good cause." A sly grin lifted Amanda's red-painted lips. "Since Jasmine obviously has some paranormal talent, and the Fates brought her to us, we have an obligation to check whether she's a Dormant. I have a strong hunch that she is."

Kian surprised her by nodding. "I agree. Even I like her, and you know me. I rarely take a liking to new people."

Amanda snorted. "Generally, that's true, but in the case of gorgeous ladies, you are a bit more flexible."

"What are you talking about?" He glared at her. "Her looks have no effect on me. How can you even suggest that?"

"Relax." She put a hand on his arm. "I'm not suggesting that you are attracted to her, only that you find her pleasing to look at. It's natural, and you don't need to get defensive about it. Even little kids prefer pretty teachers to the ones less fortunate in the looks department. That's how humans are wired, and given who our ancestors are, you shouldn't be surprised. Gods are obsessed with beauty and physical perfection."

Kian dismissed Amanda's theory with a wave of his hand, not because it was untrue but because it was irrelevant to their discussion. "The cruise is almost over, so I don't see the point in sending Edna to test Jasmine. Before she disembarks, we will thrall her to forget about us, and while we are at it, we can take a look at whatever she is hiding."

"You forget the Doomers," Amanda said. "We can't just send Jasmine home, and we can't let her return to her job. We need to get her somewhere safe for a couple of weeks until we are sure that the coast is clear."

"True." He sighed. "I did forget about that. I'll talk to Edna, but it still won't change the fact that we have only three days left."

"We can do a lot in three days, even if you don't allow Jasmine to go up. I'm going to tell Max that he needs to keep an eye on her up close and personal."

"Why Max?"

Amanda shrugged. "He's been a groomsman but never the groom for too long, and it's his turn. Jasmine might not be the one for him, but he deserves first dibs."

6

JASMINE

J asmine sat on the toilet and waited for her full bladder to empty, but instead of the gush she'd expected, there was only a trickle.

"Oh, crap. I hope I don't have a UTI or a bladder infection."

An intense urge to pee without much to show for it was a sure sign of one of those.

Nah, that was unlikely. She had drank plenty of liquids and hadn't been intimate with anyone since Alberto.

She was just nervous.

It wasn't smart to get the big boss annoyed, which would surely happen if she won again. Men didn't like losing to women, even more than they didn't like to lose to other men.

Fragile egos, one and all.

When she was done, Jasmine washed her hands, combed her locks with her fingers, and smacked her lips to plump them up.

Kian was a married man, and he wasn't interested in her, but it was always good to leave a good impression.

Satisfied with her appearance, she headed back to the lounge.

"I'm sure the queen would have loved to see her grand-daughter and her great-grandchildren," Kian was telling Amanda as Jasmine entered. "It's a shame that's not possible."

"I'm not sure about that at all," his sister said. "The royals are a stuck-up bunch who won't approve of us."

Jasmine's heartbeat accelerated. No wonder they were so secretive about the passengers. There were royals on board.

The tarot had been right after all, and her prince was on board the ship.

"Which royals are you talking about?" She tried to sound nonchalant. "Anyone I know?" She walked over to the couch and sat down at the same spot she'd occupied before.

Amanda waved a dismissive hand. "Oh, it's a small, unimportant monarchy you have probably never heard of."

"Are they on board the ship? Is that why such extreme security measures are being employed?"

The brother and sister exchanged looks, and then Amanda shook her head. "I'm sorry, but it's confidential information."

"Oh, please." Jasmine rolled her eyes. "Who am I going to tell?" She leaned closer to Amanda. "Is there a single prince looking for a bride? Tell me just that, and I won't bug you anymore." *For now.*

Amanda laughed. "No, there are no single royal princes on board."

Jasmine tried to conceal her disappointment with a joke. "Of course not. Why would there be a prince for me?" She sighed dramatically. "Poisonous frogs seem to be my lot. It would have been nice to get a prince for a change. I mean, not a literal royal prince. Just, you know, a prince of a man. Someone kind and brave and true. Not like that scumbag Alberto who only pretended to be that kind of man." She lifted her gaze to Amanda. "Do good men even exist?"

"Sure they do." Amanda wrapped her arm around Kian's broad shoulders. "My brother is one of the best men I know, and so is my husband and many of the other men on this cruise. I should introduce you to some of them."

Jasmine's eyes widened. "You would do that for me? That would be awesome. I need someone sweet to wash away the rotten taste left over from Alberto."

Amanda grinned. "I have just the guy for the job." She leaned closer and whispered conspiratorially, "I won't tell him that I'm setting him up. I'll just tell him to keep an eye on you, and the rest is up to you."

If the tarot were right, her prince was awaiting her, but that didn't mean she couldn't have fun with a nice guy until she found him.

"That would be wonderful. Who is he?"

"Someone I think you will like, but if he's busy, I might have to send someone else, so I don't want to use any names."

"Understandable. Thank you." Jasmine took the card deck and started shuffling. "Are you up for another game?"

Amanda glanced at her watch. "I should have returned to the party by now, but I guess I can squeeze in another short game."

7

KIAN

The wistfulness in Jasmine's voice and the hope in her eyes tugged at Kian's conscience. She must be very lonely if she was so excited about Amanda's matchmaking, and in that moment, she looked young and innocent, a far cry from the confident, flirtatious woman who had been bantering with him and Amanda and handing them their asses at poker.

He also couldn't shake the feeling that she was important somehow and that the Fates had brought her into the clan's path for a reason.

When Jasmine had dealt the cards, Kian cleared his throat. "I'll consider your request to be allowed on the upper decks."

Amanda's head whipped toward him. "Who are you, and what have you done with my brother?"

He smiled. "I took into consideration what you said before. Besides, since Jasmine is not going home at the end of the cruise, the window of opportunity is longer than three days, especially if we put her up in the keep."

A smile spread over Amanda's face. "Good plan, brother of mine. I like it."

"I'm not going home?" Jasmine asked, looking surprised.

"I might not have been clear before, but the cartel thugs who are a potential threat to you and your family might come looking for you at your residence. We have a place in the city where you can stay until the danger is over."

Jasmine swallowed. "I have a job that I need to return to. It's not much, but it pays the bills, and I can't afford to lose it."

Kian leaned forward. "I was told that you work in customer service between the occasional acting jobs in commercials. How much do they pay you?"

She swallowed, looking embarrassed. "A little over minimum wage."

"Do you enjoy your job?"

"Not really."

He leaned back. "Then don't worry about it. If you lose it, I will find you something better."

Her eyes sparkled. "I would love to work at Perfect Match. Being a spokeswoman in their commercials would be a dream, but any other job would be great. I heard that employees get to be beta testers, and I would love to have access to the service without having to pay for it."

Kian smiled. "I happen to be very close to one of the owners. I can ask her on your behalf."

"Thank you." She reached for his hand. "Thank you so much."

He let her clasp it for a split second before pulling it out of her grip. "Don't thank me yet. Wait until I get you the job."

"Oh, my goddess." She fanned herself. "Perhaps I read the cards all wrong, and you are my prince."

Kian recoiled. "I am definitely not. I'm a married man."

"I didn't mean it that way." She squeezed her eyes shut for a moment. "Would you at least let me explain before biting my head off?"

Kian took a steadying breath. "I'm listening."

"I sometimes consult tarot cards for fun, and lately, I've been getting the prince card a lot. I thought it meant I was going to meet my Prince Charming, but I might have interpreted it wrong, and the prince was not meant to be my romantic interest, but someone who would help me get a leg up in life."

"I see. Yes, well, I don't know much about tarot." He looked at Amanda. "Do you?"

"I don't know how to read them, but I've been to a fortune teller once or twice for a reading."

"Really?" Kian frowned at his sister. "Why would you consult someone who pretends to see the future in cards?"

She gave him a haughty look. "The cards are just a tool, a way for the gifted to channel their power. There are many charlatans, of course, but here and there, you can find real talent." She turned to Jasmine. "Are you a Wiccan?"

"Sort of. I don't belong to any coven, and the only Wiccans I know are in my social media worship group."

"Do you worship the goddess?"

Jasmine clutched the cards in her hand. "We are not idol worshipers or anything like that. We just revere the feminine aspect of divinity."

"That's very cool." Amanda put her cards down. "I dabbled a little in Wicca too, and I would love to chat more about it. But I should get back to the party before Cassandra sends out a search party for me." She pushed to her feet.

Kian glanced at his watch. He had less than an hour to get ready. For him, it was plenty of time, but not for Amanda. Also, Edna wouldn't be able to see Jasmine today.

Jasmine put her cards down as well. "Thank you," she said to Amanda, and then turned to Kian. "It was nice meeting you, and I'm sorry if I made you uncomfortable. I really didn't mean anything by it. You are very handsome, but I would never flirt with a married man." She scrunched her nose and looked at him from under lowered lashes. "Not seriously, anyway. Sometimes I just can't help myself."

"I know the feeling." Amanda patted Jasmine's shoulder. "You remind me a lot of myself a few years back, when I was still a single lady." She laughed. "I loved to flirt, and I loved the power I had over men, but I don't miss those days. Having Dalhu and Evie is so much more fulfilling than the endless chase after new thrills." She turned to Kian. "Are you coming?"

He'd hated the hunt, but then he was much older than Amanda and had been at it for too many years to count. Syssi was a boon from the Fates, for which he thanked them daily.

"Yes, I am." He looked at Jasmine. "I might send over a lady who has a talent similar to Kevin's to examine you. She has the ability to assess a person's intentions, and if she clears you, I will allow you to come up to the upper decks."

Grinning like she had just won the lottery, Jasmine reached for his hand but then reconsidered. "Thank you. I have nothing to hide, and I will do almost anything to be allowed to mingle with the guests. I can sing if you need additional entertainment."

They didn't have any entertainers other than the DJ. "I'll take it into account."

"Awesome." Jasmine clasped her hands, maybe to avoid reaching for his again. "What's the lady's name? The one who will come to assess me?"

"Edna. She will not have time to see you today, though. It will have to wait until tomorrow."

"Oh." Some of Jasmine's exuberance dimmed. "I hoped to attend tonight's wedding. Oh, well, there are two more to go, right?"

"That's right." Amanda hooked her arm through Kian's. "We need to go."

8

PETER

P eter adjusted his bowtie in front of the full-length mirror in the cabin's small foyer. Beside him, Jay did the same.

"I love weddings, but I hate these penguin suits," Jay grumbled, stretching his neck. "How about we suggest a new wedding tradition with no tuxedos, no suits, and no starchy white shirts?"

Peter cast his roommate an amused sidelong glance. "At least we don't have to wear high heels and tight dresses, so stop complaining and man up. Besides, you look dashing." He batted his eyelashes and put a hand over his chest. "Larissa is going to swoon."

Jay looked a lot like the young Beckham, and women went gaga over him.

His roommate snorted. "Instead of commiserating with our female partners, we should liberate them as well. No high heels and no corsets."

Peter frowned. "Do they still wear those? I mean, aside from wedding gowns."

Jay shrugged. "Sure they do. They are just made with better fabrics now. Don't tell me that you've never bedded a girl wearing Spanx."

"If I did, I didn't know what they were."

The brand name, which he assumed Spanx was, evoked memories of women's undies with cutouts for the ass cheeks to make them easily accessible for spanking. Naturally, thinking about it had a predictable effect, and he adjusted himself.

"They are not sexy," Jay said as he noticed what Peter was doing. "They make women's bodies look like sausages, and they are really hard to take off. I hate them."

"Are you okay?" Peter turned to face his friend. "You are usually not this grumpy."

Jay was a ladies' man, so it couldn't be because he was nervous about his date with Larissa. If anyone should feel nervous, it should be the girl.

It would be her first time attending a party as a guest, not a server, and there was also the language barrier. She spoke very little English, and Jay spoke even less Russian.

"I'm fine." Jay collected his phone from the table and put it in his pocket. "I hope Larissa will have a good time. Marina was a nervous wreck when she accompanied you to Vlad and Wendy's wedding, and she's much more confident than Larissa."

"Marina and I will stay close in case you need a translator."

"Thank you." Jay's lips curved up on one side of his mouth. "But I might not need help. I took a crash course in Russian over the past three days. I'm far from fluent, but at least I will understand what she's saying."

Peter hadn't known that. "That's a lot of effort for a girl you are not going to see after the cruise ends."

Jay shrugged. "Knowing another language is an asset. Besides, many of the Kra-ell are still struggling with English, and knowing Russian will help me communicate with them." He opened the door. "I can't wait to see Larissa's face when I greet her in Russian."

"Good luck." Peter followed him out the door.

When they reached the girls' cabin, Jay rang the doorbell, and a moment later, the door swung open to reveal Larissa, looking lovely but a little overwhelmed in a flowing purple dress and a pair of sensible black flats.

"Hello," she said with a bright smile as she stepped out of the tiny cabin.

Jay immediately launched into a string of Russian phrases, his accent passable, if a little overly enthusiastic, and Larissa's eyes widened in surprise and delight.

Craning her neck to look at Jay, she responded in English, "I can talk a little bit, too."

"Larissa needs to practice." Marina stepped out from the cabin in a figure-hugging, short black dress that showcased her long, toned legs. "She finally has an incentive to learn English, so don't start talking Russian to her."

Peter knew that dress. It was a loaner from Jessica, and he made a mental note to thank his cousin again for her generous donation to Marina's evening wear arsenal.

Jay's face fell. "I studied so hard so I could communicate with Larissa, and now you are telling me that it was for nothing?"

As Larissa's eyes darted between Marina and Jay, her smile turned strained, and she clutched her small fabric purse while shifting from foot to foot.

"It wasn't for nothing," Peter said, wrapping his arm around Marina's waist. "You can teach each other." He started toward the elevators.

"You look incredible," he whispered in her ear.

Her vivid cobalt-colored hair looked like a bolt of electric energy against the backdrop of her pale skin and black dress, and the red lipstick provided another vivid splash of color.

A self-conscious smile tugged at her lips. "Thanks."

Was it his imagination, or was there a tension in her jaw and a tightness around her eyes?

"Hey," Peter whispered, leaning closer. "Is everything okay? You seem a little out of sorts."

Marina's smile faltered, just for a second, before she hitched it back into place. "I'm great," she assured him. "Just excited about the wedding tonight. Onegus is an important guy, right? The chief Guardian and all that."

Peter doubted that was the reason. "Did you speak to Amanda about your wish to move into the village?"

She nodded. "She told me to wait until I get back to Safe Haven and ask either Eleanor or Emmett to request the transfer on my behalf."

"That's what I suggested."

"I know. I just hoped that Amanda being Kian's sister could wave a magic wand and make it happen instantaneously, so I was a little disappointed."

As Peter pressed the button for the elevator, Jay and Larissa caught up to them.

"Onegus's wedding will be just like all the others," Jay said.

"Not necessarily." Peter held the door open for everyone before getting in. "Cassandra is a hotshot art director, so she might have put her own spin on the decor."

That seemed to pique Marina's interest. "An art director? For what company?"

"Some big cosmetics brand," Peter said with a shrug. "Something with fifty shades, like the movie."

A blush colored Marina's cheeks. "Did you see it? I mean, the movie?"

"No. I heard it was awful."

"It was," Jay confirmed. "I heard that the books were much better."

9

MARINA

Marina's stomach was churning as she walked alongside Peter, her arm linked through his. She knew she needed to come clean, to tell him the truth about her initial motivation for pursuing him, but it was so damn hard. Larissa was right, though. Secrets had no place in a relationship.

On the other hand, Peter had made it very clear that he was not interested in having a relationship with her when she moved to the village, so why bother?

On the remote chance that he would change his mind?

But why would he? She had maybe two more decades of being attractive, if that, and then she would look old.

It was so damn depressing.

Why couldn't she be like Sofia?

Sofia's mother was a hybrid Kra-ell and her father was a human, which was a rare combination. In fact, she was the only human whose mother was a hybrid Kra-ell, and as it turned out, the longevity came from the mother's side.

Well, in Marina's case both her parents were human, so she had nothing of the kind.

Besides, Peter might never forgive her and dump her even before the end of the cruise.

Oh, dear Mother above. It was almost over. They were almost over.

"Are you okay?" Peter asked. "You seem tense."

Marina forced a smile, hoping it didn't look as brittle as it felt. "I'm fine. You know how uncomfortable I am mingling with your kind."

He frowned. "I thought you'd gotten over that. You survived one wedding and even got to enjoy yourself. Why the sudden nerves?"

She scrambled for an answer. What she'd told him hadn't been entirely untrue. She still felt like an imposter, playing dress-up in a world she didn't belong in. But that wasn't the reason she was so tense.

"It's the chief Guardian's wedding. Are you sure he won't mind having an uninvited guest at his party?"

Peter lifted her hand to his lips for a kiss. "You are an invited guest. You are my plus one."

Marina stopped. "What do you mean? What's plus one?"

He chuckled. "I keep forgetting that you know so little of the outside world. When people receive an invitation to an event, they need to respond and inform the host whether they are coming or not and how many people are in their party. When it's just the guest and their partner, they respond with plus one."

Marina looked confused by his explanation, but she nodded. "I think I get it. But you couldn't have responded with a plus one because you didn't know about me."

"I was speaking metaphorically." Peter led her to the main promenade bar and swiveled a stool for her so it was easier for her to slide on top of it.

Vasyli, who was the barman on duty tonight, gave her and Larissa a bright smile. "You both look so beautiful," he said in Russian.

"Thank you," Larissa said in English. "Can I have a glass of vodka with orange juice, please?"

Marina had had her memorize that one sentence, and she'd said it perfectly.

Vasyli's eyes widened. "When did you learn to speak English?"

Larissa's cheeks got red. "Only a little bit."

He turned to Marina. "What can I get for you?"

"The same."

He looked at Peter. "And for you, sir?"

"Nothing for me or my friend. We have to leave shortly." He lifted his wrist to look at his watch. "The ceremony will start in ten minutes." He leaned in to kiss Marina's forehead. "I'll come get you as soon as the doors open."

She nodded.

Humans were not allowed in the dining room during the ceremony, and Marina tried to imagine what secret stuff was happening behind the dining room's closed doors. Were the immortals conducting some sacred ritual that no one was allowed to see?

She would have preferred to wait for Peter in the kitchen like she had done the first time he had taken her to a wedding. Being elbow-deep in dirty dishes and preparing canapés would have kept her occupied and distracted from the gnawing anxiety in her gut.

It was better than sipping on her cocktail and trying not to fidget while the weight of her impending confession pressed like an anvil on her chest.

"You're making a mess of that napkin," Larissa remarked, nodding at the shredded paper beneath Marina's restless fingers. "What's going on with you?"

Marina took a fortifying sip of her drink, but the burn of the alcohol did little to calm her nerves. "I'm scared," she admitted, her voice barely above a whisper. "I'm a gutless worm who is terrified of telling Peter the truth." She sighed. "I don't even know why. It's not like what I did was so terrible. Women do those things all the time. Men too."

Larissa's eyes softened with understanding. She reached out, covering Marina's hand with her own. "If Peter truly cares for you, he'll understand, and he'll forgive you. And if he doesn't, then he's not worth your love."

The word love prompted her to take another fortifying sip from her drink and then another. She loved Peter, but he didn't love her back. Not enough, anyway.

"Hello, darlings." Amanda glided into the bar with her husband, looking like a movie star in a silver floor-length gown. "I have five minutes before I need to escort the bride to the altar, but I'm in desperate need of a drink." She cast Vasyli a charming smile. "I need something quick. Apple martini?"

"Coming up, miss."

While Amanda was all charming smiles, her husband was an intimidating mountain of a man, with bulging muscles that strained against the confines of his tuxedo and a stern, almost forbidding air about him.

"You two look absolutely stunning," Amanda drawled. "Stand up so I can get a better look at you."

"Thank you." Marina pushed to her feet. "You look as amazing as always."

The immortal was the most beautiful woman Marina had ever seen, and she was also super nice, which was surprising on several counts. Amanda was not only gorgeous, but she was also the leader's sister and a council member. People like her were usually stuck-up and condescending, but she wasn't like that at all.

In fact, Marina had expected all the immortals to be as haughty and full of themselves as the Kra-ell pure-bloods had been, but most were nice and friendly and treated the staff serving them with respect.

Amanda waved off the compliment and snatched the martini from Vasyli.

Taking a sip, she fixed her gaze on Larissa. "You, my dear, are a vision in that dress," she said in Russian. "I knew that you would look marvelous in purple."

Larissa blushed, smoothing a hand over the fabric. "I can't thank you enough for lending it to me. I feel like a princess."

"You look like one, too," Amanda reached for a lock of Larissa's hair. "Did you style it, or did Marina do it for you?"

"Marina did my hair and makeup," Larissa said.

"I must say, Marina, you've done an exquisite job." Amanda put a hand on her shoulder. "You can sit back down." She smiled at the bartender. "The martini is excellent, thank you."

"You are welcome, miss." Vasyli bowed his head.

Amanda's husband didn't ask for anything and remained standing behind her like a protective boulder.

A pang of jealousy pierced Marina's heart. She wanted a man like him who would stand guard over her. Not that she needed a guard now that she'd been liberated, but back when she'd been in the compound, helpless to object to any demand from the Kra-ell, she'd often fantasized about having a strong protector like that.

Amanda turned to her husband and offered him a brilliant smile. "Would you like a drink before we have to go?"

"No, thank you." He looked at her with so much adoration in his eyes that Marina's jealousy inflated into a big, ugly, dark balloon.

10

NEGAL

"There is nothing for miles around," Margo's mother said. "Your father and I have just taken a walk, and the air was so fresh and crisp. It's good to get out of the city once in a while."

"I'm glad that you are enjoying your time off," Margo told her mother.

After her family had been given a secure line, Kian had also allowed their new contact information to be added to Margo's phone so she could call them.

The problem was that her family had been given her contact information as well, and so far, her mother had called five times and her future sister-in-law had called twice, putting Margo's brother on the line for all of thirty seconds to ask how she was doing.

Her mother sighed. "It's nice for a day or two, even a week, but we don't know when we will be allowed to go back. Do you have any updates on how long we will have to hide out here?"

"I've already told you. Hopefully, less than two weeks. I have to go, Mom. Someone needs to talk to me."

Negal smiled at the small lie and moved his lips, pretending to be talking, and making Margo choke on a chuckle that came out sounding like a cough.

"Are you sick?" Margo's mother sounded worried. "Why are you coughing?"

"Just a dry throat. I need to drink something."

"Okay. Call me when you can."

"I will." Margo ended the call and dropped the phone with a sigh. "I love them to pieces, but they are driving me crazy. I'm tired and achy, and I don't have any patience, but if I tell my mother how I feel, she will start freaking out, and I really don't have the patience for that either."

Smiling, Negal gathered her into his arms so she was nestled against his chest. "Rest, Nesha. If they call again, I will answer for you and tell them that you are asleep."

Margo chuckled softly. "Then they will want to know who you are." She turned to look up at him. "What do I tell them about you?"

"That I'm your fabulous new paramour, and that you are madly in love with me, and that we are going on an expedition to Tibet."

She snorted. "Yeah, and that will fly so well with them. They will think that you are manipulating me and demand to meet you." She sighed. "I'm never that rash, and they know it. I take weeks to plan a weekend in Vegas."

Negal hadn't known that about her, but he should have. Margo was cautious in every aspect of her life, not just who she took to her bed.

"I hope Aru gets an extension from your commander," she said. "He promised that he would try if I start transitioning, and I have." She scrunched her nose. "At least, I think I am. I hope I am. Otherwise, I will get really worried about what's wrong with me."

"You are transitioning, my love. Even Kian said so, and he's the biggest skeptic I know."

The truth was that Negal was almost certain that Margo was transitioning, but he wasn't a hundred percent sure. He was waiting for Frankie and Dagor to leave for the wedding and for Margo to doze off so he could give her a transfusion of his blood.

Dagor had told him where he'd stashed the rest of the disposable syringes he'd pilfered from the clinic, so all that was required now was the right opportunity.

As Dagor and Frankie's bedroom door opened and the two stepped into the living room, Margo tried to whistle, but all that came out was a whoosh of air.

"You two look hot," she said. "I wish I could come with you."

"You can." Frankie patted the elaborate up-do she'd created. "You can put on something comfortable and spend the evening sitting in a chair. You don't have to do anything strenuous."

"It's okay." Margo smiled. "Negal and I will watch the wedding from here. They are broadcasting it live."

"I know." Frankie grinned. "I was in your shoes not too long ago."

Dagor wrapped his arm around his mate's waist. "We need to go, or we will be late. They lock the doors as soon as the bride walks in, and we will not be allowed in."

"Yeah, I know." Frankie cast one last sad look at Margo. "Feel better, bestie." She blew her a kiss and then flounced toward the front door with Dagor.

When the door closed behind them, Margo pulled the blanket up to her chin and yawned. "I'm so tired."

"Then sleep." Negal shifted her so her head was on the pillow, and then lifted her legs so she was supine.

"I don't want to miss the ceremony." She waved a feeble hand in the direction of the television. "Can you please find the channel they are broadcasting it on?"

"Of course."

She'd dozed off several times during the afternoon, but she'd refused to go to the bedroom and get a proper sleep as long as the others were around, and since her family had kept calling her, she wouldn't have gotten much sleep anyway.

Negal perched on the edge of the couch beside her. "I'll wake you up when it starts. You've been taking catnaps for the past couple of hours, and they seem to help you."

Margo nodded and then yawned again. "It's about to start shortly. I can sleep after it's done."

That was true, but he wasn't sure she would be able to keep her eyes open for much longer. Besides, he was itching to be done with the transfusion. The sooner she got it, the sooner she would get better.

"I wish Jasmine could at least watch the weddings on the screen." Margo curled on her side, facing the television. "She must be going out of her mind down there, all alone without even the staff to keep her company."

"I'm sure not everyone is working, and some people stayed behind." He reached for the remote and turned the television on. "She'll be fine."

Margo's concern for those she cared about was one of the many things he loved about her, but in this case, her worry was misplaced. Jasmine was safe in the staff area, and if Negal was being honest, he wasn't entirely sure he trusted the woman with her overly charming smiles and calculating eyes. Her scent was fresh and devoid of any undertones of deceit, but emotional scents were not the equivalent of a truth detector. Sometimes, they lied.

Margo didn't look entirely convinced that her friend was fine, but she allowed herself to be distracted as the screen filled up with a sweeping shot of the dining room.

"Wow, look at that," Margo breathed. "The place looks completely different every night. It's amazing what a transformation they can create with just the help of colorful lighting."

More than that went into decorating the ship's grand dining room and turning it into a space worthy of a gala, but she was right about the strategically placed colorful beams of light being the most impactful.

As the camera panned over the glittering tables and the array of immortals in their finest attire, Negal's thoughts drifted to the transfusion.

It wouldn't be enough for her to fall asleep for him to do the deed. As soon as he injected her, she would wake up from the needle jab, and he would have to explain what he had done and why.

Negal needed to thrall Margo whether he liked it or not, and the thought made his stomach twist with unease.

It was a betrayal of her trust, even though it was necessary.

Kian was not willing to compromise on the issue of letting any more people know about the miraculous healing powers of a god's blood, and even though Negal didn't answer to Kian, he answered to Aru, and Aru had promised Kian to guard the secret.

Besides, Kian was the Anumati heir's son, and even though he could never become an heir himself because he was a hybrid, he still deserved Negal's deference.

Mind made up, Negal took her hand and looked into her eyes. "Margo, my love."

She turned to him. "Yes?"

"Nothing." He smiled. "I just love looking into your eyes."

He reached inside her mind and gently wove the suggestion to sleep into her thoughts, his mental voice a soothing whisper against the edges of her consciousness.

"You're so tired, my love," he murmured aloud while making her feel her eyelids growing heavy, her limbs slacking and relaxing.

Nothing would rouse her from this slumber save a sweet kiss from her mate's lips.

He watched Margo's eyes flutter shut and a small, contented smile curve her lips. She looked so peaceful, so serene, that he was tempted to lean down and kiss her, but his kiss was what would wake her up, so he had to stifle the impulse and continue with his plan.

Retrieving the syringe from Frankie and Dagor's room, he tore the wrapping off on his way back to the couch.

Negal sat down, uncapped the needle, and positioned it against his inner elbow. By now, he was a veteran at this, and as he jabbed the needle into his vein, he didn't even flinch. After withdrawing about half an ounce, he took Margo's hand and moved the needle to the same spot on her inner elbow.

One quick prick, and it was done. Negal watched as the small quantity of his blood flowed into Margo's vein, and when there was nothing left, he withdrew the needle and pressed his finger to the spot. Then he licked it, sealing the tiny puncture, and was happy to see that the spot in Margo's inner elbow looked pristine.

With the procedure done, he collected what he had used and took it to his and Margo's bedroom. He couldn't risk anyone discovering the evidence in the trash bin, so he put the syringe back into its wrapping and stashed it in a pocket of his suitcase to discard later.

The transfusion was a small deception, a white lie told in service of a greater truth, but it still sat heavy on his chest.

Pushing the feeling aside, Negal returned to Margo's side. As his hand ghosted over her cheek in a feather-light caress, she stirred slightly at his touch, her lips parting with a soft sigh. He leaned down and brushed his lips against hers, the contact sending a jolt of electricity humming through his veins.

Her eyelids fluttered open. "Mmm," Margo murmured, her voice husky with sleep. "Did I miss anything? Has the wedding started?"

Negal forced a smile, hoping it didn't look as strained as it felt. "Not yet, my love. You dozed off for only a few minutes."

Margo lifted a hand to her face and rubbed her eyes. "That's strange. It felt like such a deep sleep. I've never slept so deeply for such a short time before."

A pang of remorse lanced through him, but he pushed it down, burying it beneath a layer of practiced nonchalance.

"Your body is going through a major change, and it needs rest, but you are fighting it because you are adamant about watching the wedding ceremony in real time. You know that you can watch it later, right?"

"I know, but it's not going to be as impactful as seeing it as it happens. I'm so curious to hear Onegus's vows. He's such an enigmatic guy."

Negal's jealousy flared. "In what way?"

Margo shrugged. "He's the chief Guardian, which I assume is like a general, but he looks and acts like a politician, charming and smiling and all that."

"Yeah, you're right. I've never thought of that. I think he's also a council member, so maybe he has some political aspirations."

"Is the clan a democracy? Could he run for office and replace Kian?"

Margo sounded worried, which was interesting. She didn't know either of the males well, but she'd spent some time in their presence, and it seemed that she had a preference for Kian.

"I don't think so, but I'm not part of the clan, so I don't know its inner workings."

Margo's gaze drifted to the television screen, and Negal's followed just as the camera panned over the assembled guests.

"They are all so pretty," she murmured. "Look, that's Frankie and Mia."

"I see them." He shifted his eyes to his mate, whose face was alight with excitement. "And I see you, my beautiful Nesha. My soul."

11

ONEGUS

Onegus stood at the altar, waiting for the female he loved more than anyone and anything in the world to enter and join him in front of the goddess.

He still remembered his reaction to her the first time he'd seen her at the fundraiser gala. She'd stood out from the crowd in every way possible. Confident, elegant, statuesque, and with ferocious eyes that could pierce through armor. They had certainly pierced through his.

Up until that moment, he had never believed in love at first sight, but he was a believer now. With one look, he had fallen head over heels, but it had taken him a few days to convince his brain of what his heart had known from that first connection formed from a distance in a crowd of over one thousand guests.

Come to think of it, the gala had been a much grander venue than his and Cassandra's wedding in the ship's converted dining room, but what it lacked in luxury and opulence, it made up with heart, and there was no competition. He would choose to be here a thousand times over. Almost his entire clan was present, their familiar smiling faces turned toward the entrance through which his bride was about to walk in.

As the music swelled and the guests rose to their feet, Onegus felt his breath catch in his throat. There, at the end of the aisle, Cassandra stood tall in a one-of-a-kind gown that seemed to have been crafted from liquid pearls. The dress lacked any of the embellishments so many of the other brides had favored. There was no lace, no tulle, no beading, just simple satin that flowed over Cassandra's gorgeous statuesque frame. Barely-there straps held a cowl neckline, and although he couldn't see the back, it seemed like it was exposed.

Her hair was swept up in an elegant twist, with a few wayward tendrils left loose to frame her beautiful face, and her luminous, expressive eyes held Onegus's gaze.

There was joy, love, and determination in her big brown eyes, and as her lips lifted in a smile that seemed to be just for him, he lifted a hand to his heart and patted the spot, letting her know without words what seeing her on the other end of the aisle was doing to him.

Cassandra glided toward him with her mother on one side and her sister on the other, and as she reached the altar, Geraldine placed her daughter's hand in his. He squeezed her fingers gently, and she rewarded him with a radiant smile before turning to face the Clan Mother.

Annani regarded them with a serene smile, her ancient, wise eyes, which belied her youthful appearance, shining with affection and approval.

The goddess raised her glowing arms and waited until the guests' excited murmurs quieted.

When the hall was utterly silent, she lowered them. "My beloved family and friends," she said in her melodious voice. "Tonight, we are gathered to celebrate the union of two souls, two hearts that have found each other across a room not much different than this one." She waved a hand over the dining hall. "Onegus never imagined that the gala he chaired would not only raise millions for our charity but also bring him the love of his life."

As Onegus felt Cassandra's fingers tightening around his, he ran his thumb over her knuckles in a soothing caress.

His groomsmen were worried about her getting overly emotional and unintentionally blowing something up, but he knew his bride well, and positive emotions did not cause her inner power to rise.

Hopefully, all of tonight would be joyful for her, and nothing would irritate her.

Annani shifted her gaze to the two of them and smiled. "Onegus and Cassandra. You are both highly accomplished, powerful people, and together, there is no limit to what you can achieve. I have no doubt that your love story will be told for generations to come." She smiled brightly. "And I cannot wait to see the children your union will produce."

As laughter mingled with murmurs of agreement, Onegus cast Cassandra a sidelong smile, which she returned. They were too busy to have children anytime soon, but when they did, he knew that they would be spectacular.

"Onegus," Annani said, drawing his attention. "You have given selflessly to the clan for many centuries, leading the Guardian force with a strong hand but also with devotion and compassion. Your people love you, and that is the highest honor a commander could hope for. You have more than earned the boon of a fated mate the Fates have bestowed upon you. None other than the granddaughter of my cousin Toven."

Onegus dipped his head.

Cassandra was even closer to her godly source than he was, but he never really thought about it. He loved her for who she was and not the blood coursing through her veins.

"Cassandra." The Clan Mother turned to his bride. "Your strength, resilience, and your dedication to those you love is as inspiring as that of your mate. You have faced challenges that would have broken a lesser woman, and yet you have emerged stronger, brighter, and more successful. You are a true winner."

As Geraldine sniffled, Cassandra gracefully inclined her head. "Thank you, Clan Mother."

Annani smiled. "Cassandra and Onegus. You have each made sacrifices to support those you care about and have proven that love can conquer all. Love knows no boundaries, it can overcome any obstacle, weather any storm, and emerge victorious on the other side."

She paused, signaling to their guests that it was okay to clap, cheer, and hoot, and when she lifted her arms, everyone quieted again. "Before I bless your union and pronounce you bonded for life, would you like to recite your vows to each other?"

"Yes, we would," Cassandra said.

CASSANDRA

Cassandra had never considered herself overly emotional. She'd prided herself on being pragmatic, assertive, and as far from a softie as could be. And yet as she stood at the altar with her hand clasped firmly in Onegus's, she was overwhelmed, and not just because she was officially marrying the male she loved above all.

So much had happened since that first meeting at the gala. She had discovered that her forgetful mother, whom she had been taking care of since she was a young girl, was a demigoddess who had suffered a traumatic brain injury that would have killed even an immortal. She also discovered that she had an older sister, a grown-up nephew who was a gifted hacker, an uncle who was a demigod who had been helping her and her mother since day one, and, to top it all, her grandfather was a god.

It was all so unbelievable that she often expected to wake up one morning and realize that it had all been a dream because stuff like that just didn't happen to normal people. But then, Cassandra had always known that she was different. Normal people couldn't blow things up with a thought or stop someone's heart, but she could, and she had done both.

Oh boy. Talk about inappropriate thoughts at a time like this.

Turning to her groom, her mate, the love of her life, she saw the same emotions reflected in his smiling, blue eyes.

"Onegus, my love. When I first met you, I thought I had you all figured out. I thought I knew exactly who you were—just another rich, charming playboy looking for his next conquest."

A ripple of laughter went through the crowd, and Onegus's lips twitched with amusement, his eyes sparkling with mirth.

"But you are so much more than that. You are kind and generous and so unbelievably patient. When you decided that I was the one for you, you took the time to get to know me, to understand me, and to love me for all that I am, flaws and punch bowls blowing up and all."

She paused as another wave of laughter swept through the crowd. "You have become my sanctuary and my home. You believe in me, support me, and you love me with a fierceness that takes my breath away."

Onegus's hand tightened around hers, his eyes shining with love.

"And so, today, I vow to be your partner in life, to stand by your side through every triumph and every challenge, to love you with every fiber of my being, and to cherish every moment we have together. You are my heart, my soul, and my forever. And I promise to spend every day of our forever showing you just how much you mean to me." She pulled her hand out of his and extended it to her sister, who handed her a ring. "I, Cassandra, daughter of Geraldine, granddaughter of Toven, take thee, Onegus, son of Martha, as my forever mate, to love and to hold in this world and the next." She slipped the simple gold circle on his finger. "I'm never letting you go."

As she finished, a single tear escaped down her cheek.

Onegus reached up with his free hand to brush it away. "Cassandra, my love, my light. From the moment I first saw you, I knew that you were unlike anyone else I've ever encountered, and given how old I am, that's saying something." A few chuckles sounded from the crowd, but he continued. "I knew that you were a force to be reckoned with, a woman of strength, intelligence, and incredible beauty, inside and out."

Cassandra smiled as she felt her heart swell with love and gratitude for this incredible male who had swept into her life and changed everything.

"Winning your heart has been the greatest adventure of my life. Our love was explosive from the very start." He paused to let the crowd clap and cheer. "You've brought so much excitement to my life, and given what I deal with day in and day out, that's saying something as well." He cast a sidelong glance at the crowd. "Being with you is a joy and a blessing that I thank the Fates for every day." He lifted their joined hands to his lips, pressing a kiss to her knuckles. "And so, today, I vow to be your husband, your mate, and your best friend. I vow to support you in all your endeavors, to catch you when you stumble, and to celebrate every victory by your side. I vow to love you fiercely, passionately, and unconditionally for all the days of our lives."

Cassandra's vision blurred with tears, her heart so full she thought it might explode.

Oh boy. Don't think about explosions.

"You are my everything, Cassandra. My reason for being, my guiding star, and my home. And I promise to spend every moment of forever cherishing you, honoring you, and loving you with every beat of my heart." He pulled a ring out of his pocket. "I, Onegus, son of Martha, take thee, Cassandra, daughter of Geraldine, granddaughter of Toven, as my forever mate, to love and to hold in this world and beyond." He slipped the ring on her finger.

As he finished, Annani stepped forward once more. "By the power vested in me by the Fates and in the presence of your loved ones, I pronounce you bonded mates, partners in life, in love, and in all things. You may now kiss."

As Onegus pulled Cassandra into his arms, his lips meeting hers in a passionate kiss, she hooked her arms around his neck and kissed him back.

13

PETER

Peter cast a sidelong glance at Jay, who was clapping, whooping, and whistling, enthusiastically adding noise to the ruckus the Guardians were making in honor of their chief's nuptials.

Not wishing to be outdone, Peter stuck two fingers in his mouth and emitted a whistle loud enough to rouse a firehouse.

The cheering went on during the kiss that the newlywed couple performed for their audience, and it didn't quiet down until Onegus took Cassandra's hand and led her to the dance floor for the first dance of the evening.

Peter glanced at the doors to the dining room, and when he saw them open, he clapped Jay on his back. "Let's go. Our dates are waiting for us."

The Clan Mother had departed through a secret passage that took her to one of the staff elevators that had been blocked off just for her.

Jay shook his head, looking like he'd awoken from a daze. "Yeah. Wow, that was something else." He shook his head. "I would have never imagined Onegus could deliver such a mushy speech."

"Mushy?" Peter arched a brow. "It wasn't mushy. Compared to the others, it was damn funny. I laughed so hard when he talked about Cassandra blowing up the punch bowl. At first, he covered up for her, but later, they both admitted that it was her doing." He started toward the exit.

"I remember." Jay fell into step with him. "I wasn't fond of Cassandra at first. She seemed a little standoffish, but later I realized that it was a defense mechanism. She lived in constant fear of accidentally blowing things up and harming people."

"Yeah, must have been tough. She didn't know what the hell was wrong with her."

Peter still thought that Cassandra was a little snooty, but if she made Onegus happy, which she obviously did, then he had absolutely no problem with her. He thought about Marina and her shifting moods. She'd been a little off today, probably shaken by her admission that she wanted more from him than he could give her.

He would have loved nothing more than to invite her to live with him in his house, but what would be fun in the short term would be excruciatingly painful in the long run, and he had to be smart about it.

As they approached the bar, the sound of laughter drifted to meet them. But there was an edge to it, a brittle quality that set Peter's teeth on edge.

Rounding the corner, they found Marina and Larissa, where they had left them less than an hour ago. They were still perched on the same barstools, but now their cheeks were flushed, and their eyes were a little too bright.

"Peter!" Marina's voice was screechy and loud. "And Jay! You are finally back." She leaned over to her friend. "Larissa and me, we thought that you forgot about us."

"Never," Peter said.

As he walked over to her, Marina started to slide off the stool, but wobbled precariously, and as he caught her, she fell into his arms with a giggle and a burp. "Sorry." She put a hand over her mouth and giggled again.

"Someone had a glass or two too many," he murmured. "How many have you had?"

Marina waved a dismissive hand. "I don't know. Ask Vasyli."

Beside them, Jay was helping Larissa off her own stool. He looked concerned even though his date didn't look half as inebriated as Marina.

Peter turned to the bartender. "How much did Marina have?"

"A lot." Vasyli smiled sheepishly. "I tell them both it was too much," he said in heavily accented English. "But they don't listen."

Marina's head whipped around, her eyes narrowing into a glare. "You're such a lousy bartender," she accused, her words slurring slightly. "You just broke the sacred trust between a customer and their barman. You released confidential information to a third party."

Peter bit back a smile at her drunken indignation. Even three sheets to the wind, his girl was a firecracker.

"I'm hungry," Larissa announced, leaning heavily against Jay. "Let's go inside and have dinner," she said in Russian, probably forgetting that Marina wanted her to practice her English. "The kitchen is serving beef Stroganoff tonight, and it's my favorite."

Jay seemed to understand what she'd said and started toward the dining hall but then stopped and looked over his shoulder. "Are you coming?"

"You two go ahead. We'll catch up in a bit."

Peter tightened his hold on his unsteady date. "Hey." He brushed a strand of blue hair off her forehead. "How about we step outside for a little bit? Some fresh air will do you good."

"Great idea." She nodded. "It might help, or I might puke over the railing. One of the two."

Peter chuckled. "Throwing up will be good for you too. You will feel better after that."

He glanced over at Vasyli, who was watching the exchange with amusement in his eyes. "Do you have any bottled water back there?"

When the bartender nodded and reached beneath the bar, Peter held up two fingers. "I'll take two, just in case. And a bunch of napkins, please."

He hoped Marina wouldn't throw up, but if she did, he wanted to be prepared.

As Vasyli handed over the bottles and the napkins, Peter stuffed the items into the pockets of his tuxedo jacket.

"Come on, sweetheart," he murmured, wrapping an arm around her waist and guiding her towards the terrace doors. "Let's get you some fresh air."

As they stepped out into the cool night and leaned against the railing, the salty tang of the ocean filled their lungs, and the night breeze caressed Marina's flushed cheeks.

The tension in her shoulders eased, and she tipped her head back to gaze up at the star-strewn sky. "It's beautiful out here," she whispered. "Peaceful."

Peter hummed in agreement, his own eyes drinking in the soft glow of the moonlight on her face. "Not as beautiful as you," he said, the words slipping out before he could stop them.

Marina's gaze snapped to his, her eyes wide and shining in the darkness. For a long moment, they stared at each other, the air between them crackling with tension.

He lifted a hand to cup her cheek. "What's wrong, sweetheart? Are you nervous about attending the wedding party?"

Marina opened her mouth to answer but then lurched forward, her hand flying to her mouth. "I'm gonna be sick," she mumbled, her words muffled behind her fingers.

Springing into action, Peter spun her towards the railing, one hand gathering her hair back while the other rubbed soothing circles between her shoulder blades.

Marina retched, her slender frame shuddering as she emptied the contents of her stomach into the dark water below.

When she was done, he turned her to face him, fishing a napkin out of his pocket and wiping her mouth as gently as he could and handed her a bottle of water to drink from.

"Thank you." She gurgled with some of the water, spit it out over the railing, and then drank the rest.

"Feeling better?" he asked.

Marina nodded, her eyes glassy with tears and something that looked a lot like shame. "I'm sorry." Reaching into her purse, she pulled out a box of mints and popped a bunch of them into her mouth.

Peter shook his head. "It's not a big deal. Happened to me on more than one occasion." Actually, he'd never gotten drunk enough to puke his guts out, but he didn't want her to feel embarrassed.

"You don't understand," Marina murmured. "I ruined everything."

He frowned. "What are you talking about? You didn't ruin anything."

Was she referring to her earlier admission that she wanted to move in with him?

He pulled her into his arms, tucking her head beneath his chin and running a soothing hand down her back. "You couldn't ruin anything even if you tried."

The truth of his words reverberated in his mind against the backdrop of the distant strains of music drifting out from the dining room and the crash of waves against the hull filling the night air.

Peter wanted Marina in his house just as much as she wanted to be there. He just hadn't had the guts to admit it or to act on it.

14

MARINA

The cool night air washed over Marina, helping clear her mind while Peter's arm around her waist provided a steadying presence. She leaned into him, grateful for his solid strength, for the way he seemed to anchor her even as the world tilted and spun around her.

She hadn't meant to drink so much. She hadn't planned on drowning her sorrows in endless glasses of too-sweet cocktails. But watching the gorgeous bride and her bridesmaids get ready to enter the dining hall, resplendent in their designer gowns and glowing with joy, had triggered an ache inside of her that was too difficult to overcome.

She'd hoped the alcohol would help, which was stupid because it never did. It only made things worse.

Marina was happy for the bride and groom and wished them all the happiness in the world, but she wanted what the bride had—the beautiful dress that was precisely what Marina would have chosen for her own wedding if she could afford it, and the wonderful, loving groom waiting for her at the altar and feeling like the luckiest man alive because this amazing woman had chosen him.

But that wish felt further out of reach than ever before, a distant mirage shimmering on the horizon of a cloudy future.

Marina didn't have a wonderful groom waiting for her at the altar. Her fiancé had dumped her for another woman, and she didn't even have a boyfriend. What she had was a web of lies and half-truths, a house of cards that was about to come tumbling down the moment she confessed her scheming to Peter.

And she would confess because she had to, and not just because she'd promised Larissa she would do it. A sort of morbid curiosity urged her to tell Peter the truth and witness his reaction.

Would he forgive her?

Or would he use it as an excuse to dump her right now?

The thought of watching the warmth in his eyes turn to hurt and betrayal was terrifying, but evidently, she was a masochist, and not just in bed.

Mother of All Life, help me do the right thing.

Tears stinging her eyes, Marina blinked them back furiously. She was tired of crying, tired of feeling defeated and unworthy.

Peter's arm tightened around her, his fingers splaying over her hip. "Hey," he murmured, his breath warm against her temple. "What's going on in that head of yours?"

Marina shivered, not because she was cold but because it was time, and she was terrified.

"You're shivering." He slipped out of his jacket and draped it over her shoulders.

The fabric was warm from his body heat, the scent of his cologne clinging to it, and Marina had the silly urge to bury her nose in it like a lovesick fool.

"Talk to me, Marina." Peter hooked a finger under her chin and turned her to face him. His hands came up to frame her face, his thumbs sweeping over her cheekbones. "Are you angry at me? Disappointed in me? What did I do?"

Marina squeezed her eyes shut. "I'm not angry or disappointed at you." A ragged breath left her lungs. "I'm angry at myself."

Peter's brow furrowed. "Why?"

"I'm scared that if I tell you, you'll hate me."

A shadow of apprehension crossed his handsome face, but he didn't pull away and didn't release her from the shelter of his arms.

"Try me," he said.

"I lied to you," the words tumbled from her lips in a rush. "When we first met, when I first approached you, it wasn't because I was attracted to you. Or, well, I was, but that wasn't the only reason."

Peter went still, his fingers tightening fractionally on her face. But he remained silent, his eyes fixed on hers with an intensity that stole her breath.

"I wanted to get out of Safe Haven. I told you that part. I was desperate to start over somewhere far away from the memories and the heartache, and I came up with a plan. If I could find an immortal who would fall in love with me, he might invite me to the village to live with him, and I would be set. I scanned the dining room during every meal, searching for the perfect candidate, and you caught my attention because you looked sad like I was. You needed someone to shower you with love and attention, and I figured that you wouldn't be too discriminating and might accept a human with blue hair and a nice smile."

She trailed off as shame and self-loathing rose like bile in her throat. Mother of All Life, saying it out loud made it sound even worse, even more manipulative and cruel.

"I used you," she whispered, hot tears spilling down her cheeks. "I used your kindness and open heart for my own selfish ends. And I am sorry for that, but in the end, I was the fool because I fell in love with you, and you don't feel the same about me. So once again, I'm the one holding the short end of the stick."

A sob tore from her throat, and Marina buried her face in her hands, her shoulders shaking with the force of her anguished confession. She waited for Peter's arm to fall away from her, waited for him to say something polite but final, but neither happened.

Instead, his arms tightened around her, pulling her into his warm, solid chest. "Oh, Marina," he murmured, his voice a low rumble against her ear. "My sweet, beautiful Marina." His heartbeat thrummed beneath her cheek as he stroked a hand down her back in long, soothing passes.

She lifted her head, blinking up at him through a veil of tears. "You're not mad at me?"

Peter's lips curved in a rueful smile. "Oh, I'm angry, but not at you." He brushed his fingers over her cheek. "I'm angry at the circumstances that made you feel like you had to resort to deception. I'm angry at your ex-boyfriend and the Kra-ell before him who made you doubt your own worth. But most of all, I'm angry at myself for pushing you away."

Marina shook her head. "None of this is your fault. I'm the one who schemed and deceived, who..."

"Who did what she had to do to make her life bearable," he finished for her. "I understand why you did it, and I'm not mad at you for that. We all have our ulterior motives for going after someone. Have you stopped to consider that all I wanted from you was a few tumbles in bed? Is that any better than what you wanted? More noble? If anything, it's worse. And just like you, I fell prey to my own scheming. Instead of seducing a sexy, beautiful woman, having my wicked way with her, and then forgetting all about her when the cruise was over, I fell in love with her, and I don't want to let her go."

Fresh tears spilled down Marina's cheeks, but this time, they were tears of relief.

He was right, but that didn't diminish the sweetness of his admission.

"Do you really mean it?" she whispered, curling her fingers into the fabric of his shirt. "Do you love me enough to keep me even though I'm just a human?"

He leaned down, his forehead pressing against hers. "I love you, Marina. That's all I can say. I don't know how we will make it work, but we have to try because I can't think of life without you."

The sob that escaped Marina's lips was part relief that he wasn't pushing her away and part despair because they really didn't have a future together. Surging up on her toes, she captured Peter's mouth and poured every ounce of her love for him into the kiss.

Peter banded his arms around her waist and lifted her off her feet, kissing her like a man possessed.

When they finally broke apart, chests heaving and hearts racing, Marina felt lighter than she had in years. The weight of guilt had lifted off her shoulders, replaced by the buoyant, effervescent joy of love requited. Her happy cloud had a big rock tied to it, but at this moment, the buoyancy was strong enough for her to soar despite the weight dragging behind.

"I love you so much," she whispered. "I will spend every day trying to be worthy of you."

Peter's eyes shone with a happiness that took her breath away. "You already are, Marina." He pulled her into another kiss, this one softer, sweeter, a promise of forever sealed with the press of his lips.

Marina felt a sense of peace settle over her. She was where she was meant to be, which was in the arms of the man she loved, or rather the immortal who, against all odds, loved her back.

15

AMANDA

When Onegus had swept Cassandra into his arms, the cheering and hooting had gone for much longer than it had for Amanda and Dalhu, and even though Alena and Orion hadn't gotten that much applause either, it still irked.

Amanda hated feeling petty and jealous, but she couldn't help it. So yeah, Onegus was the chief Guardian, and his people respected and appreciated him, but she was the princess, the clan's darling, the one who had set them on the path of finding Dormants who, in turn, had become life-long partners. If not for her, Onegus would have never suspected that Cassandra could be a Dormant, and she would have become just one more conquest in the endless string of them.

Oh, well. Amanda let out a sigh. She had a job to do and another happy couple to match.

Her gut was telling her that Jasmine was a Dormant, and even though Amanda had been wrong about that before, this time she was sure she was right because of the extraordinary circumstances of Jasmine finding her way to the clan. The more bizarre and unlikely the path was, the stronger the indicator for the Fates' intervention.

Craning her neck, she swept her gaze across the crowded ballroom, searching for Max. She spotted him by the bar, his blond head and boisterous bearing setting him apart from the other patrons waiting to be served by Bob.

He was so perfect for Jasmine. She seemed like a fun-loving, easygoing person, and that was Max to a tee. Opposites might attract, but similar personalities made relationships stick. The best ones had a little bit of both.

Her Dalhu hated attention while she thrived on it, but they both had an eye for art and shared similar views about the world at large. In fact, the only thing they had ever argued about was how to raise Evie, but they had sat down, had a talk, and reached a compromise like a civilized couple should, so it was all good.

Leaning toward her mate, she cast him a bright smile. "I love you." She planted a kiss on his cheek. "I'm going to have a quick chat with Max and come back. Do you want me to get you something from the bar?"

"I'll come with you." He stood and offered her a hand up. "I'll order us drinks while you have your chat."

"Good plan." She let him pull her to her feet.

He wrapped his arm around her waist and started toward the bar. "Are you going to talk to him about Jasmine?"

"Why else would I want to talk to him?"

Dalhu shrugged. "I don't know. You don't tell me everything."

She arched a brow. "That's not true. I don't keep any secrets from you."

"It's not intentional. Sometimes you think that I'm not interested in this or that, so you skip over the things you think bore me, but you shouldn't. I find everything you say and do fascinating." He leaned and brushed his lips over the side of her mouth. "I just love listening to your voice and seeing the sparkle in your eyes when you get excited about something. You are so full of life and energy. So passionate."

"Oh, darling." She leaned into him. "You say the nicest things to me."

"I love you." He let go of her as they reached the bar. "Make it quick." Leaving her standing next to Max, Dalhu strode to the other end of the bar.

"Fates, I love this male," she murmured, taking a moment to admire the breadth of his shoulders and his tight ass. "Perfection." She tore her eyes away from her mate, plastered a smile on her face, and turned to the Guardian she'd come over to talk to. "Max, darling. I need a word with you."

He inclined his head. "I'm always at your service. What can I do for you?"

She shifted her weight to her other stiletto-clad foot. "I'll cut right to the chase. I think that our rescued damsel in distress is a potential Dormant. I've spent some time with her, as have Syssi and even Kian, and we all believe that she has a paranormal talent. In fact, I'm sure of it." She leaned closer and whispered conspiratorially, "I thought I should tell you first that there is an available Dormant on the ship before it becomes widely known and there is a stampede of males vying for her attention. You've been the groomsman for too long. It's time you became the groom."

"I'll pass." Max surprised her. "If Jasmine needs guarding, I'll go, but I'm not interested in her otherwise."

Amanda blinked. "Have you seen her?" she asked, not even trying to stifle the incredulity in her voice. "She's a stunning woman, and she's lonely, just waiting for someone to talk to. Right now, she's all alone in the staff lounge. You can go, have a little chat with her, and see if there is any attraction. If there is, great, and if not, someone else will gladly take your place."

Edgar, who was standing next to Max, turned around and lifted his hand. "If he won't, I will. Jasmine is one hell of a catch. She's beautiful, friendly, and not full of herself as so many beautiful women are."

Had his remark been directed at her?

Amanda pursed her lips. "I'm not stuck-up."

Edgar blanched. "I didn't mean you. Never. I meant human women, and it was a generalization."

She waved a dismissive hand. "You don't need to apologize. I might not be stuck-up, but I can admit to being vain." She smiled. "If I didn't have any flaws, I would be perfect, and that's boring." She shifted her gaze back to the obstinate Guardian. "Last chance, Max. If you don't want to go, Ed will."

Max shrugged. "I've seen Jasmine through the surveillance cameras, and she's beautiful, but she also reminds me of someone who I lost a friend over, someone who wasn't very discriminating with her affections and chose to indulge me when she knew my friend was in love with her. I was an ass for not realizing the depth of his feelings for her, but she wasn't blameless. I know that Jasmine is not her, but she is similar enough in character and looks that I can't help the aversion I feel."

It was silly to think that just because Jasmine looked like that woman, she was like her in other ways, but Amanda had to admit that Jasmine was a major flirt, so there could be more to the similarity than met the eye.

"I would love to go," the pilot said. "I would have visited Jasmine before, but we were told to stay away from the crew quarters because of the rescued women and their fear of men."

That was true, and she'd forgotten about it, but the rescued women had their own section of the staff quarters, and as long as Edgar didn't go to that area or to the staff dining room, it should be okay.

"Jasmine spends most of her time in the staff lounge, and the rescued women never go there. If you stay away from the staff dining room and their section of cabins, it should be fine."

Ed rubbed a spot behind his left ear. "What if I go down there and Jasmine is not in the lounge? She could have gone to bed already."

"Then you can try again tomorrow. She doesn't have a phone. Otherwise, I would call her and ask her to meet you there."

"I can check for you." Max pulled out his phone. "We have surveillance cameras in the lounge." He typed on his screen and then nodded. "She's there, watching television, and Amanda was right. She's all alone."

Edgar's face lit up. "Awesome!" He practically bounced on his feet. "I'll go right now."

Chuckling, Amanda held up a finger. "Don't you want to stay for the wedding dinner?"

Edgar's eyes widened, a look of inspiration crossing his face. "That's a great idea!" He snapped his fingers. "I'll load up two plates and take them down to the lounge. Jasmine and I can chat over dinner and get to know each other."

"Just be careful," Amanda cautioned. "Jasmine still doesn't know who we are, and it needs to stay that way, at least until Edna probes her. I was supposed to wait until after Edna had a chance to get a read on Jasmine's intentions, but I got excited by the idea of making another match." She cast an accusing look at Max. "I didn't expect my gesture to be refused."

"I'm sorry." Max smiled apologetically. "I can't help it. Just looking at her irritates me."

"Don't sweat it." Amanda let him off the hook and turned back to the pilot. "Jasmine thinks that this cruise has been organized by Perfect Match for its management and top employees, and that the secrecy surrounding it is to protect the privacy of some high-profile clients who met through the service and are getting married on the ship."

"Got it," Edgar said. "I can talk a mile about Perfect Match. I've been on six solo adventures so far, and it was amazing."

Max clapped a hand on Edgar's shoulder. "I hope Jasmine is the one for you."

"Alright." Amanda waved a hand at Edgar. "Go forth and conquer, Romeo."

"Thank you." The pilot sketched a mock salute. "Wish me luck!"

16

EDGAR

E dgar discovered that loading up two plates at the buffet table required careful maneuvering, and it also annoyed the people standing in line behind him because he was taking so long to decide what to load for Jasmine.

Succulent slices of roast beef or beef Stroganoff, creamy mashed potatoes or Persian rice, crisp green beans or mushrooms with onions. He didn't know what Jasmine liked, but he figured variety was the key. The problem was that he had only two hands and could maneuver only two plates.

He loaded each plate with different things with the intention of letting Jasmine choose what she wanted, and he would eat the rest. Edgar couldn't care less what she left for him to eat as long as she didn't dismiss him.

She wouldn't be rude, he knew that, but she could come up with a polite excuse that she wasn't hungry, or that she was bone tired and on her way to bed, or any other gentle letdown she could think of.

Ed wasn't like the hulking Guardians that women found irresistible, but being a pilot had its own allure as well. A civilian helicopter pilot was not as sexy as a jetliner captain or a military fighter pilot, but it was still better than having a boring desk job.

Hopefully, Jasmine would remember him fondly from the boat ride, and would welcome his company.

Ed had been lusting after Jasmine from the moment he'd first laid eyes on her back on Modana's yacht.

Those lush curves and that dazzling smile…

Fates, she could make any male salivate.

Well, except for Max, who was acting like an ass, but his loss was Edgar's gain.

With her long, olive-toned limbs, ample hips, flowing dark hair, and flirtatious eyes that sparkled with mischief and intelligence, Jasmine was a knockout. And that seductive voice of hers that had wrapped around him like warm honey…

As his erection punched against the zipper of his slacks, getting lodged in an uncomfortable angle, Edgar groaned.

With a loaded plate in each hand, he couldn't adjust himself, which meant that he was going to show up at the staff lounge with tented pants.

Dear Fates, have mercy on me.

Jasmine was every male's sex dream come to life, and he'd been the lucky guy who had happened to be in the right place at the right time.

Walking out of the dining room, he headed to the bar instead of taking the elevator down to the staff decks or the stairs. Now that the party had started, no one would be there, so he could put down the plates and adjust the angle of his shaft.

When it was done, he let out a sigh of relief, hefted the plates, and headed down to the staff lounge.

The truth was that Ed didn't care whether Jasmine was a Dormant or not. He was young, and he wasn't looking for his one and only. He had centuries stretching out before him and endless opportunities to find his fated mate. All he cared about right now was seducing or being seduced and spending the night between those lush thighs.

He found her curled up on one of the plush couches with a book in her lap, and as he entered, she lifted her head and smiled.

"Edgar." She set the book aside and rose to her feet. "Are you lost? Or are you looking for me?"

"I'm not lost." He lifted the plates he was carrying higher for emphasis. "Amanda told me that you were all alone down here, and I had the brilliant idea to share dinner with you. I hope that's okay."

"It's more than okay." She reached for one of the plates. "I'm so glad to see you. I wondered why you didn't come to visit." She cast him an accusing look and walked over to the nearest table. "I thought that you forgot about me." She put the plate down.

"You are unforgettable, Jasmine. I was told to stay away from the staff area because of the rescued women who occupy several cabins down here. They are scared of men."

"Oh, yeah. I've been told to be super gentle with them. The women eat in the staff dining room, and some of the staff are men, but I guess the rule applies only to the guests. It's easier to ensure that the staff behaves than the guests, right?"

If they were human, she would be right. But that wasn't the reason.

Jasmine looked at him with anticipation, and only when he put his plate down did he figure out why.

"Damn it. I forgot to bring silverware. I need to go back and bring some, along with napkins and glasses and something to drink."

He'd been so excited about the opportunity Amanda had given him that he hadn't thought about all the details. Or, more accurately, he'd been too busy imagining Jasmine naked.

She laughed. "We have everything we need down here." She rose to her feet and sauntered over to the bar area of the lounge.

He had to force his mouth to close as he watched her ass sway enticingly from side to side, her dark locks reaching just above the start of the curve, and what a curve it was. He'd never thought of himself as an ass man, but he was now.

Jasmine collected all the missing items from behind the counter and returned to the table.

"Now we can eat."

As she put down a napkin next to his plate and put a fork and a knife on it, Edgar took a deep inhale, and her scent almost knocked him out.

Was she aroused just from being near him?

That was how it worked for males, but usually not for females. They needed much more than the sight of a handsome male to get all hot and bothered.

Perhaps she'd been entertaining naughty thoughts before he got there?

He remembered that she had been reading a book when he'd walked in. Was it one of those raunchy romances with lots of sex in it?

As she finished setting up the table, he cast a quick glance at the book that was lying splayed open on the couch, both the front and back cover visible but not clearly from the angle he was looking at it. Still, he could discern a woman in a Victorian dress with a dark-haired guy standing behind her.

"What are you looking at?" Jasmine asked.

"Your book. What is it about?"

She laughed. "It's a silly romance. Nothing a manly man like you would be interested in."

17

JASMINE

Ed had interrupted a particularly steamy part in the book when he'd arrived in the lounge, but Jasmine didn't mind. She would rather have the real thing instead of reading about it any day of the week and twice on Sunday. It was Saturday, so perhaps twice on Saturday as well.

The pilot didn't emit the bad boy vibes that usually were her Achilles heel, but he was handsome and charming enough to compensate for the lack of spice.

She'd learned a long time ago that appearances could be deceptive, but he just didn't have that aura. Kian had it in spades, but he was taken, and Kevin even more so, but he was taken as well. Jasmine wondered what type of women managed to lasso such dangerous men. Syssi seemed mellow and shy, so maybe the old adage about opposites being attracted to each other was true. Then again, Jasmine didn't have a mellow or shy bone in her body, but she still liked edgy men, so maybe it wasn't true.

Edgar grinned. "A manly man? I hope you meant it as a compliment."

"Of course. Why wouldn't it be?"

He shrugged. "Nowadays, it's hard to tell. As long as manly man does not mean toxic masculinity, I guess I'm good."

She laughed. "There is nothing toxic about you. In fact, the only danger I could think of is you being too sweet."

His face fell. "That for sure is not a compliment. Sweet is not sexy."

"I disagree." She smiled suggestively. "Give me a fresh creampuff, and I'll show you how sexy it is to me."

As a pained groan escaped Edgar's throat, his eyes started glowing.

Was he crying?

Some men experienced excruciating pain when their arousal couldn't be immediately relieved, but usually that afflicted only very young men, and Edgar was in his late twenties or early thirties.

Perhaps she should take mercy on him and ease up on the flirting. "Let's dig in before this lavish feast gets cold." She lifted her knife and fork.

"Yes, indeed." He swallowed. "I didn't know what you like, so I piled different things on each plate. If there is something you like on mine, it's yours."

"I'm not a finicky eater," she said. "I'm perfectly happy with what's on my plate." She scooped some of the buttery mashed potatoes on her fork and found herself sighing with pleasure at the first bite.

The roast was also divine. "This is perfect," she murmured around a mouthful.

Glancing up at Edgar through her lashes, Jasmine expected to find him equally engrossed in his meal, but to her surprise, he was just watching her with those strange, glowing eyes.

"What is it?" she asked, suddenly self-conscious. "Do I have mashed potato on my nose?" She lifted a napkin and dabbed at it.

Edgar shook his head, his smile widening. "I just enjoy seeing you eating with such delight. It's so rare to see a beautiful woman with a healthy appetite. Food should be savored and enjoyed. It's one of life's pleasures, but so many women think that they should look like sticks and starve themselves." He leaned in closer. "Me? I love a woman with curves."

"You are like a decadent sundae, Edgar. You know all the right things to say to me."

Jasmine had every intention of inviting Ed back to her cabin once they were done with dinner, but first, she needed to pump him for information about Perfect Match and the mysterious guests whose privacy was so tightly protected.

"Those are not come-on lines," he said. "I'm just saying what's in my heart."

"I know, and that is what makes them even more precious to me." She set down her fork and fixed him with a coy smile. "Amanda and Kian visited me earlier, and Kian said something about sending a woman named Edna to probe me. Do you know what that's about?"

She watched Edgar closely, looking for any sign of recognition, any hint that he knew more than he was letting on. And sure enough, there it was—a slight tightening around his eyes, a barely perceptible stiffening of his shoulders.

"Edna, huh?" he said, his voice carefully casual. "Yeah, I know her. She's one of our special consultants."

Jasmine leaned forward, her eyes wide with feigned innocence. "Special how? What kind of probe does she use? Is it some kind of high-tech compatibility test?"

Edgar hesitated, and for a moment, Jasmine thought that he might clam up and change the subject, but then he shook his head. "Edna has a gift. She doesn't need any fancy equipment to see into people's hearts and souls. It's like a sixth sense. She can determine a person's intentions and innermost desires, and I'm not talking about desires of the flesh. I'm talking about desires of the soul."

Jasmine's breath caught in her throat, a thrill of something that might have been fear or excitement or both zinging through her veins. Was Edna a seer or a psychic?

Could it be that she was a fellow witch?

Would Edna be able to help her with the tangle of answers her divination had produced?

Jasmine had tried to connect online with other practitioners, and most had been eager to help, but their advice didn't improve her results. Some tried to give her alternative meanings, which had been somewhat helpful, but in her gut, she knew that the prince was not an idea but someone real that she had to find.

18

EDGAR

E dgar wondered where he had come up with that crap. Well, come to think of it, intentions and aspirations were desires of the soul, right?

Still, Jasmine looked much too shaken by his description of Edna's ability than was merited.

"Desires of the soul?" she whispered. "What do you mean by that?"

He remembered her talking about her acting career and how she only got to play a few minor parts in commercials.

"If you are consumed by a burning need to become a movie star, Edna will see that in your soul even if you don't tell her anything about yourself. She might not know precisely what you want, but she will know that you desire fame, acceptance, recognition, or whatever else your inner motives for wanting to be a famous actress might be."

There was disappointment in Jasmine's eyes, as she picked up her knife and fork again. "That doesn't sound as scary as a probe. I was afraid that she could read my thoughts." She cut off a piece of roast beef and put it in her mouth.

Edgar was having a hard time formulating his thoughts as he looked at her mouth and imagined all the things he wanted her to do with it.

When she was done chewing, she regarded him with a small smile. "I've never thought about what motivates me to want to be an actress, and the funny thing is that it's none of the things you mentioned. Well, that's not true. I want to be famous and make a lot of money, but that's not the main reason."

"Then what is it?"

She shrugged, forked a few green beans, and put them in her mouth, probably to give herself a few minutes to think.

"When I auditioned for the first musical production in middle school, it was because a friend of mine convinced me that I had the perfect voice for the part, and since the person who was supposed to play that part had dropped out, it was a sure thing. The thought of performing on stage terrified me, but I went to the audition anyway, not really expecting to get the part. I must have impressed the drama teacher, or maybe she was desperate because it was so late in the production, and I was in."

She smiled, her eyes assuming a distant look as she walked down memory lane. "I found a home in the theater club, a community of like-minded people. I loved the camaraderie and the grueling schedule of rehearsals, and I loved finally being good at something. I wasn't a brilliant student, but I was a good singer and actress, and people who hadn't given me a second look before were suddenly smiling at me, congratulating me on my performance, and wishing me luck. I became addicted to the rush." She sighed. "Regrettably, my amazing career didn't extend beyond high school. I got accepted to one of the most prestigious acting programs in the country, but my father didn't have the money for the insanely expensive tuition, and he said that there was no way he was taking on debt for a degree in acting."

"That's harsh, but I can understand his reasoning."

Jasmine nodded. "Yeah, so did I, but it didn't make it any less disappointing. Anyway, I went to a community college that had a drama program and continued my studies, but I was no longer the star of the show the way I was in high school." She speared a bite of roast beef with her fork. "But enough about me. Tell me about yourself and why Perfect Match Virtual Studios need a helicopter pilot."

Ed suppressed a groan. He wasn't really an employee of the company, but he had gone on enough virtual adventures to talk about it with a degree of expertise.

The only problem he had was lying to Jasmine. He didn't mind skirting the truth, but he didn't enjoy fabricating tales from thin air as he was about to do.

"Some of the virtual adventures involve piloting a helicopter, and that's where I come in. They record hours of footage of me flying the simulator, and this footage is later used by the artificial intelligence to create realistic scenarios for clients. They are developing adventures that are all about piloting a helicopter, a fighter jet plane, a commercial airliner, a submarine, etc."

Perhaps he could suggest that they actually do that, so it wouldn't be a lie.

She looked at him with awe. "That sounds like a dream job."

"It is. But I still love the real thing more." He leaned closer to her. "There is one adventure I want them to develop, which you would be perfect for."

"Oh yeah? Do they use real people in their simulations?"

"Of course. The two participants, but that's not what I'm talking about. You would be a perfect avatar for Aladdin's Jasmine." He chuckled. "You even have the same name." He reached for her hand. "But if they ever make an Aladdin Perfect Match adventure, I would love for you to partner with me as yourself, no avatar needed."

She grinned. "Let me guess. You'd be Aladdin."

He arched a brow. "Would you prefer Jafar?"

Jasmine laughed. "No, not Jafar, but I kind of had a thing for the genie."

19

JASMINE

Edgar's eyebrows shot up. "The blue balloon-like cartoon genie? No way."

Jasmine shrugged. "He made me laugh, and he had really big biceps. Aladdin looked like a sixteen-year-old boy."

"So? How old were you when you first saw the movie?"

"The first time, I was a little girl, and I was so excited that I was named after the main character and also looked a little bit like her. Then I watched it a couple of times as a teenager, and I didn't really click with Aladdin. As an adult, I kept dreaming about finding the magic lamp and having the genie at my command."

Ed shook his head. "Do I want to know what you wanted to ask the genie for?"

Jasmine leaned forward. "I'll make you a deal. You'll tell me your preferred version of the story, and if I like it,

I'll tell you mine."

He made a face. "That's not fair. I asked first."

Jasmine affected nonchalance. "Take it or leave it. That's my final offer."

He huffed out a breath. "You are a tough negotiator."

"So I've been told." She cut off another piece of meat and lifted it to her mouth.

"By whom?"

Jasmine paused with the fork suspended in midair. "Stop stalling. I won't tell you anything until you enchant me with your story first."

At this point, she was more curious about that than what Edgar could tell her about Perfect Match. Besides, if everything went well, he was going to spend the night with her, and she could ask him more questions over breakfast.

Her core twitched pleasantly at the thought.

Edgar was a delicious morsel of maleness, with clear blue eyes, a chiseled jaw, and a sensuous mouth that promised sinful kisses in all kinds of places.

Edgar smiled, the mischief and mirth in his eyes making him look even more handsome. "Princess Jasmine…"—he spread his hands theatrically—"is the most beautiful and desirable woman in all of Agrabah. Her sultry eyes and luscious curves have men falling at her feet, but she's bored with all the stuffy princes and dignitaries vying for her hand. She craves adventure and a man whose hands are callused from hard work and not smooth like a baby's ass."

Jasmine laughed. "Let me see your hands."

He shook his head. "This is my fantasy, not my reality. I don't have any calluses. I'm a pilot, not a woodcutter."

Jasmine smirked. "Oh, so you are Aladdin, the dashing street rat who's going to sweep me off my feet and show me the world?"

"Exactly." Edgar winked. "I'm the charming rogue who catches your eye in the marketplace. There's an instant spark between us, an undeniable chemistry that makes the air crackle with tension."

"Ooh, I like it."

Jasmine felt a thrill run down her spine and heat pooling low in her belly. Edgar was a good storyteller, but his story would have probably been less effective if Jasmine hadn't been reading a steamy book only moments earlier. She was still primed.

"Wait, the good bits are yet to come." He leaned back and crossed his arms over his chest. "When we meet in the market, I promise to visit you at the palace. You tell me not to come because it's dangerous. You reveal that you are extremely well guarded, and you are worried that I will get caught and executed on the spot. You can't stand the thought of losing me when you have only just found me."

Jasmine pushed the plate aside and leaned her elbows on the table. "So, it was love at first sight?"

"Of course." Edgar uncrossed his arms and leaned toward her, so their noses were almost touching. "I tell you that I would rather die than never see you again, but not to worry. I am an accomplished thief, and I won't get caught."

Jasmine smiled and picked up the storyline. "I wait for you every night, yearning for you to come but also dreading it. But as the nights pass and you don't show up, I start to worry that something has happened to you. I tell my handmaiden to bring me a commoner's cloak so I can slip away from the palace again, and just as she leaves to get it, I hear a knock on the terrace doors." She extended her hand, motioning for him to continue.

"Your room's balcony overlooks an inaccessible and therefore unguarded cliff, but I have a magic carpet that I got from the genie, and I use it to fly onto your terrace." Edgar's voice dropped an octave, taking on a seductive edge. "You open the doors for me and fall into my arms, sobbing with happiness. As I lift you into my arms and carry you to your enormous circular bed, you pepper my face with kisses."

Jasmine canted her head. "Why would a princess need a huge round bed?"

He rolled his eyes. "It's my fantasy, so let me tell it."

"Fine." She waved a hand. "Please, continue."

"You are draped in silks and a sheer gown that leaves very little to the imagination, and as I lay you down on the bed, your eyes darken with a hunger that matches my own."

Jasmine swallowed, her mouth suddenly dry. "And then what happens?"

Edgar's breath ghosted over her cheek. "My hands roam over your lush curves, caressing you through the thin fabric until you're trembling with need and begging me to undress you."

A soft moan escaped Jasmine's throat as his words conjured up vivid images in her mind. Tangled limbs, sweat-slicked skin, her pleasure coiling tighter and tighter.

"I tell you to have patience while I worship your body with my mouth and hands, and you are moaning my name. You tell me to lock the door so your hand-maiden won't be able to come in, and when I do, you take off your clothing and wait for me naked, so magnificent that I'm frozen in place for a moment."

"I call your name," Jasmine said. "And I cup my breasts, teasing my nipples. I tell you to get rid of your clothes and join me in bed."

As Edgar's breathing became labored, he reached for her hand and brought it to his lips for a kiss. "I do as you command, and when you see me naked, you lick your lush lips and tell me that I'm a dream come true. I climb onto the bed and dip my head between your spread thighs, asking your permission to taste you."

Jasmine clenched her thighs together, her core throbbing insistently as desire pulsed through her veins.

"I grant your wish."

"I pleasure you with my tongue and fingers until you're writhing beneath me and begging me to take you. When I finally slide deep inside you, joining us as one, it's like magic, like flying over an endless diamond sky."

"You paint a vivid picture." Jasmine could practically feel everything he'd described, and she wanted it. She wanted his hands on her, his hard body pressed against hers.

"You're my muse." The words were low and rough, laced with raw desire that made her shiver. "Say the word, Princess, and I'll show you a whole new world."

She lifted her eyes to the surveillance camera mounted near the ceiling, which was pointed right at Edgar's head. "Should we continue the story in a more private setting?" With a smoldering look, she rose to her feet and offered Edgar her hand.

She had no idea if he would be as skilled a lover as his fictional Aladdin, but she couldn't wait to find out. After all, every princess deserved to be thoroughly ravished by her street urchin at least once in her life, and if Edgar's performance was half as good as his imagination, she was in for a wonderful magical ride.

20

PETER

As Peter led Marina inside the grand dining room, the music and laughter seemed oddly distant, a muted backdrop to the storm of emotions raging in his heart.

He had surprised himself when he told Marina that he loved her and couldn't live without her. It was the truth, but he had never intended to voice it, not to himself and not to her.

Now that it was done, though, he felt at least a hundred pounds lighter. Keeping his feelings locked inside had been as bad for him as the guilt Marina had harbored had been bad for her. They had both lied to themselves and to each other, trying to protect their hearts but only hurting themselves more.

Admitting the truth and accepting the consequences was so incredibly liberating, but it was also daunting, because now what?

Hope for a scientific breakthrough that would make Marina immortal?

The notion wasn't as farfetched as it sounded. Perhaps over the next two decades, Kaia and Bridget would uncover the secret of immortality.

They found Jay and Larissa seated at the table and enjoying the wedding dinner. Their heads were bent close together as they talked and laughed, and Peter couldn't help but smile at the sight. They were somehow managing to communicate with her broken English and his rudimentary Russian and were having a good time together.

As he and Marina approached, Larissa's head snapped up, her eyes widening with concern as she took in Marina's disheveled appearance.

Marina was still wrapped in his jacket, which looked like a coat on her, and her hair was a mess.

He should have told her that she needed to fix it before they went inside, but he'd been too busy freaking out inside his own head to think straight.

"*Chto sluchilos'?*" Larissa asked in Russian, her brow furrowed. "*Ty v poryadke?*"

Marina waved off her friend's concern with a somewhat shaky smile. "*Ya v poryadke,*" she assured Larissa. "*Luchshe, chem v poryadke, na samom dele.*"

At Larissa's questioning look, Marina elaborated in English. "Everything's fine, Larissa. Better than fine, actually. I just had a little too much to drink on an empty stomach, that's all." She reached for a piece of bread from the basket on the table, tearing off a small chunk and popping it into her mouth. "I think I'll stick to bread and olives for now," she said to Peter. "And water. Lots and lots of water. But you should fill your plate from the buffet before your friends and family finish it all."

Peter squeezed her hand under the table. "I'll get both of us plates."

Marina shook her head. "I don't think it's a good idea for me to eat anything other than bread. Maybe later, I'll try something else." She smiled up at him. "When you go for seconds."

"As you wish." He pushed to his feet.

"I'll come with you." Jay looked at Larissa with affection in his eyes. "Do you want me to bring you another serving of beef Stroganoff?"

Her eyes sparkled. "Yes, please."

As Peter made his way towards the buffet table, Jay fell into step beside him. "I love watching Larissa eat. It's so erotic. She eats so daintily, and she looks like she's orgasming after every bite. I've been as hard as a rock the entire time you were outside."

Peter shook his head. "TMI, my friend. TMI."

Jay laughed. "Yeah. I have no filter. Is everything okay with you two?" he asked quietly, his gaze darting back to where Marina and Larissa were sitting, heads bent close together as they talked.

Peter hesitated for a moment. Soon, Marina would move in with him, so their love wouldn't be a secret anyway. Besides, he was a male in love, and he wanted to shout it from the rooftops, not hide it just because everyone he knew was going to think that he had lost his fucking mind.

"We're good." He let out a sigh. "Better than good, actually. We're in love."

Jay's eyebrows shot up, his expression shifting from surprised to skeptical. "You are in love with a human?"

Peter ran his fingers through his hair. "When it hits, there isn't much you can do about it. I don't know why the Fates chose a human for me, but I hope they know what they are doing and that it's not punishment for something I have done." He looked over his shoulder back to where Marina sat, her blue hair gleaming like a beacon. "She wants to move in with me."

Jay's eyes widened. "Kian will never agree."

"Why not? Marina knows who we are, and she wouldn't be the only human in the village. Several of those who served the Kra-ell moved into the village from Safe Haven, and Kian is contemplating inviting more. Atzil needs people to work in his bar, Callie needs servers and assistant cooks for her restaurant, and there are many other jobs that our people don't want to do."

Jay remained silent for a long moment. "What about you, Peter? What happens when she grows old? There is a good reason we don't form long-term relationships with humans, and it's not that we think of ourselves as superior."

Peter closed his eyes, a dull ache blooming in his chest. "I'll take whatever time she can give me, and I'll cherish every moment. And who knows? Maybe we'll decide to part ways after a while. It's not like we are fated mates. We can't be. So, it might end like it ends for many humans."

Even as he spoke the words, Peter was aware of the lie. Deep down, he believed that Marina was his one and only truelove mate.

Kagra's words echoed in his head again, "You are enamored with love, Peter. You are lying to yourself."

Was he?

Not really. He would be lying to himself if he denied what he felt for Marina.

There would be no parting ways, no amicable split. He was hers and she was his, and they were bound together by a force that transcended their differences, but he couldn't say that, not yet.

Instead, he clapped Jay on the shoulder. "Let's get some food. I'm starving."

21

MARINA

As Peter and Jay made their way to the buffet table, Larissa put her fork down, leaned back and regarded Marina with a knowing look. "Okay, talk. What happened?"

Marina leaned in close. "I followed your advice, and I confessed everything."

Larissa's eyes widened. "And? What did he say?"

Marina felt a smile bloom across her face. "Peter forgave me and told me he loved me and didn't want to let me go, no matter what. He wants me to move in with him. Can you imagine? It's everything I wanted."

A squeal of delight escaped Larissa's lips, and she reached across the table to embrace Marina. "I knew it! I told you he would forgive you. Peter is so in love with you that anyone could see it besides you."

Marina ducked her head. "I hoped so, but I didn't dare to believe. Heck, I still can't believe it."

"I'm so happy for you," Larissa whispered. "But what's next? You need to plan for the future."

Knowing what her friend was going to say, Marina grimaced. "What future? I'd rather not think about it."

Larissa sighed. "You can enjoy a few years with Peter, but you shouldn't stay with him for more than five years. Save up some money, maybe even study in an online university, and when you are ready, leave and find a human man to marry and have kids with. You don't have much time if you still want to have them."

Marina felt like she'd been doused in ice water, the harsh truth of Larissa's words hitting her like a physical blow despite having the same thoughts herself.

Somehow, it felt more real when someone else voiced them. Humans were very good at shoving unpleasant thoughts and consequences to the back of their minds. It was a coping mechanism, and right now, Marina would have loved to do that, but Larissa was right about the life she had imagined with Peter being a beautiful but fleeting dream.

Mother of All Life, have mercy on her soul. The thought of leaving him, of walking away from the most perfect relationship she'd ever had with a male, was like cutting her heart in half.

She just wouldn't survive it. To be with Peter, she had to give up other dreams.

"I'm not stupid. I had the same thoughts, but then I realized that not everyone has to have kids. We don't get to have everything we want, Larissa. And if I want to keep Peter, maybe I need to give up the idea of having children." She took a deep breath. "Did you know that in the Western world, as well as most countries in Eastern Europe, there aren't enough live births to keep the population from shrinking? Many people are not having kids at all. On average, women only have one and a half kids, which is way below the replacement ratio needed. The world population is going to decrease significantly in the next few decades."

Larissa rolled her eyes. "So what? You can't change that, and having kids isn't going to reverse the trend. You need to do what's good for you, not what's good for the planet."

"I want to have children," Marina said, even as the words rang hollow in her own ears. "For me, not for the planet."

Larissa threw up her hands, a look of frustration passing over her face. "A moment ago, you said you didn't want kids, and that many women chose not to have any. Then you said that the planet needed women to have more children, and that you want that too. Make up your mind."

The truth was that Marina didn't know what she wanted. The only certainty she had was her love for Peter.

Her gaze drifted to where he stood in line, his broad shoulders and tousled hair making her heart ache with longing, "I just want to be with him. I don't want to worry about anything else, about the future or the consequences or anything. I just want to live in the moment and not think about the future." She looked back at Larissa. "Is that so wrong? To want to be happy, even if it's just for a little while?"

Larissa's expression softened. "It's not wrong at all. The Mother of All Life knows how little joy we get in our miserable existence, and we need to grab whatever sliver of happiness we can get our hands on. If this sinfully handsome immortal makes you happy, then hold on to him with both hands for as long as you can."

22

EDGAR

E dgar had had easy conquests before, but never with a stunning beauty like Jasmine. And yet, here he was, holding her hand as she led him down the narrow corridor leading to her cabin.

Seducing her had taken almost no effort.

Hell, who was he kidding? He hadn't done the seducing, she had. Well, they both had.

Could she hear the pounding of his heart?

If Jasmine were immortal, she probably could, but she was human, so his secret was safe.

Well, not for long. He would have to thrall her soon so she wouldn't notice his fangs and glowing eyes, which he was barely managing to hold control of.

Edgar hadn't been with a woman in over two weeks, which was a long time for an immortal male, especially since he wasn't a fan of self-pleasuring. It was no fun having to bite a pillow or a towel to empty his venom.

It would take a lot of restraint for him not to harm Jasmine when he was going in that hot.

When they reached her cabin door, she gave him a bright smile as she fished the keycard from out of her purse. Her hands were steady as she pressed it to the reader and opened the door.

"Welcome to my humble abode." She waved at the tiny interior.

Edgar wanted to reach for her, wrap her in his arms, and kiss her until they were both breathless, but he held himself back, waiting for her cue.

Jasmine was in charge, and given his experience with her so far, she had no problem with that. The lady knew what she wanted, how she wanted it, and she wasn't bashful about her needs and wishes.

He admired that more than words could convey.

The cabin was tiny, with barely enough room between the narrow single bed and the desk and chair on the other side of the room. It couldn't be more than eight by ten feet.

"Most of the staff cabins are not as small as this one, but they are doubles, and this is a single." She put her purse on the desk and waved at the narrow bed. "This is a far cry from the princess's enormous round bed, but the mattress is surprisingly comfortable, and most importantly, there are no cameras in here. I checked."

So, was that why she'd said they should move to somewhere more private to continue their story? The surveillance cameras in the staff lounge bothered her?

Perhaps she had meant it literally, and all she wanted was to continue the story?

"Yeah. That's good." He suddenly felt too hot, claustrophobic.

Removing his tux jacket, he pulled out the lone chair and draped the jacket over its back. Not sure what he should do next, he sat down.

How had he expected her to invite him to her bed when they hadn't even kissed yet?

He'd been delusional.

As Jasmine looked at him, though, her eyes sparkled with mischief, and Edgar felt a surge of molten lust course through his veins. Fates, she was stunning, all lush curves and golden skin, her dark hair tumbling around her shoulders in soft waves that he couldn't wait to rake his fingers through.

Tilting her head, Jasmine put a hand on her hip and bit her lips. "It has been a long day of doing nothing, but I feel like showering. Would you like to join me?"

Fuck me. Edgar swallowed hard, his erection swelling to uncomfortable proportions in his pants. "I would love to." He rose to his feet and pulled her into his arms. "But I have a rule."

"What is it?"

"Before I get naked with a woman, I have to kiss her first."

She laughed, a throaty sound that sent shivers skittering down his spine. "I like your rules. Do you have more?"

"A few." He raised his hand and wrapped his fingers around her neck, threading them through her luxurious ebony locks. "But let's start with this one." He tilted his head and leaned into her, hovering his mouth a fraction of an inch away from hers.

Jasmine closed the last of the distance, fusing her lips to his, and then he took over, lashing his tongue against the seam of her lips and being granted immediate entry.

As he dipped his tongue into her mouth, he sent a light thrall into her mind, making her ignore the sharp points of his fangs and his glowing eyes.

Her arms closed around his body, and she brought him closer, her hardened nipples rubbing against his chest through two layers of fabric.

Three, if she was wearing a bra.

Jasmine pulled away, breathless and a little dazed. "You are one hell of a kisser, Edgar."

23

JASMINE

What had just happened?

Why was she feeling dizzy?

The kiss had been spectacular, and the hard muscles Jasmine had felt under Edgar's shirt had her blood pumping, but she wasn't prone to fainting spells like Margo, and she rarely felt dizzy.

Was the ship swaying more than usual?

"Are you okay?" Edgar steadied her with a hand on her hip.

"Yeah. I've never been bespelled by a kiss before." She licked her lips. "You didn't slip something into my water, did you?"

The horrified look on his face was the best answer he could have given her. "I would never do something like that." He reached for his jacket. "If you think I'm capable of such a despicable act, I'd better leave."

"Relax. I was just joking." She took the jacket from him and draped it over the back of the chair. "You are taking everything much too seriously."

"How can you say that? You were a victim of such a travesty only a few days ago."

Jasmine grimaced. "You are nothing like Alberto. I know that you would have never taken advantage of me." She reached for the hem of her top. "Let's play a game to lighten the mood. For every piece of clothing I take off, you have to take one off too. Deal?"

Edgar nodded, a sly smile making his handsome face look boyish.

"I'll go first." Jasmine pulled her top over her head in one smooth motion and tossed it over the desk.

Left with her lacy black bra on, she waved a hand at him. "Your turn."

"You are breathtakingly beautiful," he murmured as his eyes roamed over her exposed skin.

"I'm waiting." She playfully tapped her foot on the floor. "I'm not getting any younger here."

The dizziness had passed by now, and she was enjoying the game she'd come up with, even though it was tormenting them both by prolonging the anticipation.

Edgar started on the buttons of his shirt, going slowly and dragging it out as she looked on with fire burning in her eyes.

When he finally shrugged the shirt off, she sucked in a breath. "How many hours a day do you spend in the gym to look like that?"

The look of smug satisfaction on his face was priceless. "None. I spend a few minutes every day training at home."

"I hate you." When the horrified look returned to his eyes, she lifted her hand and laughed. "You are so literal. I'm just envious, that's all."

"Why?" He closed the distance between them with one step, wrapping his arms around her and pulling her to his bare chest. The feeling of skin on skin was incredible. "You are perfect." He kissed her.

When he let her up for air, she pushed on his chest. "Next item."

They continued their seductive game of strip poker, each revealing more and more skin until they were both completely naked.

Edgar seemed to have trouble breathing. "You are a goddess." The reverence in his voice did something to her chest.

Something eased inside.

Why had she allowed Alberto to erode her self-confidence with his snide comments about her hips being too fleshy, her stomach too rounded, and her nipples too big and too dark?

As always, she had shoved those uncomfortable thoughts into a corner of her mind where all the dark moments of her life were imprisoned, but Edgar's appreciative gaze had released them and then pulverized them.

He made her feel beautiful.

"You are not so bad yourself." She let her eyes roam over his body, stopping at the enormous erection jutting from between his hips.

Thankfully, she wasn't a dainty woman, and the size of him titillated her rather than worried her.

Edgar's skin was so much lighter than hers, and other than his head, he was almost hairless. If she hadn't gotten all of her body hair removed with laser treatments, she would have been more hairy than him.

Stop it. No self-deprecating remarks from you today. Or ever.

She walked into his arms, his skin hot and smooth against hers, and as their mouths met in another searing kiss, passion rose swiftly and sharply between them.

Somehow, they managed to stumble into the tiny bathroom without breaking the kiss. Fumbling blindly for the taps, Ed turned the water on, and the spray of water was so shockingly cold at first that Jasmine screeched and clung to his hot body until the water warmed up.

In the confines of the narrow stall, their bodies were pressed together from head to toe, slick and slippery as they explored each other with eager hands—soaping, massaging, stroking.

"I want you," she panted against his lips. "I want you now."

24

EDGAR

J asmine was just as gorgeous in the nude as Ed had imagined, but the reality of her was even headier—the hot silk of her skin, the intoxicating taste of her mouth, the way she moved against him, her lithe body straining closer, seeking more.

"I want you," she breathed. "I want you now."

He groaned, his erection throbbing almost painfully between them, and as she dipped her hand between their bodies and wrapped her palm around his shaft, his hips bucked into her hold as if they had a mind of their own. He nearly came right then and there.

That wasn't how he'd envisioned the encounter. If he climaxed now, he wouldn't be able to refrain from biting Jasmine, and that would send her on a euphoric trip that could last hours. He could wait for her to wake up and then have her again, but he didn't want to wait, and he didn't want to shortchange their pleasure by ending their shower interlude in under thirty seconds.

"Don't." He placed his hand over hers on his shaft. "I don't want it to be over before it begins."

She looked into his eyes, gold flecks swirling hypnotically in her irises, and after a moment, her grip on his happy handle slackened, and her lips curved in a smile. "Should I switch the temperature to cold?"

"No need, beautiful." He started going down to his knees, his hands sliding down her sides, caressing the smooth, silky, golden skin. "Just let me worship you first."

"Oh, goddess." She let out a throaty groan and leaned against the fiberglass wall.

"Yes, you are." He smoothed his hands back to cup her bottom and leaned in to plant a soft kiss on the top of her hairless mound.

She must have had her pubic hair professionally removed because the skin was flawlessly smooth, and her scent…

Fates, her scent.

He was getting lightheaded.

"You smell divine."

She emitted a throaty chuckle. "That's because I'm a goddess, right?"

"To me, you are." He slid a finger inside of her while pressing his mouth over her clit to suck it in.

"Fuck me!" Jasmine hissed.

He let go of her clit and looked up at her with a grin. "I will, just not yet." He wedged a second finger inside her.

Her hips churning, she lifted her hands to cup her ample breasts, rubbing her thumbs over her nipples as she gyrated over his fingers.

He berated himself for not giving them the proper attention and vowed to remedy the neglect as soon as he was done getting his fill of her feminine nectar.

Clamping his hands on her ass, he held her in place as he kissed her tender bud, soft kisses that were more teasing than satisfying. She tried to grind herself over his fingers and his mouth, and even though his hold on her was unyielding, she kept fighting despite the futility of it.

Stubborn woman.

He liked strong females, and her stubbornness only spurred his arousal.

As she burrowed her fingers into his hair and tugged hard, he groaned against her throbbing clit and rewarded her with a flick of his tongue.

"Yes, just like that," she encouraged. "It's so good."

It was, but it would be even better in bed. The shower had seemed like a good idea, but it was way too small. On the other hand, it meant that everything was within reach.

It was the work of a moment for him to turn off the water, grab the towel, and wrap Jasmine in it.

"What are you doing?" she finally croaked when he lifted her into his arms.

"The bed will be much more comfortable."

"I've never seen anyone move so fast." She wrapped her arms around his neck.

"Pilot training." He laid her on the narrow bed using one hand while tugging the towel with the other.

Her large amber eyes grew even bigger. "How come you are so strong?"

Toweling off, he laughed. "Next, you'll ask why my teeth are so long."

Hopefully, his thrall made sure that her brain couldn't process seeing his fangs, but she must have sensed that something was off and that she was in the presence of a predator because a shudder went through her.

"Are you cold?" he asked, tossing the towel into the small bathroom.

She shook her head. "I'm serious. I'm heavy, and you lifted me with one arm like I weighed no more than a feather."

He prowled over her. "Lots of weightlifting." He cupped her breasts and then lightly pinched her nipples.

Jasmine narrowed her eyes at him. "You said that you don't go to the gym."

If she was this coherent, he wasn't doing a good job of pleasuring her.

"You said that you only…"

Lifting her by her waist, he twisted her around before the last syllable left her mouth.

His hand on her nape, he pushed her down so her face was on the mattress and her ass was high in the air.

Jasmine turned her head and looked at him over her shoulder. "What are you doing?"

"What does it look like I'm doing? I'm still worshiping my goddess."

Bending down, he extended his tongue and gave her wet slit a long lick. "Delightful." He smacked his lips before diving in for more.

25

JASMINE

As Edgar's tongue speared into her from behind, Jasmine gasped. It was so erotically wicked to be licked like that, and so was the feel of his strong fingers digging into her fleshy bottom.

It didn't take long until she was spiraling toward an orgasm, and as much as she tried to hold on so it could climb even higher, she was powerless to do anything about it. The climax erupted from her like a volcano, and she screamed something incoherent into the mattress.

Edgar kept gently licking her quivering flesh and pumping his fingers in and out of her until her tremors subsided, and then he flipped her over and looked into her eyes.

"Gold," he whispered.

Still dazed from her climax, she wasn't sure what he was talking about, but then it occurred to her that he was referring to the gold flakes swirling around her pupils.

He closed a warm palm around her breast, feathering his thumb over her nipple. "Are you ready for more?"

She reached between their bodies and took hold of his length. "Does that answer your question?" she purred, stroking him softly and maddeningly slow. "I need you inside me, but first..." She stretched her arm and retrieved a condom packet from her nightstand. "Protection."

With deft fingers, she tore the wrapper and sheathed him with practiced ease. "Now."

He entered her in one smooth thrust, his shaft sliding inside her wet heat with ease and sheathing himself to the hilt.

They both gasped at the intensity, the incredible feeling of being joined.

The fit was so perfect that she had an absurd thought about Edgar being her promised prince.

He surely looked and made love like one.

Even his weight on top of her felt perfect, his smooth, muscled chest pressing into hers and flattening her breasts. At first, his hips retreated and surged forward slowly and gently, and as he increased the tempo and strength of his thrusts, he did so in small increments as if testing how much she could take.

Did he think she was made of glass?

She was far from delicate, timid, or shy, and she could take much more than what he was giving her.

"More." Jasmine arched up.

He didn't comply right away, exhibiting uncommon and truly admirable restraint as he ramped up his thrusting, and for some reason that brought tears to her eyes.

Well, Jasmine knew precisely why she appreciated that so much. Most of the men she'd been with hadn't been as careful with her, even those she'd been in long-term relationships with, and this stranger was gentler than those who had claimed to love her.

Pausing completely, Ed lifted his head and looked into her eyes. "Am I hurting you?"

"No. You are perfect."

"So why are you crying?"

She wasn't. She was sure that not a single tear had spilled from her eyes. How did he know that the tears were gathering before even looking into her eyes?

Intuition?

Or had she made a sound without being aware of it?

Lifting her hand, Jasmine cupped Edgar's cheek. "I'm just a little emotional. Thank you for being so careful with me."

He lowered his head and pressed his lips against her in the softest of kisses. "You are precious," he murmured between kisses. "And you deserve to be treated as such."

The man didn't know her, so if he thought that she was precious, he must think that all women were, and that made him even more special to her.

So many men thought of women as vessels for their pleasure, to be used and abused. Most were not malicious, though, just careless and selfish.

"You are a rare jewel, Edgar, a prince among men."

He smiled and then, kissing her softly, resumed his slow and steady rhythm. Watching her carefully, he soon set up a tempo that had her careening toward the edge of the cliff again.

She met him thrust for thrust, her nails raking down his back and her breathy moans and cries spurring him on.

It was raw and primal, but she still had a feeling that he was holding back. It was evident in his tense shoulders, the hard set of his jaw, and the perspiration on his brow. But as much as she tried to spur him on by churning her hips and moaning in his ear, he wasn't releasing all that pent-up power.

His tongue flicking over her neck was what drove her over the edge, and as another climax washed over her like a tsunami, she heard him hiss, and then twin points of searing pain stole her breath before fading away.

The momentary pain was replaced by another earth-shattering orgasm, and as his hot seed jetted out of him, another climax thundered through her.

When her convulsions finally eased up, relaxing her muscles and leaving her boneless, euphoria spread throughout her mind and body, carrying her on its wings to a place of bliss where nothing negative existed.

Was it heaven?

Did she just die from too much pleasure?

Jasmine couldn't care less as she soared above the clouds, light as a thought and free as a bird.

EDGAR

S tars exploded behind Edgar's eyes as he followed Jasmine over the edge and emptied himself inside the damn condom.

Still, despite the hated prophylactic, it was the best sex he had ever had by a wide margin. Clinging to Jasmine, he retracted his fangs and licked the puncture wound closed, but he didn't stop there. He pressed soft kisses to her damp temples, her cheeks, and her lush, kiss-swollen lips that were lifted in a blissful smile.

"You are incredible," he murmured, even though she couldn't hear him. "A fantasy come true."

Letting himself catch his breath and enjoy the feel of this incredible woman in his arms, he turned to his side, bringing her with him, and almost fell off the narrow bed. He knew that he couldn't stay like this forever, but for a few more minutes, she could be his

Princess, and he could be her Aladdin, and the real world could wait.

Caressing her rosy cheek, Ed chuckled. His definition of the real world was very different from Jasmine's. Would Kian allow him to tell her about their world?

He'd allowed that for Frankie and Margo just because of a few weak indicators that they might be Dormants, so why not Jasmine?

If Amanda had wanted Max to check her out, she suspected that Jasmine was a Dormant as well, and she must have a good reason to think it.

Damn, he hoped that Max wouldn't change his mind and decide that he wanted to pursue her. The Guardian was an impressive guy, and Jasmine might decide that she preferred his hulking masculinity to Edgar's more slender and less macho form.

With a sigh, Ed carefully untangled himself from Jasmine's arms and pulled out slowly while holding on to the top of the condom so it wouldn't spill inside of her.

He didn't have much practice with those, and he wondered why he hadn't thralled Jasmine to forgo it. His standard modus operandi was to thrall his partners to ignore his fangs and glowing eyes, to think that he'd used a condom when he hadn't, and to forget the venom bite. He had thralled Jasmine with all save one.

Come to think of it, his subconscious had saved him from making a huge mistake. If Jasmine was a potential Dormant, he could have accidentally induced her without her consent.

She had to be told about her potential first and then decide whether she wanted to be induced and who she wanted her inducer to be. He couldn't assume that she would choose him.

Hell, she could potentially want to sample all the eligible clan males before deciding on the one who would induce her. Something told him that Jasmine wasn't the kind of woman who settled on the first option presented to her.

Rising to his feet, Edgar discarded the condom in the bathroom trashcan and turned on the shower faucet again. The towel they had used had slipped to the floor, and when he picked it up, he realized that it was still a little damp, but it was the only one she had.

As he stood under the spray, he thought about Max. Perhaps he needed to have a talk with the guy and ask him to stay away from Jasmine. If he hurried, he might even still catch the Guardian at the wedding party.

But did he have the right to make such a request of the guy?

Jasmine wasn't his girlfriend, let alone his mate, and tomorrow, she might decide to invite someone else to her bed. After Edna cleared her, which he had no doubt she would, Jasmine would be able to mingle with all the bachelors on the upper decks and have her pick of the crop. Why would she limit herself to him?

It wasn't as if they had formed an emotional connection. As amazing as the sex was, it had been purely physical.

For the first time in his life, Edgar bemoaned not spending more time with a woman and getting to know her before taking her to bed. He should have formed a closer connection with Jasmine before engaging with her sexually.

The thing was, though, Jasmine had taken him to her bed, not the other way around.

27

KIAN

Syssi leaned her head on Kian's shoulder and whispered, "What time is it?"

He glanced at his watch. "It's five minutes after midnight. We should start making our exit soon."

The wedding party was still in full swing, and they had plenty of time until the telepathic meeting between his mother and her grandmother, but before leaving, they needed to congratulate the newlyweds and say goodnight to people. Syssi also wanted to get out of her evening gown and put on something comfortable before heading to his mother's cabin.

Scanning the room for Aru, Kian found the god dancing with his mate, and when they made eye contact, Kian lifted his wrist and looked at his watch again. Getting the hint, the god nodded.

It still boggled Kian's mind that Aru and Aria could create an instantaneous mental connection while separated by hundreds of light years. The implications were so profound that it made his head ache just thinking about them. It was proof that consciousness was not bound to the material world and its rules, at least not in the way he understood the laws of physics and space-time.

Kian put down his coffee cup, pushed away the small plate with the half-eaten cake, and put his hand on Syssi's thigh. "You look tired, my love."

It was her cue to start pretending that she was exhausted so they would have an excuse for their early departure.

The queen of Anumati expected the connection to be established by one in the morning Earth time, and the meeting would start whether he and Syssi were there or not.

The truth was that it wasn't really necessary for him to be with his mother when the meeting commenced.

It wasn't as if Kian feared for Annani's well-being when alone with Aru. First of all, she could take care of herself, as Toven had reminded him time and again, and secondly, she had her Odus with her, and not even Aru's immense strength was a match for two Odus who were charged with protecting their mistress.

Still, his mother appreciated the moral support. Besides, Syssi had volunteered to transcribe everything that was being said, and he couldn't argue with her logic that the best way of keeping the notes an absolute secret was writing them by hand.

In today's hackable world, recording things with pen and paper was the only hack-proof method, provided that the records were well hidden and well guarded, which he would take care of as soon as they got back to the village.

Syssi sighed loudly and turned to Kian. "My feet are killing me. Are you ready to call it a night?"

Across the table, Amanda lifted a brow. "Leaving so early again? What's your rush?"

"It's not that early," Kian forced a casual tone. "Syssi has been dancing for hours, and she's tired."

"So were you." Syssi grimaced. "Just not in high heels. I'm dying to take my shoes off."

"You can dance barefoot," Amanda suggested. "Many do." She waved her hand at the dance floor.

"True, but they are not shorties with giants for mates." She cast a fond look at Kian. "Kian would look like he's dancing with a little girl."

He snorted. "No one would mistake you for a girl." He leaned closer and nuzzled her neck at the spot he planned on biting later tonight. "You are all woman."

Amanda rolled her eyes. "Oh, please. You should have said that you were eager to take your wife to bed from the get-go."

Predictably, Syssi's cheeks reddened. "It's not that. I am really tired, and we also need to go pick up Allegra from your mother's. We don't want to keep her up too late."

Suspicion flashed in Amanda's eyes.

His sister was sharply perceptive, always had been. It was part of what made her such a great researcher. She never accepted things at face value and always asked why.

Kian's jaw clenched at the need to hide things from her, but Aru insisted on keeping his ability to communicate with his sister a secret, and Kian had given him his word.

"I see." Amanda's tone was carefully neutral. "Well, don't let me keep you." Her gaze cut to Syssi, a silent question in their blue depths.

Syssi leaned over the table and clasped Amanda's hand. "The decorations were beautiful tonight."

Amanda shrugged. "Not my doing. Cassandra did all that on her own. I didn't even help with the menu. Geraldine insisted on doing it. Not that I minded." She leaned forward to whisper in Syssi's ear. "It left me free to do some matchmaking." She turned to Kian. "By the way, did you remember to talk to Edna about Jasmine?"

"Not yet. I'll speak with her first thing in the morning."

Amanda's eyes narrowed. "Don't put it off too long. I've already put the rest of the plan in motion."

"You did?" He glanced at the dance floor where Max was dancing with Darlene.

Amanda followed his gaze. "Oh, not with Max. He declined the offer. Something about Jasmine reminding him of someone he disliked."

"Then who?"

"Edgar."

That surprised Kian. He hadn't seen that coming. Edgar was still a kid in immortal years, but he had a reputation for being a ladies' man. Like most immortal males, he was handsome, but in a more boyish way than Max. He didn't have the heft and swagger of the Guardian.

Kian wasn't sure how he felt about the pilot pursuing Jasmine. It wasn't that Edgar was undeserving of a mate. It was just that he was still young and there were many who were more deserving.

Jasmine being a Dormant was not a certainty, though, and at the moment, it was only a theory.

"We still don't know what Jasmine is about, and having a Guardian befriend her would have been better."

"I know," Amanda admitted. "But Ed overheard me talking with Max, and when Max declined, he jumped on the opportunity to take his place. I couldn't say no."

"You could, but I assume it's too late?"

She nodded. "He took her dinner and didn't come back up yet."

"If he returns after we leave, question him about her."

"Yes, sir." Amanda saluted him. "Goodnight, you two, and kiss Allegra for me."

"We will." Syssi pushed to her feet and stopped by Amanda to give her a hug. "Enjoy the rest of the party."

After a round of congratulations and goodnights to the groom and bride and to their families, Kian and Syssi walked out of the dining room.

The music and laughter faded behind them as they entered the elevator, and as soon as the doors closed behind them, Kian pulled Syssi into his arms. "Can I steal a kiss from my wife?"

"Always." Smiling, she lifted on her toes, cupped his cheek, and pressed her lips to his.

Kian leaned into her touch. "I hate all this damn secrecy. It feels wrong to lie to my sisters and keep this from them. They should know." He couldn't say more in the elevator that had a surveillance camera located in a discreet spot.

"I know, love." Her thumb stroked over his cheekbone. "But it's not up to you. It's Aru's call, and I can understand why he's being so paranoid about it." She waited until they stepped out of the elevator on their deck, where the surveillance cameras were off for the next few hours. "If word got out about Aru's sister and her work with the queen, it could spell disaster not just for her but for the queen, the oracle, and the entire resistance."

Nodding, Kian opened the door to their cabin and drew her into his arms. "I love you," he murmured into her hair as he held her close, breathing in the scent of her and letting it soothe his jagged edges.

"I love you, too." She kissed his cheek lightly. "But we should hurry up and change. We have five minutes to be at your mother's."

He sighed. "That's a shame. If we had fifteen, it would have been infinitely better."

Snorting, Syssi playfully slapped his arm. "Do you ever think of anything other than getting me in bed?" She started walking toward their bedroom.

"I do. I think about getting you in the closet, in the shower, on the kitchen counter..." He stopped to catch the pillow she chucked at him. "Oh, this is going to cost you, young lady."

Syssi laughed, the husky sound fueling his budding arousal. "I'm looking forward to it, big guy."

28

ANNANI

A nnani stood in front of the door to the cabin's terrace and looked up at the starry sky. Somewhere out there, hundreds of light years away, was Anumati, the home world of the gods, the corner of the galaxy her father had come from.

In the enormous, incomprehensible scale of the universe, Earth and Anumati were not only in the same neighborhood but on the same street. Maybe even in the same apartment building. She did not know enough about astronomy to know the actual scale, but since they were in the same galaxy, probably even in the same spoke of the wheel, it was considered close.

They called themselves gods and believed that they were the masters of the universe, but that was as misguided as humans thinking the same thing. Somewhere out there, in a different galaxy, there was probably a species of beings even more powerful than the gods, but the distances were so vast that there was no way to physically traverse them. The only way contact could be made was through connected consciousnesses like Aria and Aru's.

Somehow, their minds were entangled like quantum particles.

Vivian and Ella had a similar connection, probably created by the same mechanism of quantum entanglement. The question was whether beings who had never touched each other, physically or otherwise, could be conjoined.

Theoretically, it was possible.

After all, the entirety of matter and all of energy in the universe had supposedly been created in the Big Bang, so every particle in all of creation had at one time touched all others.

Everything was intertwined.

Annani lifted a hand to her temple. She was giving herself a headache by thinking and theorizing about things she did not know enough about and had no patience for learning.

Sometimes, she suspected that she suffered from what humans called attention deficit disorder. She had all the classic indicators, starting with poor impulse control and continuing with a dislike of learning anything that required concentrating for a long time.

Oh, well.

No one was perfect. Not even the royal heir to the throne of the Eternal King. Annani was a powerful goddess, the most powerful being on Earth, and deep down she knew that she had not explored the extent of that power.

Toven kept telling her that, and she kept dismissing him, saying that after five thousand years she knew perfectly well what she was capable of, but it was a lie. The truth was that she was afraid to look too deeply inside herself and discover that she was more powerful than her father or even more than her grandfather.

It was terrifying.

Annani did not want to rule Anumati any more than she wanted to rule Earth. She had not even wanted to rule her own clan, entrusting her children to manage it for her, and they did that splendidly without her.

As for humans, even if she was interested in governing them, they would never accept her as their ruler, and by taking over she would do more harm than good, which was the reason why she had never considered it.

Working from the shadows and trying to improve their condition as much as she and her clan could was the best option for the divided and fiercely tribal humans.

But Anumati was different, and it was possible that she was the only one who could liberate trillions of beings from the oppressive rule of her grandfather.

Or conversely, cause mass loss of life and destruction.

A soft sigh had her turn to look at her sleeping grand-daughter. Allegra shifted in the portable crib that Parker had brought to Annani's cabin with Okidu's help.

The sweet child always brought a smile to her face.

Annani had hundreds of grandchildren, great-grand-children, and many times removed great-grandchil-dren, but Allegra had a special place in her heart.

When the doorbell rang, the child whimpered in her sleep but did not wake up.

As Kian and Syssi entered along with Aru, Annani walked over to them and welcomed each one with a warm embrace.

"Are you okay?" Kian regarded her with a frown.

"I am very well, my son. I have been pondering the universe, and it has made me feel melancholy for some reason. But then I gazed upon the face of my grand-daughter, and my heart swelled with so much love that I became emotional. But do not mind me." She waved her hand at the couch. "Let us all get comfortable before the meeting begins." She turned to Aru. "Is Aria ready?"

"She has not opened the channel yet, but I assume that she will at any moment."

"Indeed." Annani offered him a fond smile. "In the meantime, please help yourself to the refreshments my Odus have prepared."

"Thank you, Clan Mother."

As Aru reached for a teacup, Ojidu immediately rushed to lift the carafe and pour into the young god's cup.

When each one of them had a cup in hand, Aru closed his eyes, and Annani's heartbeat accelerated.

There was something she desperately needed to ask the oracle, and hopefully, her wish would not be denied by her grandmother or the seer.

29

QUEEN ANI

Ani settled into her cushioned seat, excited anticipation filling her chest as she prepared for another telepathic meeting with her granddaughter. The connection, which was made possible through the extraordinary abilities of the twins Aru and Aria, had become a lifeline for her, a bridge over the vast distance between Earth and Anumati so she could get to know her beloved son's daughter and share the wisdom of her years with Annani, the young goddess who might be the answer to the future of their people.

Sofringhati slanted a look at her. "You look amused. Care to share?"

Ani smiled. "I was thinking of Annani, and to me, she is a young goddess, but she thinks that she is ancient at her mere five thousand Earth years."

"It is a matter of perspective, my dear friend. She lives among humans whose lives are so short that they are a mere blink of an eye to us. And yet, they pack so many experiences into their short lives to take with them to the beyond."

Ani frowned. "You said that you cannot see beyond the veil. So how do you know that?"

Her friend's lips twitched with a smile. "I cannot see, that is true, but sometimes I get impressions." She leaned closer to whisper in Ani's ear, as if anyone could hear them.

Aria was there, but she was already privy to all of their secrets, so there was no need to whisper around her. Sometimes, Sofri just liked to be dramatic.

"The mighty gods would not like to hear this, but beyond the veil, they are no different than the created species they look down their noses at. In the realm of the spirits, no one being is worth more than another." Sofri leaned back.

Ani nodded. "That is what the scriptures say, but I doubt it. Do you know why?"

"Enlighten me."

"Patterns. The universe is made of patterns, and things repeat themselves. So, if there is a hierarchy in the physical world, there is also a hierarchy in the spirit world. They might not use the same criteria for who is better than whom, but I am sure they have them. Besides, can you imagine how boring it would be without any intrigue and backstabbing?"

Sofri shook her head. "You are as incorrigible and irreverent now as you were when we were girls. You just mask it with a lot of royal attitude."

Ani canted her head. "I am a free thinker, Sofri. I never accept dogma."

"I know." Sofringhati reached for her hand. "That is why you are the unofficial leader of the resistance; its beating heart."

Ani squeezed her friend's hand. "That was very nice of you to say." She glanced at Aria. "Is it time?"

The young goddess dipped her head. "Yes, my queen. I will check if Aru and the heir are ready."

"Annani likes to be called the Clan Mother," Ani said. "I think it says a lot about her."

Sofri nodded. "It does. She is a shepherd at heart."

Ani hoped that she and Sofri were not projecting their wishes onto Annani and making her out to be someone she was not. What if she was more like her grandfather than they realized?

They did not need another Eternal Queen who would do everything to stay in power, no matter who she needed to murder to do that.

From what Aru had told them, though, Annani had left the leadership of her clan to her children and functioned more as a spiritual figurehead than an active ruler. It indicated that she was not power-hungry.

But who knew?

She might develop a taste for it like her grandfather had. El had been a brilliant leader who had united Anumati's factions and brought peace and prosperity before his heart had turned to stone.

"They are ready, my queen," Aria said.

"Send my warm greetings to Annani, her son, and his mate if they are with her."

Aria closed her eyes for a moment. "They are, and they send their warm greetings as well. Your granddaughter awaits her first lesson on Anumati's history."

There was so much to tell, so much history and knowledge to impart. But where to begin? How to condense the complex, often turbulent story of their world into a narrative that would both inform and inspire?

Ani took a deep breath, casting her mind back to the earliest days of Anumati, to the tales passed down through the generations of gods and goddesses, some of them recorded by oracles from the past, some by scribes and scholars.

"Not much is known of the early days of our kind's creation. There are legends, of course. The Kra-ell believe in the Mother of All Life who created every living being in the universe, and they claim that we believed in her as well before we lost our way and severed our connection to the land, deciding that we were gods—the creators of our world and many others."

She sighed. "But I am getting ahead of my story."

"When our civilization was young, millions of years ago, our lifespans were not endless like they are now. On average, we lived about a thousand Earth years, which is long compared to your humans, but a blink of an eye compared to our lifespans now. There were conflicts, as in any civilization, power struggles, and wars, but there were also long periods of peace, during which we lived in harmony, exploring the boundaries of our abilities and shaping the world around us. As the eons passed, our numbers grew, our technology advanced, and space travel became a necessity, first for the harvesting of resources and later for colonization. Naturally, power struggles and differences in opinions created division. Factions arose, each with their own vision of what Anumati should be and how its people should live and govern themselves."

Ani twined the chain of her pendant around her finger. "Most of the struggle was political and economic, and the leading families who owned the large manufac-turing conglomerates became the royalty of Anumati. They controlled the genetics labs and dictated who got which traits. Those who had the means invested in their children's future, giving them a genetic advantage over those with lesser resources, and over time, a huge divide formed between those who called themselves royals and those who they called commoners."

ANNANI

"So that was how it began," Kian murmured as Aru paused to listen to his sister Aria's telepathic relay. "The divide between the glowing and non-glowing Anumatians."

"I wonder if that schism was the start of the resistance," Syssi said.

Annani had a feeling that even more complex political machinations had been at play in those early days of their ancestral civilization. Regrettably, it seemed to be a universal constant that in every society there were leaders and there were followers. And more often than not, those who rose to power came from the privileged echelons, even when they claimed to champion the cause of the downtrodden masses.

It was almost never about the masses. It was always about power and wealth.

The simple truth was that the underprivileged were usually far too preoccupied with the daily struggles of earning a living and providing for their families to have the time or resources to organize a rebellion.

"Each of the royal families amassed their own power bases," Aru continued. "Alliances and coalitions were forged, consolidating their power primarily through strategic marriages between the leading houses. It was an imperfect system, but it worked."

Aru went on to relay the queen's explanation of how the ruling families installed vast networks of administrators who were tasked with overseeing public affairs and enforcing the dictates set forth by their masters. While each dynastic conglomerate had its own particular set of laws and customs, there was a great deal of commonality between them. By and large, the system functioned adequately, and the majority of the population, commoners included, enjoyed a reasonable degree of prosperity.

"But periodically, the leaders of one faction or another would grow dissatisfied with their allotted share of wealth and power." Aru paused for a moment. "Or they would feel slighted by some real or imagined offense from their rivals. In such cases, localized conflicts would erupt, disrupting the peace. In an effort to break the cycle of internecine violence, the heads of two of the most influential royal houses convened a summit, where they conceived of a governing council intended to serve as a forum for the peaceful resolution of disputes. They presented their idea to the heads of the other families, who agreed to the proposition, and thus the first Anumati Council was born.

"Each family was granted the right to appoint a single representative to the Council, regardless of their relative wealth, territorial holdings, or the size of the population under their dominion."

"A surprisingly egalitarian provision," Annani said, "given the generally oligarchic nature of the power structure. I wonder how effectively it worked in practice."

Aru nodded. "Her Majesty believes this is a suitable place to conclude for today. She has provided you with a broad overview, which she will continue to expand upon in the subsequent meetings. After that, she intends to circle back and delve into more specific aspects of Anumati's sociopolitical evolution. Are there any other questions you would like to present before we adjourn?"

Annani glanced at her son, knowing that he would not like what she was about to ask next, but she was going to ask it anyway. "Actually, my question is more in the nature of a request. I was hoping that the Supreme Oracle might be able to shed some light on a particular event from our own history, one that has haunted me for millennia."

She braced herself as she awaited the response, hoping against hope that the oracle might be able to help her.

"The oracle would love to help, but regrettably, Earth is shielded from her sight," Aru relayed. "She cannot penetrate the barrier to glimpse its past or future."

Annani's heart sank, but she had expected as much. The queen had said so last night, but Annani had hoped that there was a loophole she could use. "Is it certain that this limitation applies to all of Anumati's oracles?"

"I am afraid so, my dear granddaughter," Aru relayed the queen's answer. "But I am curious to hear what you wanted Sofringhati to divine for you."

Annani cast another glance at Kian, and given his somber expression, he knew what she wanted to ask. "After your revelation about the assassins the king sent to kill my father and the realization that Mortdh might not have been the one responsible for the annihilation of my people, it occurred to me that perhaps he was not responsible for my Khiann's death either. For five thousand years, I have been haunted by the horrific account of my mate's supposed demise at Mortdh's hands, an account I have never before had any cause to doubt. But now I cannot help but question it."

She closed her eyes against the sudden sting of tears. "My father made numerous attempts to placate Mortdh and defuse his hostile intentions. When all of those overtures failed, I fear Ahn may have resorted to a far more ruthless stratagem. He dared not have Mortdh assassinated outright, for it would have been all too clear who was behind the act. But if he could convincingly lay the death of a god at Mortdh's feet, the effect would be much the same in terms of neutralizing the threat."

Annani's hands curled into fists. "Ahn was a cold and calculating ruler, as you well know. But I refuse to believe that he would have conspired to murder my mate solely for the purpose of framing Mortdh. What I suspect is that the witnesses who originally reported Khiann's death to my father may have simply informed him that my love and his retinue had fallen victim to the catastrophic earthquake that cleaved the desert. My father might have seized the opportunity and compelled the witnesses into claiming Mortdh had murdered Khiann in cold blood. That is what I hoped the Oracle could ascertain. Because if Mortdh did not, in fact, behead my beloved, then there is a chance, however small, that Khiann still lives. He might be in stasis, trapped beneath the desert sands, waiting for me to find him and bring him home."

Annani's voice broke on the last word, and in her peripheral vision, she registered Kian shaking his head.

If Kian had known Ahn, he would have realized that exploiting his own daughter's devastation for political gain was absolutely consistent with his character.

She could just imagine her father rationalizing it to her mother, saying that Annani's grief would make the deception all the more believable. He would have added that he had raised his daughter to be resilient and that, in time, she would recover from the loss.

It was even possible that he had intended to send a search party for Khiann once the threat of Mortdh had been eliminated but never got the chance to do it because of the assassins the Eternal King, his own father, had sent to kill him.

Such an ugly tangle.

"The Supreme Oracle sends her deepest regrets," Aru said. "She would gladly scour the desert sands in search of your mate were such a thing within her power, but the veiling of Earth has ever been an inviolable barrier to her sight."

Annani swallowed past the lump in her throat and nodded. "I understand. Please convey my gratitude to Queen Ani for the fascinating lesson in Anumati's history and let her know how eagerly I await our next session."

31

KIAN

As Aru's telepathic connection with his sister ended, Kian turned his gaze to his mother. She avoided his eyes, but he could see the stiffness of her shoulders and the stubborn tilt of her chin.

Annani feared that he would dismiss this latest theory of hers as more wishful thinking and quash her hope again.

The prophecy she'd gotten five thousand years ago had kept that flicker of hope alive in her throughout the millennia, despite all the evidence stacked against it. He knew that, even though his mother didn't talk about it. Or maybe she did, just not with him. Perhaps she'd confided in Alena.

The thing was, she should have trusted him to be open-minded and listen to her because what she had told the queen actually made perfect sense. In fact, he couldn't understand how none of them had ever considered the possibility of Ahn manipulating the witnesses.

His grandfather had been a powerful compeller and a ruthless leader. If he wanted to eliminate the threat of Mortdh, Khiann's untimely demise in the earthquake would have provided him with the perfect opportunity to frame Mortdh as his murderer.

Kian couldn't understand how Ahn could have been so cruel to Annani, but then he himself was very different from his grandfather. He would never have sacrificed his own daughter on the altar of politics.

Hell, he would have killed Mortdh himself and screw the consequences.

Syssi reached out and touched Annani's arm. "I know you are disappointed that the oracle couldn't help you, but perhaps I can help search for Khiann. If there's even the slightest chance that he is alive, I will do everything I can to find a clue to his whereabouts. After all, if I could find David's parents by inducing a vision, I might be able to find out the truth about Khiann's fate as well."

Kian hated it when Syssi did that. It was one thing when the visions came to her unbidden and another thing when she forced herself into a trance and invited them.

Every time she delved into the mists of time and possibility, she emerged drained and disoriented, sometimes taking days to fully recover. The thought of her

subjecting herself to that again made his protective
instincts surge to the fore.

True, he told himself that she wasn't pregnant now and
that there was no risk to her health, but he was still
wary of the damn visions. Where did they come from?
Was it from the Fates or from some malignant force
that could leave its residue on Syssi's soul?

Kian didn't like anything that he didn't understand, and
out of all the paranormal abilities, seeing events that
hadn't happened yet or even past events that were
unconnected to the seer had no logical explanation.

Still, he didn't say a word.

The desperate hope his mother was trying to mask
slew him, and if Syssi could help her, he would never
stand in her way.

Annani turned a grateful smile at Syssi. "If you wish to
try, by all means, but there was a reason I did not turn
to you first, my sweet child. Your visions are about the
now or the future, not the distant past. Jacki might
have been able to take a peek if I had anything of
Khiann's I could give her to hold, but regrettably, I have
nothing of his."

Kian frowned. "Why not? Didn't you take some
mementos from your time together when you fled to
the north?"

"There was no time. I knew that I would need to start a
new civilization and to do that, I would need knowl-

edge I did not possess. My first priority was to find Ekin's tablet and steal it." She sighed. "I took some jewelry to barter with, and I used it wisely over the years. Keeping my children and grandchildren fed and sheltered was more important than keeping Khiann's gifts. I have never assigned much value to possessions." Her eyes suddenly widened. "What about the Odus? They were also a gift from my Khiann. I could ask Jacki to touch them."

Syssi pursed her lips. "Jacki can definitely try, but I doubt it will work with the Odus. Then again, Jacki saw what happened to Wonder just from touching the little statue someone had made of her as Gulan, so maybe she can pull it off." Syssi cast a sidelong glance at Kian. "It's a shame the amulet is depleted of power. Jacki could have used it to amplify her ability."

Annani shook her head. "That thing was evil. Even if it still held its potency, I would not resort to using it for this purpose. My Khiann was all bright light and love. To seek him through an instrument of darkness would be an affront to his memory."

Kian nodded in agreement. "I wouldn't use that thing either. I hope that Kalugal stored it somewhere safe so no evil can find it and use it to amplify its darkness."

His mother cast him a loving smile and reached for his hand. "You might not be Khiann's son, but I named you after him not just because I wanted to honor his memory, but because I saw so much of him in you, even when you were still a baby. You grew up to be just like him in so many ways. Your strength, compassion, and sense of justice, even your sense of humor. You also love your wife as fiercely as he loved me."

Kian felt his throat tighten with emotion. "Thank you. I'm honored to carry his name, and I hope Syssi or Jacki can help find him or at least find out what fate befell him."

Annani squeezed his hand. "I know it is not easy for you to watch your mate surrender to the visions, and I appreciate it."

Syssi leaned back in her chair. "If it wasn't so late, I would do it now, but I'm tired, and it's never good to summon visions when I'm not fully rested."

Aru, who had listened to the exchange without saying a thing, pushed to his feet. "If my services are no longer required, I would like to retire for the night."

"Not yet," Kian said. "There is a matter I need to discuss with you before you go."

32

ANNANI

A nnani had not expected Syssi to volunteer to induce a vision about Khiann, so she was not disappointed that her daughter-in-law did not wish to do so right away.

Well, not majorly disappointed.

When Annani had asked the oracle for help, she had been aware that Earth was obscured from her vision, but she had hoped that some events from the distant past were accessible to the Supreme Oracle of Anumati, and hearing that they were not had been deeply disappointing. In comparison, Syssi's delay in doing so was inconsequential.

Annani had no doubt that her son's mate would do everything in her power to assist her. In fact, she would probably do more than she should and exhaust herself.

Leaning over, Annani took Syssi's hand. "Promise me to pace yourself and not force too many visions. If

Khiann has waited five thousand years for me to realize that he might be alive, then he can wait a few more weeks."

Syssi nodded. "You know me too well, Clan Mother. I promise not to overdo it. If the Fates are willing, they will show me Khiann, and if they are not, no amount of pressure will force them to do so."

Aru had waited patiently for her to finish talking before turning to Kian. "What did you want to discuss?"

Kian raked his fingers through his hair. "It's late, so I will cut straight to the chase. I'm not comfortable hiding things from my sisters and sneaking around behind their backs. This connection is monumental on so many levels, and they are the leaders of this community as much as my mother and I are. If you want us to someday house the headquarters of the resistance, they and everyone else in my clan will have to be told, but everyone can wait. Right now, I just want to tell my sisters."

Aru's eyes blazed with anger. "I thought that I was clear on that. You've already betrayed my trust by telling your mate, and now you want to tell your sisters?"

"If I'm talking with you about it, I'm not betraying your trust. I know that you want to protect your sister, but you are being irrational. At some point, we will have to share this with them, and you know it. Does it really matter if we do it now or in a few months? The only thing we will achieve is mistrust. My sisters will not be happy to discover that they have been kept in the dark for so long."

Closing his eyes, Aru let out a breath. "What about their mates?"

Kian met his hard gaze with an equally hard one of his own. "My sisters and their mates are one and the same. None of them will betray you."

Indecision clouded Aru's eyes. "I did not tell my mate about my connection with my sister. If we are to include your sisters and their mates, then I will have to tell Gabi as well. She is my partner, and I cannot in good conscience keep this from her while sharing it with your entire family."

"Of course," Kian said. "I don't know why you kept it from her so far."

Aru's brows went up, and the look he gave Kian had her son avert his eyes. What was that about? Was it about Kian keeping from Syssi the knowledge of what a god's blood could do?

Annani would find out later, but right now she needed to find a compromise that would keep Aru from losing his mind. "I have an idea," she said. "If it would set your mind at ease, I could use compulsion to ensure the silence of my daughters and their mates on the matter. I do not like controlling the minds of others, least of all my children, but I am willing to do so to alleviate your concerns."

"That is an interesting proposition," Aru said. "How strong is your compulsion ability, Clan Mother?"

"Strong," Kian answered for her.

"What about Toven?" Annani asked. "He might be crucial to the success of our future goals, and he should be in the know as well."

Aru's expression turned pensive. "Can you compel Toven?"

"I've never tried," she admitted. "But he is a very strong compeller in his own right, so I probably have no power over him, but I trust him implicitly. Ultimately, however, I leave the decision in your hands."

Aru was silent for a long moment. "Let's keep Toven in the dark for now. We can always include him later when we actually need him. The same is true for your daughters, Clan Mother, but I understand that family dynamics might become problematic if we keep this from them."

"It is not about family dynamics," Kian said. "In the grand scheme of things, this affects everyone in the clan."

"I could host a family lunch tomorrow," Annani suggested before turning to Aru. "You and Gabi are invited, of course, but perhaps it would be a good idea for you to inform Gabi beforehand. She is your mate, and she might feel slighted at not being told first."

"You are right, Clan Mother. I will speak with Gabi beforehand."

"Is there anything else we need to discuss?" Syssi glanced at her watch. "It's nearly three o'clock in the morning."

"I believe we are done." Annani looked at Kian, and when he nodded, she added, "I will make the arrangements for lunch tomorrow. Will one o'clock in the afternoon work for you?"

When Aru nodded, Kian turned to Syssi. "Did you make any plans for tomorrow?"

She smiled. "Other than chasing a vision of Khiann? No. I didn't." She walked over to Annani and embraced her. "If he's alive, we will find him. I promise."

33

JASMINE

J asmine woke up alone.

She hadn't expected Edgar to spend the night in her narrow bed, but she'd hoped he would stay despite the cramped space. He could have spooned her or held her to his chest, and in the morning, they could have shared breakfast in the dining room.

With a sigh, Jasmine turned on her back and draped her arm over her eyes. She was no stranger to disappointment, and as usual, she found a way to look on the bright side.

Edgar couldn't have joined her for breakfast because he wasn't allowed in the staff dining room, where the rescued women ate. Not that it made any sense to her since the male staff members used the place, but that was the rule, and he couldn't break it.

Poor women, though. It wasn't hard to see that something terrible had happened to them. Their eyes were haunted, hopeless, and Jasmine found it painful to look at them.

Thank the goddess that she hadn't chosen a career as a therapist or a social worker. She would have sucked at it. There were only two ways Jasmine knew how to make people happy. One was acting or singing, and the other was sex.

She also sucked at finding love, but that was beside the point. She should be glad for everything that the goddess had given her.

With a sigh, Jasmine dragged herself out of bed and went through her morning routine, trying to shake off the lingering sense of melancholy. As she made her way to the dining room, she wished she had a phone, just so Edgar could call her and tell her that he missed her or that he had a great time last night and couldn't wait to see her again.

She would have even settled for a half-assed excuse explaining why he hadn't stayed with her.

After getting dressed, Jasmine stepped out of her cabin and headed for the dining room, but then decided to skip it and go to the lounge instead. Her mood was low enough without seeing the poor women and getting nauseous thinking of what had been done to them or getting chest pains from trying not to think about it.

There was so much evil in the world, and there was so little she could do to make things better.

Besides, she wasn't hungry, probably because of the late dinner she'd eaten last night, and she could get coffee at the lounge.

The place was quiet when she got there, the usual bustle of activity conspicuously absent. After pouring herself coffee from the commercial pot, Jasmine settled herself on one of the plush couches and grabbed a glossy magazine that someone had left behind. Flipping through it, she looked at the celebrities caught on camera doing this or that and tried to ignore the hollow feeling in her stomach that wasn't about hunger.

From the corner of her eye, she saw a couple enter the lounge, but since neither of them was Edgar or one of her friends, she ignored them and kept flipping through pages of gossip about the rich and famous.

Jasmine would have loved to be on those pages, but that was a dream that she had given up on a long time ago. Now, she just wanted to act in quality productions and get paid enough to make a decent living. Except, even that modest dream was out of reach for most actors, including her. The best she could hope for was getting a part in the occasional commercial and satisfying her acting bug performing at community theaters for free.

When the couple approached her couch, she couldn't ignore them any longer and shifted her gaze to them. The woman looked a little drab but was pretty in a forgettable kind of way, and the man was a hunk who looked like he could bench-press a car. She hadn't seen either of them before, so they were either lost guests or they were looking for someone.

Jasmine put on a charming smile. "Can I help you?"

"Hello," the woman said. "My name is Edna. Kian sent me to talk to you."

Oh, crap. The one with the probe, whatever that meant. She'd forgotten all about it.

Jasmine rose to her feet and offered the woman her hand. "I wasn't expecting you so early in the morning."

A tight smile lifted the edges of Edna's thin lips as she shook Jasmine's hand. "It's after ten in the morning, so I wouldn't call it early." Her pale blue eyes bored into Jasmine's, but there was no malice in them, just curiosity and piercing intelligence.

Wow, she hadn't encountered anyone with quite that look before. Later, she would practice it in the mirror. Was it possible to act out an intelligent look, though?

Jasmine shook her head. "I didn't know that it was so late. I don't have a phone, and it's difficult to assess the time down here." She waved a hand at the windowless walls.

Edna scanned the room and nodded. "I would be uncomfortable in these surroundings." She glanced at the hulking man next to her. "Does the lack of windows make you uncomfortable, Max?"

"Not at all. It's cozy down here."

The man was the very embodiment of masculine beauty, and his deep voice sent a shiver down Jasmine's spine. Except, he hadn't spared her a look yet, so he was either gay or one of those dudes who thought that they were all that and that women should fall at their feet and worship them.

Not this woman. She was the one who should be worshiped, and Edgar had.

"Hello, Max." A coy smile tugging at her lips, Jasmine offered him her hand. "Are you here to make sure that I don't escape Edna's probe?"

He finally looked at her. "You've got it. Are you going to run?"

The dude was looking at her as if she had something nasty stuck in her teeth.

Turning to Edna, she asked, "Do you always travel with a bodyguard?"

"No, not always." She lowered herself to the couch. "Please, sit down, and let's get it over with."

Perhaps Max was Edna's boyfriend? The two didn't look like they even liked each other, but perhaps they had gotten into an argument on the way.

"How long have you been together?" Jasmine asked as she sat down next to Edna.

"We are not together," Max said. "I'm just an escort."

A chuckle bubbled up from Jasmine's throat. "I bet you are pricey." She waved a hand at him. "What with all the muscles, you must be in high demand."

As Edna snorted, sounding like a donkey, Max's neck went a very satisfying shade of red.

"I'm not a bodyguard," he clarified. "Nor am I Edna's boyfriend or her paid escort. I'm here as a representative of the clan, and my job is to ensure that you behave."

Jasmine had to bite her lip not to pick up that line and run with it.

But then it occurred to her that he'd said 'clan.' What clan?

Before she could inquire further, however, Edna lifted her hand to put a stop to the banter.

"Before we begin, tell me a little bit about yourself."

Edna's pale blue eyes were unnerving, and Jasmine wondered if she was a powerful hypnotist like Kevin. Come to think of it, why hadn't Kian sent Kevin to talk to her?

If the guy could convince Modana to be born again, he could get her to tell him anything he wanted.

Maybe she wasn't important enough to bother Kevin with.

The truth was that she had nothing to hide except her witchy ways. They were harmless, but some people thought that they were evil or dangerous, while others scoffed at all Wiccan practitioners, regarding them as lunatics.

Come to think of it, Kian had decided to send Edna to probe her after Jasmine had admitted to him and Amanda that she was Wiccan. But then Amanda had also admitted to dabbling a little with the occult, so maybe they had no problem with it.

Still, maybe it was better to preempt any potential criticism by explaining why she'd chosen that path to follow and the solace and comfort it provided her with. She should tell Edna about that in her own words instead of the woman picking up some odd ritual and thinking that Jasmine was a devil worshiper because she saw a pentagram in there.

"First and foremost, I'm an actress," Jasmine said. "Acting is my passion and what I enjoy doing the most. I'm not famous, and I can't make a living doing what I love, so I work in customer service to pay the bills. I'm also a Wiccan. I know that some people have negative preconceptions about Wiccans, but for me, Wicca has been a blessing and a solace. The embrace of the Mother of All Life, the connection to nature and the divine feminine have helped me through some tough times." She smiled. "The life of an actor is full of rejections, and everyone deals with that in their own way. I think mine is healthier and more nurturing than most."

To her surprise, Max suddenly seemed very interested in what she had to say. "Did you say Mother of All

Life?" It sounded like an accusation.

Jasmine nodded, taken aback by his tone. "Yes, she's one of the central deities in Wicca. Why?"

Max shook his head. "Nothing. Go on."

He sounded dismissive, which was so aggravating because so many people made fun of witches.

"Wicca is listed as an official, legitimate religion by the government, with recognized holidays that practitioners can claim." Jasmine's tone was a little sharper than she'd intended. "It's not some fly-by-night cult."

Max snorted, his expression turning derisive. "Yeah, because the government is always such a great arbiter of what's real and what's not. Your so-called religion is just another sham organization that calls itself a faith to get tax-exempt status."

Why was he being so hostile?

What had she ever done to him?

Jasmine bristled, anger and indignation coursing through her veins. "Wicca has no churches," she snapped, "and no one makes money off of it unless they run a store, which wouldn't be tax-exempt anyway. We don't have any central authority or hierarchy. It's a personal, individual path."

There were covens, but they were usually small, ten to fifteen people, and Jasmine didn't belong to any. She was still a rookie witch who didn't know enough to even ask the right questions.

Max looked like he wanted to argue further, but Edna held up a hand, silencing him with a pointed look.

As she turned back to Jasmine, the woman's expression was one of gentle curiosity, with no trace of judgment or condemnation. "Tell me, Jasmine, has your practice ever produced any tangible results for you? Any instances where you felt like your spells or rituals had a real, measurable impact on your life?"

Jasmine nodded, a smile tugging at her lips as she remembered the countless times her incantations had seemed to work in her favor. "Absolutely. I always do a special ritual before going on auditions, and more often than not, I end up getting the part. It's like the universe is conspiring to help me succeed."

Edna's expression turned thoughtful, her head tilting slightly as she regarded Jasmine with a piercing gaze. "So, would it be fair to say that you've never auditioned for any truly major roles? No leading parts in big-budget productions or anything like that?"

Jasmine felt her cheeks heat up, a twinge of embarrass-ment mingling with the ever-present sting of self-doubt. "Well, no," she admitted. "But that's because I knew those parts were out of my reach."

"From divination?" Edna asked.

Jasmine nodded.

Something like understanding flickered through Edna's eyes, shaded by a hint of sadness or pity. "Perhaps it would have been better if you hadn't consulted your cards or your crystals whether you should audition for bigger parts. It's possible that you channeled your doubts and lack of belief in your own abilities into your divinations, producing the results you expected to see. And those results, in turn, only fed back into your insecurities, creating a self-fulfilling prophecy."

Jasmine stared at the woman as the truth of her words sank in. She had never stopped to think that her own fears and doubts might be influencing the very tools she relied on for guidance and reassurance.

"I've never thought of it that way, but you might be right. Do you really think that my own mind could have been sabotaging me?"

Edna reached out, her hand coming to rest on Jasmine's arm. "The mind is a powerful thing, and our beliefs, whether positive or negative, have a way of shaping our reality in ways we might not realize."

Max, who had been watching the exchange with a skeptical expression on his infuriatingly handsome face, leaned forward, his elbows coming to rest on his knees. "So, what else?" he asked, his gaze darting between Jasmine and Edna. "If her divinations were just a reflection of her own doubts, does that mean there's nothing to this whole Wicca thing? No real magic or power at all?"

Before Jasmine could jump to the defense of her beliefs once more, Edna spoke up again.

"I wouldn't be so quick to dismiss the validity of Jasmine's beliefs," she said. "Just because her divinations may have been influenced by her own thoughts and emotions doesn't mean that there isn't real power or truth to be found in the Wiccan path. The divine feminine, the connection to nature, the belief in the inherent sacredness of all life, are all powerful ideas with roots that go back thousands of years."

Jasmine felt like hugging the woman, but instead, she glared at Max. "Yeah, what she said."

Edna smiled. "The key is to learn to quiet the mind and trust your intuition and inner strength rather than relying solely on external tools for validation. Your power comes from within, Jasmine. You need to learn to tap into that."

As Edna's words washed over her, Jasmine felt a sudden sense of clarity. All this time, she had been looking outside herself for answers, for guidance, for proof of her own worth and value. But the real magic had been inside of her all along if only she knew how to reach it.

But wasn't that why she had turned to the occult in the first place?

She'd always felt that there was a reservoir of something powerful inside of her, but she didn't know how to tap into it.

Jasmine let out a breath. "That's the trick, isn't it? To learn how to use what's inside. The thing is, I don't even know what I've got inside." She put her hand on her stomach.

Edna reached for her hands and clasped them. "I can help with that. Look into my eyes and let me in. Don't try to fight me, or this will be more difficult than it needs to be."

As Jasmine looked into Edna's strange, wise eyes, she felt the world recede. "Are you going to hypnotize me?"

"Something like that."

34

ARU

The weight of the secret Aru had been keeping from his mate sat heavily on his shoulders.

It was strange how it hadn't bothered him before. He and Aria had been hiding their abilities since the day they realized that their connection was more than the typical twin intuition. They had kept their telepathic communication from their parents, their teachers, and their friends, and if the oracle hadn't discovered them, they would have kept it a secret from everyone still.

Having a truelove mate was a game changer, though.

It wasn't just about the fairy tales claiming that bonded mates could not keep anything from each other. For Aru, it had been a physical strain to keep the secret from Gabi, and in a paradoxical way, he was grateful to Kian for forcing his hand.

Now he had no choice, and it was like a two-ton boulder had been removed from his chest and he could finally take a deep breath.

"What time is the lunch at Annani's?" Gabi asked as she removed a freshly brewed coffee cup from the machine.

"One." Aru sipped on his tea. "Why?"

"Karen was released from the clinic last night, and she is back in her cabin. I want to visit her."

She sat on the stool next to him. "I'm not going to stay long. Just a few minutes to see how she's doing."

"Did she have her test yet?"

Gabi shook her head. "Karen doesn't want one. She says that all she has to do is look in the mirror to know that she's immortal. The fine lines around her eyes are gone."

He chuckled. "Smart woman. Although I have to say, rituals have their place. Maybe she should have the test done anyway just so it's videotaped, and she can show it to her grandkids one day."

Gabi rested her head on his shoulder. "Not everyone is sentimental, and apparently, Karen is not."

Taking a deep breath, Aru wrapped his arm around Gabi's shoulders, pulling her attention back to him. "There is something I need to tell you. A secret that I've been keeping from you."

She lifted her head, and the look of worry that flashed across her face made his gut clench. "Is something wrong? Do you need to leave?"

He hurried to reassure her. "It's nothing bad, but it's important, and I need you to vow that you will not tell anyone. Not even Dagor and Negal know, and it's important that it stays that way."

Gabi nodded. "Just tell me. The anxiety is killing me."

"First, I want you to know that I kept it from you not because I didn't trust you but because I was protecting my sister. It is something that Aria and I have been hiding our entire lives, but I was forced to share our secret with the Clan Mother, and, by extension, Kian. And now, with recent developments, I must also share it with Kian's sisters and their mates. But you deserve to know first."

Gabi swallowed. "What's going on, Aru? You are scaring me."

He tightened his grip on her hand. "Aria and I share a telepathic connection that allows us to communicate instantaneously regardless of distance. Over the past two nights, we've been facilitating contact between Queen Ani of Anumati and her granddaughter Annani. That's why I needed to leave the weddings every night to be at the Clan Mother's cabin at precisely one o'clock in the morning for the nightly meeting."

"That's incredible, Aru. Why is it such a dangerous secret, though?"

He sighed. "I told you about my home world and the king ruling it. His wife is not his fated mate, and she is not his ally. She is the heart of the resistance, and she's grooming her granddaughter, the only legitimate heir to the throne, to one day take his place."

"Oh my." Shock rippled across Gabi's face. "Now I get why your sister is in so much danger. But Dagor and Negal are part of the resistance. Why do you need to hide this from them?"

"So no one can pluck the information from their minds. The Eternal King's spies are everywhere, and they might even infiltrate the resistance. Some of them are rumored to be mind readers. No one is safe, not even inside their own minds, unless they keep their shields up at all times, the way Aria and I have learned to do. Telepathy of any kind is a rare and highly sought-after skill on Anumati, and even rarer is the ability to communicate verbally mind-to-mind like Aria and I can. If we had been discovered, we would have been either eliminated or conscripted to the king's spy service. That's why we hid it from everyone, even our own parents."

Gabi's fingers tightened around his. "If you kept it a secret, how did you end up working for the queen? Did you and your sister offer the queen your services?"

"I wish we were that brave or that altruistic." Aru's mouth quirked in a sad, wistful smile. "The Supreme Oracle found us. Queen Ani tasked her with finding people with our specific talent, and as soon as our abilities manifested, the Supreme sensed us. But she waited, biding her time until we were old enough to be properly brought into the fold."

He went on to explain how he and Aria had been recruited into Ani's service. "We were brought to the sacred temple that stands as one of the only bastions of safety from the King's spies. Aria was hired to become the Oracle's personal scribe, her telepathic bond with me allowing her to relay messages and information instantly and securely. I was drafted into the interstellar fleet, and my posting on the patrol ship tasked with monitoring the sector where Earth resided was not a coincidence. It was all part of the queen's plan, a gambit to find a trace of the exiled gods. Again, Negal and Dagor have no clue about any of that. They wonder why I was chosen to be the team commander despite my youth and inexperience, and they suspect some nepotism, but that's it. It's crucial that they never find out."

"This information will never leave my lips." Gabi reached up to cup his cheek, her thumb brushing gently over the curve of his jaw. "If you want, you can thrall me to forget all of this. I don't need to know."

He shook his head. "There should be no secrets between bonded mates. Telling you has lifted a heavy weight off my chest."

Gabi's eyes suddenly widened. "Did the Queen know that you would find her granddaughter on Earth? Did the oracle tell her that?"

Aru shook his head, a rueful smile tugging at his lips. "For some reason, Earth is veiled from the Oracle's sight. That is why the queen needed to have boots on the ground, so to speak. She hoped to find out if any of the exiled gods had survived and made a life for themselves on Earth. Discovering that the beloved son she had lost had fathered a daughter and his legacy lived on was as much of a surprise to the queen as it was to us. A very joyous surprise, I might add."

"Naturally." Gabi's eyes shone with tears. "That is such a tragic and heartbreaking story, but also so full of hope and love."

He glanced at his phone and noted with a start how much time had passed. "I think you will have to wait to visit Karen after the luncheon with the Clan Mother and her family. It's almost time for us to head over there."

35

KIAN

"Here you go, sweetie." Kian put the tray over Allegra's highchair while Syssi put a bowl of cooked veggies in front of her.

Allegra regarded the peas and carrots with such distaste that Kian could barely stifle a chuckle.

"Tha!" She pointed at the breadbasket.

He turned to Syssi. "Can I give her a piece of baguette to chew on?"

"Only if she eats at least some of the veggies."

Allegra slumped in the highchair with an air of resignation that would have made a surly teenager proud, gave her mother an accusing look, and then picked up a piece of carrot and stuffed it in her mouth.

"Good girl," Syssi encouraged. "Eating your veggies is important. Try the peas, too."

Struggling not to laugh, Kian turned his attention to Amanda and Dalhu, who were similarly engaged with Evie. Their daughter was much more amenable than Allegra and didn't make a fuss as Dalhu fed her some mush from the bowl. But then, she was younger than Allegra, and her personality might still change. So far, she seemed to take after Alena more than Amanda, but she still might develop a forceful personality like her mother. No one could have ever accused Amanda of not being assertive.

Shifting his gaze to his mother, Kian was happy to see her basking in the joy of her granddaughters.

Good times.

If only all the moments of their lives could be so peaceful and happy. Some might say that would be boring, but Kian would have welcomed it with open arms.

There was always something to keep him on edge. Now it was the developing saga with the Doomers in Mexico, and Syssi's promise to his mother to induce a vision about Khiann.

She hadn't yet, but she planned to do so when Allegra took her afternoon nap. The problem was that their daughter was not always cooperative in that regard, and sometimes instead of sleeping, she chose to rest in her crib awake.

He wondered what she thought about when she lay quietly with her wise eyes open and her blanket clutched in her small hands. Was she pondering the mysteries of the universe? The meaning of existence?

"Did Edna probe Jasmine already?" Amanda's question pulled him out of his reveries.

Turning to his sister, Kian nodded. "She did."

"And? What did she find? Did Jasmine click with Edgar?"

"According to the guys in security, Jasmine took Edgar to her cabin, and he stayed there for a couple of hours before returning to the wedding party." Kian wasn't happy about sharing that information with his family, but he knew that Amanda wouldn't rest until she got it out of him. Resistance was futile, and it was faster and easier to just report things as he knew them.

Amanda grinned. "I hope that it was more than just sex, and they clicked. Did Edna say anything about it?"

"She didn't report anything about Jasmine having feelings for the guy, but she might not have looked for them, or they might have been absent. I didn't ask."

"I like how assertive Jasmine is," Amanda said. "She knows what she wants, and she isn't afraid to take it. What else did Edna say?"

"Edna seems to think that Jasmine is harmless. There are some painful shadows in her past, probably childhood traumas that Edna didn't explore, and she's a Wiccan, which we already knew, and she believes in the Mother of All Life, which we did not know." He chuckled. "I wonder if that's another influence of one of the Kra-ell's early settlers."

Amanda's eyes sparkled with excitement. "That's probably a coincidence. Many of the ancient civilizations worshiped the Mother. Anyway, I'm so happy that Jasmine is a practicing witch. If she turns out to be a Dormant and joins the clan, I'll have someone to play with."

Syssi groaned. "Promise me that even if Jasmine joins the clan, you won't start a new tradition of forming witch circles and chanting in the nude inside the village. The place is not big enough to ensure your privacy, or rather to ensure that those who shouldn't see a bunch of ladies dancing in the nude under the moon are not exposed to it."

"I don't mind who sees me." Amanda leaned back in her chair. "It's liberating, and it works."

Dalhu wrapped his arm around Amanda's shoulders. "The Fates work in mysterious ways, and it seems like they chose to deliver you a playmate." He leaned and kissed her temple. "You can chant in the nude as much as you want, just not without proper safety measures. While you and your lady friends are busy having fun, I and the other mates should secure the perimeter."

Kian shook his head. "I can't believe that you are taking this so seriously, Amanda. Doing it for fun is one thing, but to actually think that it's effective is crazy."

"Oh, really." She gave him a haughty look. "It worked every time."

"Coincidence."

Amanda looked down her nose at him. "If it makes you more comfortable to think that, be my guest."

"Thank you." He mockingly dipped his head.

"You're welcome. So, are you going to allow Jasmine on the upper decks?"

"In light of Edna's findings, or rather lack thereof, I don't see why not. And if Jasmine bonds with Edgar, I will allow him to tell her the truth so he can ask her consent to be induced. In the meantime, though, I'll instruct everyone not to talk about immortals and gods around her, and I'll have her kept under close watch."

Annani, who hadn't said much until now, nodded. "In case Edgar is not the one for her, it will be good for Jasmine to interact with more people."

"Precisely." Amanda dabbed at Evie's mouth with a napkin. "You still didn't tell us what this lunch is about. You wouldn't have asked us to come earlier if it was just a regular family get-together."

His mother's idea was for the two couples with young children to come a little earlier so the girls could finish eating before the rest of the adults arrived.

"Patience, my daughter." Annani leaned over and patted Amanda's hand. "We have important issues to discuss, and I did not want us to be interrupted. Once the girls are done with their lunch, Ojidu can watch over them in the bedroom while the adults talk, but we need to wait for your sisters and their mates and for Aru and Gabi to join us. It concerns all of you."

"Now, I'm really worried." Amanda crossed her arms over her chest. "Can you at least give me a hint?"

Annani smiled. "It is big, but no one is in any immediate danger."

"Thank the merciful Fates." Amanda let out a breath. "By the way, how is Margo doing?" She looked at Kian. "Is she really transitioning?"

"I don't know," he admitted. "I haven't checked on her this morning."

"Perhaps you should call her before the others get here," Amanda suggested. "She'll be so happy to hear about Jasmine being allowed on the upper decks."

Kian turned to their mother. "Is it okay with you if I call Margo now?"

"Of course. I am also curious about her transition."

Kian pulled out his phone and scrolled through his contacts until he found Margo's. He could have used a voice command like all the young gods were doing, but he liked doing things the old-fashioned way.

Margo answered on the second ring, sounding breathless. "Hello, Kian. What a nice surprise. How can I help you?"

"I have some good news, and I also want to know how you are feeling. Did you experience any changes? Are there any new developments?"

"I'm feeling great. Bridget came to check on me earlier, and she said my fever and blood pressure have both gone up, which, according to her, are good signs that the transition is progressing as it should. Surprisingly, though, I don't feel weak or dizzy anymore."

Kian had a strong suspicion regarding Margo's sudden improvement. Negal had most likely given her his blood, and he just hoped that the god had exercised discretion.

"That's fantastic news, Margo. Is Bridget moving you to the clinic, or is Karen still there?"

"Bridget said that Karen is doing well enough to be released and that I can move in whenever I want, but I'm not in any rush. I told Bridget that Negal had been glued to my side, fussing over me and functioning like my own personal nurse, and she agreed that I could stay in the cabin for now. If things get worse, Negal will take me to the clinic."

"That's good." It was unusual for Bridget to agree to leave a transitioning Dormant in the care of her partner, but she must have had her reasons.

"So, what's the good news you were calling about?" Margo asked.

"I cleared Jasmine to roam around the upper decks. She can visit you, spend time on the Lido deck, and she can attend the weddings, but only after the ceremonies are concluded. I want to keep her exposure minimal, so we won't have as much to thrall away in two days."

"That's wonderful. When can she come up?"

"As soon as she wants, but she doesn't know yet. I need to send someone to inform her. Regrettably, we don't have a spare phone we can give her."

"I can ask Frankie to go down there and get her if that's okay with you."

"Of course. It will save me the trouble. But you need to remember not to say anything about your transition. You will have to tell her that you are just sick. As I said before, the less she knows, the less we will have to erase."

"Don't worry," Margo said. "I totally get it, and I won't breathe a word about anything she doesn't need to know. Thank you for letting her out of the lower decks."

"My pleasure." He ended the call.

36

AMANDA

Once Kian was done with the call and had slipped his phone back into his pocket, the sound of the door chime announced the arrival of more guests. Amanda pushed to her feet as Ojidu opened the door and greeted her sisters and their mates with hugs and kisses. When the greetings were done, everyone took their seats at the table, which was now complete save for the two empty chairs reserved for Aru and Gabi.

It was like the game 'find the Thing That Doesn't Belong.' Why were Aru and Gabi invited to a family lunch?

Usually, when the close family got together, it was for more than just the feels. News and updates were delivered in an unofficial manner, and advice was provided just as unofficially.

The reason that Aru and Gabi had been invited was probably that they had news that pertained to the family, which meant something about Anumati.

Oh, well. Amanda would have to wait and find out, along with the others, what this was all about.

When the doorbell rang again, and Ojidu opened the door for Aru and Gabi, their pinched expressions made Amanda's hackles rise.

She leaned over to Syssi. "Something big is about to happen," she murmured conspiratorially, her eyes darting between her mother, who had lost her easy smile, and the anxious-looking couple. "I can smell it in the air."

Syssi's only response was a slight nod.

"Good afternoon, Clan Mother." Aru bowed to Annani. "I apologize for us arriving last."

"No need to apologize, Aru. You are right on time. The others have arrived a little early."

"That's good to know," Gabi said. "Thank you for inviting us."

As Annani inclined her head magnanimously, the couple followed Ojidu to their seats and sat down.

Annani scanned the faces of her guests with a soft smile lifting her lips. "Now that everyone is here, we can start."

Amanda held her breath as she waited for her mother to reveal what the meeting was about, but Annani just lifted her hand to signal to her Odus that it was okay to bring out the food. The babies had been situated in the bedroom with a kids' show to entertain them and an Odu to watch over them.

As the Odus began to serve the fragrant dishes, the adults dug into the delicious pesto pasta and Caesar salad, and the conversation around the table turned to the latest developments, with Kian filling the others in on Karen's and Margo's progress.

"It's a pity that Frankie and Margo are going to leave right away," Alena said. "I bet Mia is disappointed. She hoped they would join her in the village."

"It's problematic." Kian spread a napkin over his knees. "Negal and Dagor can't join the clan for security reasons, and the same is true for you, Aru." He looked at the god. "Nevertheless, we need to extend our umbrella of protection to them. There should be no unaffiliated immortals out in the human world even if they have three gods to protect them." He shifted his gaze to Gabi. "You need a community. Especially if and when you have children. You already have family in the village, so it's a given, but I will have to talk with Margo and Frankie about their status."

She gave him a bright smile. "I thought that it was a non-issue, and that I could visit anytime I wanted, but thank you for the official welcome."

When their mother regarded Kian with pride in her eyes, Amanda wondered if that was what they had been assembled for. Except, Kian did not need their approval to welcome new members to the clan. If he thought that approval was necessary, he should have called a council meeting and put it to a vote.

Perhaps he wanted to make sure that the family was on board beforehand?

David chuckled. "You should have a 'Welcome to Oz' banner at the glass pavilion for the newcomers, and a yellow brick road painted on the floor."

Amanda lifted her hand. "I volunteer to be the witch, but I don't know which one, the Wicked Witch of the West or the Wicked Witch of the East, or one of the good witches. I need to read up on them again." She had read the original book version, which had four witches, two good and two wicked, but Amanda didn't remember who was who and what each was responsible for.

Kian groaned. "Again, with the nonsense about witches?"

Sari narrowed her eyes at him. "What nonsense?"

"Turns out that our rescued guest fancies herself a witch." Kian shook his head. "Jasmine is an active Wiccan who is convinced that she's destined to meet a prince. I wonder if Edgar fits the bill or if he's just a placeholder until she finds her dream royal."

Amanda snorted. "Edgar is a sweetheart, but he's no Prince Charming. I mean, he can be charming, but he is..." she glanced at her mother "not very discriminating with his affections, and very active."

That was common for young immortals, and until not too long ago, Amanda had been just as bad or just as good, depending on how one regarded raging promiscuity. She'd used to refer to herself as a slut, but it had become politically incorrect to do so because it was supposedly shaming. Except, she had always worn the title with pride.

Oh, well. She was a college professor, which meant that she was surrounded by the current generation of whiny ninnies who found every other word offensive but had no problem bullying whoever did not fit their extremely narrow and misguided worldview. The ignorance was just staggering, but thankfully, it wasn't as bad in her department. Scientifically inclined minds were a little better trained to ask questions and a little less susceptible to herd mentality, though not by much.

Amanda stifled a sigh. Her job wasn't to teach them right from wrong. That was their parents' job. She was there to teach them about the brain.

As the conversation turned to Wicca, Amanda discovered that Sari knew more about it than she did. Her sister had not taken part in any rituals, but she'd studied the subject because several of her people had gotten into it. She explained about altars, the different deities they believed in, and the tools they used to channel energy.

The soothing sounds of conversation mingled with the clatter of silverware and the clink of glasses, and even Aru and Gabi cracked a few smiles, the good mood around the table managing to break through the anxious veil that seemed to be hanging over them.

Something about Jasmine's prince quest prickled Amanda's mind, but before she could catch the string of thought, her mother distracted her with a comment about brainwaves that she had to respond to, but even though Annani nodded and smiled, it was obvious to Amanda that she wasn't really listening.

The glint of anticipation and excitement in Annani's eyes sent a shiver down Amanda's spine.

The luncheon wasn't about welcoming new immortals into the clan or even about Jasmine. It was about something else.

Leaning forward, Amanda asked, "What's going on, Mother?"

Annani smiled, the gleam in her eyes making Amanda's heart race. "Patience, my darling," she murmured. "All will be revealed soon. But first, let us enjoy coffee, dessert, and wonderful company."

37

ANNANI

As the Odus cleared the dishes and then served coffee and tea, Annani watched Amanda's growing impatience, her leg bouncing beneath the table and her fingers tapping its top.

She had always been such an inquisitive child. Annani should have known that she would one day become a researcher despite the years of partying and losing herself in the pleasures of the flesh to drown out the crippling grief that had followed her son's death.

It was any mother's worst nightmare, and Annani regretted having this in common with her daughter. She did not know what was worse, losing Lilen, who had been an adult and whom she had gotten to know and appreciate as a grown man, or losing a little boy and all the unrealized potential of who he might have been had he lived.

Death was a terrible thing, but hopefully it was not the end, and beyond the veil, Lilen and Aiden were together, perhaps they had even joined Khiann, if he had indeed been murdered by Mortdh and was not in stasis under the desert sands as she ardently hoped.

Across the table, Aru and Gabi sat in silence. Annani could not see their hands, but she was sure they were clasped tightly together under the tablecloth as they sipped their coffee and avoided the curious gazes of her children and their mates.

As the minutes ticked by and the coffee cups emptied, the tension in the room grew thicker, and Annani knew it was time.

"I can see the curious looks you're casting my way, and I know that you are all wondering why I have called you here today. There is a secret I am about to share with you, but I want you to know that I kept it from you only because it was not my secret to reveal. Kian and I have convinced Aru that you can be trusted with it, but to ease his fears, I also offered to compel you all to secrecy, but I will never force it on you. If you do not wish to be compelled, you can leave now before I speak of it."

Amanda snorted. "After such a preamble, wild horses couldn't drag me away." She waved a hand. "Please compel me and then tell me what the big secret is before I die of curiosity."

This was such an Amanda response that Annani could not help the laughter that bubbled from her throat. "Does everyone here share Amanda's opinion?"

As heads bobbed all around, Annani closed her eyes for a moment to gather her power.

When she opened them, her family were looking at her with so much awe that she knew she must be glowing like a star. Glancing at her exposed arm confirmed her suspicion.

"My dear family, my son, my daughters, and their mates. What Aru and I will tell you in a moment can be shared only between those seated around this table. The only one who can choose to share it with whomever he pleases is Aru because this is his secret."

Hopefully, she'd closed all the possible loopholes, and if modifications were needed, she could alter her compulsion as needed.

As her glow receded, Aru bowed his head. "Your power is immense, Clan Mother."

"Yeah." Alena rubbed her belly. "I hope it didn't do any damage to the baby."

"He or she will be privy to the secret and will have to keep it," Amanda teased her sister. "After all, your child is seated around this table."

"Not funny," Alena grumbled. "We don't know what compulsion does to the brain, and especially to a developing one."

"He is going to be fine." Sari reached for her sister's hand.

Alena frowned. "How do you know it's a he?"

"I don't, but I have a hunch. Kian and Amanda got girls, so it's your turn to have a boy. You also have many more girls than boys, so a boy is statistically more likely."

"It doesn't work that way," Amanda murmured. "There are many factors that determine a baby's gender."

Annani lifted a hand. "Let us not get distracted." She turned to Aru. "Would you like to share your story, or should I?"

"I will start." Aru rose to his feet.

Annani felt a flicker of apprehension twist in her gut. She knew that the revelation of his connection to the queen of Anumati and the communication that was enabled thanks to him and his sister would come as a shock to her daughters and their mates, but the bigger shock would be when they understood the implications.

"I have guarded this secret since I first became aware of it, and it has shaped the course of my life and my twin sister's. Not even our parents or my teammates know, and it's imperative that they never find out. It is not because I don't trust them but because this knowledge is so dangerous, and the king's spies are everywhere." He scanned their faces. "Except here. Earth is shielded from the oracles, and the only vessel passing through this sector is the patrol ship I arrived on."

Annani was not sure that Aru was right about that. Had the assassins who had come to destroy the rebel gods arrived on a patrol ship? Or had the King sent a smaller, faster vessel with a few well-trained, well-armed, trusted operatives?

"My sister and I have a special telepathic connection," Aru continued, his words hanging heavy in the air. "You have a similar duo in your clan, a mother and daughter who can talk to each other mind-to-mind. What you might not have realized is that distance does not affect telepathic communication. I can talk with Aria, who is on Anumati, as if I was talking to any of you on the phone. It is instantaneous."

Even though everyone was aware that Vivian and Ella possessed a similar ability, a ripple of shock went around the table, gasps and murmurs of astonishment mingling with the clatter of silverware and the hush of held breaths. Annani kept her gaze focused on her daughters, her heart preparing for their hurt expressions.

"That's amazing," Amanda said. "I understand the need for secrecy given that you are part of the resistance, and I assume that your sister is part of it too, but why was it necessary when you were growing up?"

Aru sighed. "Duos like ours are hunted on Anumati. The Eternal King does not want a mode of communication that he cannot tap into. We are either recruited to work for the king or sent to a colony to meet with unfortunate accidents. Aria and I were lucky that our connection bloomed when we were old enough to understand that we should keep it a secret. But that's just the tip of the iceberg, as the Earth saying goes. The queen of Anumati discovered Aria and me a long time ago and recruited us to work for her.

"My sister serves the Supreme Oracle, who is the queen's closest friend and coconspirator, and I was inserted into the interstellar fleet and through careful maneuvering stationed on the patrol ship bound for this sector.

"The queen hoped to find some survivors who could tell her what had really happened on Earth and how her only son had died, but she didn't expect to find a living granddaughter, her son's only legitimate heir, and therefore the only legitimate heir to the throne of Anumati."

Aru turned to Annani. "Would you like to tell the rest of the story?"

She nodded. "Thank you, Aru. I can take it from here."

38

ARU

As Aru sagged in his chair, Gabi reached for his hand and squeezed it.

Hearing himself talk about his connection with his sister had been terrifying, and his confession hadn't brought about any of the relief he had expected.

The cruise had done what Kian and the heir had hoped for, which was to bring Aru and his teammates into the fold without inviting them to join the immortals' community. By now, they were almost like family to him, and he knew he would do everything to protect them, like he had done everything he could to protect Aria, but he still felt as if he had betrayed her even though he had not.

Well, maybe he had.

He hadn't asked the queen's permission to tell all of Annani's children, their mates, and his own mate about the communications between the queen and her granddaughter, which was most likely the most important secret in all of Anumati and its countless colonies.

The resistance needed the queen, and it needed Annani to step into her grandfather's shoes after he had been forced to vacate them. But the truth was that they would need the help of all of Annani's children to achieve that, and it couldn't be done without letting them in on the secret.

The Clan Mother, as the royal heir of Anumati liked to be referred to, scanned her children's faces. "The Queen, my grandmother, was delighted to find out about me. She suggested that we meet through Aru and Aria, who would function as the channel between us. We have had two such meetings so far, both at one o'clock in the morning, which necessitated Kian and Aru leaving the celebrations before they were over." She glanced at her daughter-in-law. "Syssi knew about Aru and Aria from a vision she had about the queen and her best friend, the Supreme Oracle. Once she saw Aria's face, it was clear to her that she was Aru's twin sister, and the rest of the puzzle pieces fell into place. That is why she joined our meetings and transcribed by hand what was being said so nothing would be lost."

The heir paused, letting her words sink in.

"The queen of Anumati," Orion murmured, "hundreds of light years away, is talking to you here on Earth. What did she tell you?"

"In the first meeting, she asked me many questions, probably to assess my worth. Our second meeting was used by the queen for a broad history review of Anumati, which was a little more political in nature than what Aru already shared with us. She intends to continue the overview tonight, and then go back and describe things in more detail."

"To what end?" Sari asked. "Just for your general knowledge?"

Sari was a smart female, and she must have guessed what was behind the queen's interest in her grand-daughter. Aru's emphasis on her being the only legitimate heir to the Anumati throne must have given that away.

The Clan Mother nodded. "The queen wants me to learn all there is to know about Anumati's social structure, its politics and economy. Her plan is to impart an intimate knowledge of the main movers and shakers, so one day, when the resistance manages to take down the Eternal King, I can take over and prevent chaos from destroying Anumati. The population will accept me as a rightful ruler, and the transition of power will be smooth."

"That's insane," Alena said. "Why did you allow her to convince you to take part in this?"

The Clan Mother sighed. "I did not commit to anything yet. I do not wish to rule, but I am starting to realize that if I refuse, I may be condemning the people of

Anumati, along with all the hybrid species they have created over millions of years, to endless war and chaos, which would happen if the resistance takes down the king and there is no one to replace him who can unite them. Still, it might take thousands of years of resistance to get to that point, and in the meantime, I am worried about what my grandfather will do to Earth once humans advance beyond what he is comfortable with. This is a male who had no qualms about killing his own children. Do you think that he would hesitate even for a millisecond before he gives the order to destroy Earth?" Her voice rose in power as she got emotional. "The only way to save Earth is to take him down before he finds out, and that means that I have to push the timeline of the resistance."

"How long have you known?" Amanda directed her question at Kian.

"Not long."

"Before the cruise or during?" Amanda asked.

"During. Aru told me first."

"You should have insisted that we all learn of it as soon as you found out," Amanda said. "It was wrong to keep it from us."

"I know, but it wasn't my call."

Amanda turned a pair of angry eyes at Aru. "Thank you for finally confiding in us, but I truly don't understand why you felt the need to keep it from me and my sisters. Once you told Kian and our mother, there was no point in hiding it from us."

Kian lifted his hand. "Enough. This is not the time for accusations or recriminations. Aru has risked everything to share this truth, and we should be grateful to him and Aria for providing this channel of communication that wouldn't have been possible otherwise."

Amanda snorted, her eyes flashing with anger. "It would have been better if they hadn't. I don't want our mother to get involved in the biggest uprising in the freaking galaxy. Chances are that she won't survive it, and neither will Earth. Instead of plotting insane coups, we should adopt the same strategy that has helped us survive against the Brotherhood. We need to find a way to hide Earth and its capabilities from the freaking Eternal King."

39

ANNANI

As Amanda's words hung heavy in the air, Annani felt a ripple of unease pass through her assembled family. She could see the conflict playing out across their faces, the struggle between the desire to protect the mother they loved and the sense of duty to do the right thing.

"Amanda has a point." Sari's eyes drifted to meet Annani's. "In the grand scheme of things, we are nothing. We can't even obliterate our enemies at home. To think that we can move the needle against the Eternal King is too ambitious even for you, and frankly, it's delusional. And I mean no offense, Mother. I'm just stating the facts."

"It is not ambition, my child." Annani's heart clenched at the fear in her brave daughter's voice. "I understand your concerns, my darling, and I would be lying if I said I didn't share them. But here are the facts. This is not the clan's fight or even mine. I will have one job in this grand scheme, and it is to become a figurehead the people of Anumati can unite around." She smiled. "I do not intend to lead armies into battle or challenge my grandfather to a duel to the death."

Sari shook her head. "The moment he learns of your existence, it's game over for you and for all of us, including every human on Earth."

Annani swept her gaze over the faces of her children and their mates. "That is a valid point, but I cannot let fear dictate my actions. I cannot hide from the truth of who I am and the responsibility that comes with it."

Orion leaned forward, his brow furrowed. "But is it really your responsibility, Clan Mother? The Eternal King is the ruler of Anumati and its colonies, and he might be a tyrant, but he is out there, and you are here, and until not too long ago, you didn't even know that he existed. Why should you risk your life and ours and the safety of our entire world to overthrow a tyrant on a planet hundreds of light years away?"

Annani sighed. "Because it does not matter if he knows about me or not. Sooner or later, his gaze will turn to Earth, and when it does, he will not hesitate to eliminate this planet we call home if he perceives humans as a threat. We cannot wait and hope that he will one day disappear and that the threat will be gone. There is a reason he calls himself the Eternal King. He has all the time in the galaxy to find us and destroy us. If we do nothing, we are as good as dead."

She turned to Amanda. "Hiding was a good strategy against the Brotherhood, and still is, but it is not an option against the Eternal King. Not in the long run. The only way we can prevent Earth's destruction is to make sure humans never achieve interstellar flight capability. Do you really think we can do that?"

Kian nodded. "Mother is right. We cannot bury our heads in the sand and hope that the storm will pass us by. I've seen enough human leaders adopt that approach and get wiped out. History forgot about them."

"But at what cost?" Alena whispered, her hand coming to rest on the swell of her belly. "Are we really willing to risk everything, to put our children and our future in jeopardy, for a war that is not our own and might never get here? The Eternal King has declared Earth a forbidden planet whose name was erased from Anumatian records. He might have forgotten about us."

Aru cleared his throat. "The fact that he sends a patrol ship every seven hundred years or so indicates that he has not forgotten about Earth. In fact, he probably keeps closer tabs on it than many of the colonies that are in the records."

"It's because of the Kra-ell," Amanda said. "He's afraid of the damn royal twins..." Her eyes widened. "The prince and the princess, the son and daughter of the Kra-ell queen." She looked around the table, a smile forming on her face. "Jasmine is obsessed with finding the prince that her tarot cards keep promising her. She even hooked up with Alberto because the damn cards told her to. What if the Fates are steering her toward the Kra-ell prince?"

Syssi chuckled. "Of all of your harebrained ideas, that is the wackiest. We talked about seeing patterns where there are none. It's nothing more than projecting your wishful thinking onto things and connecting dots that don't connect."

Annani was grateful for the change of subject.

Jasmine's preoccupation with tarot cards and royalty was a much lighter topic of conversation than the threat of the Eternal King and Annani's aspirations to save the home planet of her people and Earth along with it.

Kian shifted and put his hand next to hers on the table. "Are you okay?" he asked quietly as his wife and sisters continued arguing with Amanda about her latest hypothesis.

"Yes, my son." Annani drew herself up, her shoulders squaring and her chin lifting in resolve. "I am the daughter of Ahn, the granddaughter of the Eternal King, and even though I may not have sought this destiny, it has found me, and I will not run from it. I will not hide from the truth of who I am and what I must do."

The Eternal King might be a formidable foe, a tyrant with an iron grip on the galaxy and a heart as cold as the void of space. But Annani was not weak, even though her heart was full of love. Maybe that was why the Fates had chosen her. She was all about love and hope, while her grandfather was all about cruelty and despair.

40

MARGO

Margo stretched out on the couch, feeling more energetic than she had in days. The fatigue and dizziness that had plagued her since the onset of her transition seemed to have vanished overnight, to be replaced by a sense of vitality that had her itching to do something, anything, other than lying around.

So what if she had a little fever and her blood pressure was elevated? She didn't feel it, and if Bridget was allowing her to stay in her cabin instead of hooking her up to the monitoring equipment in the clinic, she wasn't worried about her suddenly losing consciousness either.

The phone call from Kian had also been a major mood boost. She couldn't wait to show Jasmine around the ship. Well, her cabin would have to do for now, but maybe tomorrow she could take her to the Lido deck and they could share a drink.

Regrettably, there was no way Negal was going to let her go down to the staff decks to look for Jasmine, and leaving her alone to go himself was also not going to happen.

Frankie wasn't back yet from lunch, so Margo couldn't ask her to do it. Maybe instead of waiting for Frankie to come back, she could call her and ask her to stop by the staff lounge before returning to their cabin.

When she reached for her phone, Negal frowned. "What are you doing, Nesha? You should be resting."

"I'm calling Frankie. I want to ask her to find Jasmine and bring her up here."

His frown deepened, concern etching lines into his handsome face. "You should be resting. In fact, you should be in bed."

Margo waved off his concern with a smile. "I feel great, Negal. Better than I have in days. And it's all thanks to you."

He tensed, his eyes widening slightly. "Why me?"

She laughed, reaching out to pat his arm. "Your godly mojo, of course. I wouldn't be transitioning with such ease if I'd been induced by a mere immortal's diluted venom. Yours is a miracle drug."

Negal shifted uncomfortably, looking like he wanted to say something but thought better of it. "Still," he said after a moment, "hosting a party might be pushing it. You don't want to overtax yourself."

"It's not a party," Margo said. "It's just a little get-together, Jasmine, Frankie, and maybe Mia if she's free. Does it really matter if I'm on the couch watching television or talking to my friends? One does not require more energy expenditure than the other."

He looked like he wanted to argue but then nodded. "Fine, but you are staying on the couch. I'll make them coffee or tea or whatever you want to serve them. Deal?"

"Deal." Margo smiled as she pressed the star next to Frankie's number.

"What's up, Margo?" Frankie asked. "Did you change your mind about lunch? Dagor and I are on our way out, but we can stop by the kitchen and bring two packed lunches for you and Negal."

"Thanks, but we are fine, food-wise that is. I need to ask you for a favor."

"Anything," Frankie said. "Are you feeling better? Do you want me to sneak you out to the Lido deck while Dagor distracts Negal?"

Margo laughed. "I might take you up on that offer tomorrow. Today, I was hoping you could go down to the staff lounge and tell Jasmine that Kian cleared her for the upper decks and bring her here. As you know, she doesn't have a phone, so someone has to go get her, and Negal won't let me off the couch."

"No problem," Frankie said. "Dagor and I are heading down there right now. See you soon."

"I love my friends," she murmured as she called Mia.

The phone rang a few times before her friend picked up, sounding slightly out of breath. "Hey, Margo, is everything okay?"

"Everything's great. Are you busy?"

"No, not really. I was just doing a little exercising."

Trying to imagine her wheelchair-bound friend doing sit-ups or push-ups, Margo frowned. "Lifting weights?"

Mia chuckled. "Lifting one weight. Me. I brace my arms on the armrests and lift myself off the chair. It's like push-ups in reverse, if that makes sense."

"That sounds difficult. How are your feet coming along? You keep hiding them, so I don't know if you are growing toes already or not."

"I am. Bridget says they will be complete in no more than two weeks. I can't wait to walk again."

"I can imagine." Margo sighed. "I want to celebrate your first steps on your own two feet with you, but I probably won't be there." She shifted her gaze to Negal. "I'm progressing so fast through my transition that Aru won't need to ask their commander for a few more days before they head to Tibet. I will be fine to join them."

Smiling, Negal sent her an air kiss.

"I'll pray that you do, and if you have to miss my first steps on my brand new feet, I'll have Toven film it, and you can watch it live."

"That's an awesome idea. You do that."

"I will, but enough about me. How are you doing?"

"Great, and that's why I'm calling. I was wondering if you wanted to come over for a bit. Kian approved Jasmine to be on the upper decks now, and Frankie is bringing her up to our cabin. I thought we could all hang out together. I mean, as long as it doesn't interfere with your bridesmaid duties."

"Mey didn't invite me, so I don't have any. I don't really know her all that well. I'd love to come over."

"Awesome. See you soon." Margo ended the call and tossed her phone aside. "I'm so excited that Jasmine is coming." She opened her arms. "Come give me a hug."

"You're lucky you're so cute," Negal said as he leaned over her and kissed her lightly on the lips. "Otherwise, I might have tried to talk some sense into you."

She laughed, reaching for his hand and twining her fingers through his. "Admit it," she teased. "You love it that I'm stubborn."

"I love everything about you." Negal's voice dropped an octave as he lifted her hand to his lips. "Even when you're driving me crazy with your stubbornness."

41

JASMINE

The sound of the doorbell echoed through Jasmine's tiny cabin, startling her out of a very romantic part of the book she was reading.

It was the third time she was reading it, and yet she still teared up when James went down on one knee and declared his undying love to Annabel.

"I'm coming." She scrambled off the bed, smoothing down her hair and checking her reflection in the small mirror above the desk.

It was probably Margo. She hadn't seen her or heard from her in what seemed like days, and she was starting to worry about her.

Or maybe it was Edgar, come to apologize for leaving last night with not so much as a note.

Satisfied that she looked presentable, she pulled it open, a smile curving her lips. But instead of Margo or Ed, she found Frankie standing in the corridor with a breathtakingly handsome guy towering over her petite frame.

What was it with the insanely good-looking people on this cruise?

"Hey, Jasmine!" Frankie said. "I have great news. You've been cleared to come up to the upper decks, and Dagor and I are here to escort you to our cabin, which we share with Margo and Negal."

Jasmine's eyes widened, her heart doing a little flip in her chest. "Really? Did Edna clear me?"

Frankie shrugged. "Margo only told me that Kian was okay with you coming up and to come get you."

The niggling feeling of worry that had been hovering in the back of her head came to the fore. "Is Margo alright? I haven't seen her in days, and now she sends you instead of coming down here herself."

Frankie waved a dismissive hand. "She's just a little under the weather, and Negal is fussing over her and not letting her move from the couch. She wants to see you. We can all hang out together."

"Awesome." Jasmine turned back into the cabin. "Do I need to put on something fancier for the posh upper decks?"

Frankie shook her head. "Nah, you look great. We're just going to Margo's cabin. No need to get all fancy."

"Then I'll just get my shoes and my purse." Jasmine cast a smile at Frankie's boyfriend. "I'm so excited to finally be allowed up there." She chuckled. "Talk about feeling like Cinderella."

As they stepped out into the hallway, Jasmine was practically bouncing on her toes in her eagerness to get to the upper decks and see all the wonders hiding up there, but as they got to the stairs, a familiar figure rounded the corner, his blue eyes lighting up when he saw her.

"Jasmine!" Edgar grinned. "Where are you off to?"

"I've been cleared to go up to the upper decks, and I'm going to visit Margo in her cabin."

His eyes widened. "That's fantastic." He reversed direction and climbed the stairs beside her. "I can finally show you around and give you the grand tour."

"That sounds great." She reached for his hand and clasped it. "But I will have to take a raincheck. I need to go see Margo. Frankie said that she was not feeling well, and I wanted to make sure she was okay. I haven't seen her in days."

Edgar nodded. "Perfectly understandable. Mind if I tag along?"

Jasmine glanced at Frankie and then at Dagor. "Is that okay with you?"

Frankie hesitated for a moment, annoyance flickering across her face too quickly for Ed to notice. "Sure." She affected a bright smile that didn't quite reach her eyes. "The more the merrier, I guess."

An uncomfortable silence fell over the group as they made their way up the stairs, and Jasmine didn't like the tension in the air.

Ed shouldn't have invited himself, but was it really such a big deal?

"Why are we taking the stairs instead of the elevator?" she asked, to fill the silence.

"Our cabin is on deck three," Frankie said. "It's faster to climb the stairs than to wait for the elevators."

As they stepped into the lushly appointed hallway of Frankie and Margo's deck, Jasmine pushed the thought aside and took in the decor.

She approved.

It wasn't gaudy or over the top as she'd expected. Instead, the style was of understated elegance. Plush carpets, gleaming wood panels, and works of art that might have been originals or fakes—she didn't know enough about art to tell the difference.

42

AMANDA

While the discussion around the table continued to revolve around modern witchcraft, fields of energy, and how quantum physics could explain paranormal phenomena, Amanda pushed aside thoughts of her mother becoming the ruler of the galaxy because, frankly, it was just crazy.

Instead, she thought back to the fun times she'd had with leading her mostly made-up witchy rituals.

She had always been fascinated by alternative spirituality and connecting with the divine feminine, but she had only superficial knowledge of Wiccan practices and had never delved too deeply into the specifics of modern witchcraft. It had always been about fun for her—a way to bond with her female friends over something different and naughty. She'd had a blast scandalizing Syssi by coercing her shy sister-in-law into dancing in the woods in her birthday suit.

Amanda stifled a smile at the memory.

Across the table, Syssi let out a long-suffering sigh. "I will never forget how you roped me into the ritual you did for Vivian."

"I was just thinking about the same thing," Amanda admitted. "It was so much fun."

"For you," Syssi grumbled.

Amanda chuckled. "After you got over your excessive modesty, you enjoyed it too. Besides, it worked beautifully, so it was worth a few minutes of embarrassment. Vivian stopped thinking that she was cursed and embraced her relationship with Magnus."

Sari cast Amanda an amused look. "Since the curse only existed in Vivian's head, the ritual probably had a placebo effect. She believed that it worked, so it did."

Amanda pursed her lips. "Maybe you are right, or maybe the combined positive energy of fourteen females did the trick."

Syssi laughed. "It was an impressive theatrical production, so it looked convincing. Although I doubt that Vivian was impressed with the wizard robes we wore. They came from a costume shop."

"Why fourteen?" David asked. "I've heard of a circle of seven or thirteen but never fourteen. Is there more power in doubling up on seven?"

"Humm." Amanda tapped her finger on her lower lip. "I should have thought of that explanation when we ended up with fourteen instead of thirteen witches in our circle, but that wasn't it. It's actually a fun story." She looked at Syssi. "Do you want to tell it, or should I?"

Syssi waved a hand. "Go ahead. I'm sure that your version will be much more entertaining than mine."

"Fine. So the plan was to assemble thirteen females, but since I knew that not everyone would be on board with nudity," she cast Syssi a pointed look, "I got fifteen. Syssi said that there was no way she was getting naked and that she would offer her support from the side-lines. Kri, who was there in a Guardian capacity, was armed to the teeth, so she couldn't join in either because of her weapons. That left me with thirteen, which was what I needed."

"We looked so ridiculous," Syssi said. "I had my clothes on under the wizard robe, but Amanda, Carol, and many of the others were naked underneath."

Amanda shrugged. "We looked fabulous, but after we each shared our life force energy with Vivian, it was time to disrobe, and before you all think that I was being eccentric or silly or just wanted to torment poor Syssi, I will have you know that nudity is a legit requirement of the Wiccan ritual. You can look it up if you don't believe me."

Syssi let out a sigh. "You made a very convincing argument back then, and I'm often reminded of it. It was about how we clothe ourselves in customs, ideology, and comforting illusions in our everyday lives. The naked body represents the truth, and by shedding our material and spiritual garments, we proclaim our loyalty to the truth."

"Nicely said." Sari nodded.

"That's how Amanda convinced me to participate," Syssi said. "That and the speech about how we are all perfect in our own way and have nothing to be ashamed of. When I agreed to shed my clothes, I became the fourteenth female in the circle that had been supposed to have only thirteen."

Kian shook his head. "You are a bad influence, Amanda."

He'd heard the story before, probably more than once, so he was saying that to tease her. Fine, she could play his game.

She gave him a haughty look. "I beg to differ. I think that I'm a wonderful influence. All the women who participated in that ritual felt energized and empowered by it, and Vivian no longer thought that she was cursed. It was a win-win for everyone involved."

Not only that, but they had created a memory they would carry with them forever. How many of those did people have? Most of life was mundane, with one day resembling the next and nothing to distinguish it from all the others. People remembered the highs and lows. Since lows were usually unplanned and just hit them over the head at random, it was important to build an arsenal of highs, and that didn't happen without planning.

Syssi leaned toward Amanda. "Do you remember the incantation?"

"More or less." Amanda cleared her throat. "We are gathered here in a circle of fourteen powerful women to beseech the Goddess's help for our sister Vivian. With her divine light, the Goddess will destroy the malignant energy within Vivian's soul and free her from her curse. Let us all join our voices in the chant. Please repeat after me. Great mother, the supreme mistress who lives in our hearts and guides our way toward love and compassion, honor and humility, mirth and pleasure, bestow upon us your power tonight, chase away the darkness and replace it with your light, so our sister Vivian can worship and honor you by freely accepting love and pleasure without fear."

Leaning back, Syssi crossed her arms over her chest. "You totally made that up."

"I did," Amanda admitted. "But you can't deny the energy we all felt that night. That wasn't made up."

"It's true." Syssi looked at Kian. "We talked afterward, wondering if a group of males could have produced the same energy."

He chuckled. "Don't expect me to try it, and if you somehow convince thirteen males to do a witchy or wizardry ritual in the nude, there is no way I'm letting you watch it in the name of science or anything else."

"Don't worry, my love." She cupped his cheek. "The only male I want to see in the nude is you."

"Oh, wow." Amanda fanned herself. "Who are you, and what have you done with my shy sister-in-law? The Syssi I know and love would have never said that in public."

As Syssi's cheeks got red, Annani came to her rescue. "So, if I understand correctly, modern Wiccans worship the feminine."

"Not exclusively," Sari said. "Wiccans believe in a dual deity system, with a goddess and a god representing the feminine and masculine aspects of divinity, but because Wicca is about honoring the natural world and the cycles of life, it has a more feminine slant than the traditional religions, and it appeals more to females."

"What about the magical aspect of it?" Gabi asked.

Amanda lifted her hand. "I can answer that. The Wiccan magic is not the fantasy version of turning misbehaving princes into beasts or growing giant trees from magical beans. It's about focusing intention and energy to bring about positive change on the individual and global levels."

"Those are lofty statements," Aru said. "But how does that work in practice? How can a ritual or a spell influence reality?"

Sari leaned over so she could face him. "In the same way that meditation and prayers do in other spiritual traditions. Wiccans believe that by aligning their intentions with the natural energies of the world, they can tap into a deeper power and create change in accordance with their will. Given your connection with your sister, you shouldn't be so skeptical. There are forces and energies in the universe that are impossible to explain based on what we know."

Aru dipped his head. "Well said."

David, who so far had been satisfied with just listening, put his hand on Sari's shoulder to get her attention. "You don't have to work hard to convince me that this is all real, but with harnessing such power comes great responsibility. How do those who practice the Wicca religion ensure that it is used ethically?"

Sari let out a breath. "The Wiccan guiding principle is the Rule of Three: Whatever you release into the world will return to you trifold, so be sure that you do no harm."

Amanda nodded. "What it's basically saying is that everything a witch does comes back at her, so cursing someone or wishing them ill will cost the witch dearly. It's a good incentive to only cast good spells."

Kian looked like he'd had enough of the discussion. "As fascinating as I find all this talk about witchcraft, what we should focus on is what Jasmine believes in and if she can actually do what she claims she can."

"Very true." Amanda smiled at her brother, who had been very patient up until now. "I should talk to her about it."

43

JASMINE

A s they neared Frankie and Margo's cabin door, Jasmine watched Frankie pull out her phone and aim it at the lock.

"That's so cool. I only have a simple keycard." It figured that even that small convenience was reserved for the guests of the upper decks.

As the door swung open, Margo rushed over, her face split by a huge grin. "I'm so glad that you are here."

Pulling her friend into a hug, Jasmine was careful not to squish Margo, who looked a little pale. "I finally get to see where you've been living."

Margo laughed, ushering her into the spacious cabin. "This place is bigger than my apartment and much nicer. I don't know how I'm going to go back to living like a pauper."

"You won't," Frankie murmured.

Jasmine wondered what she meant by that. Was Margo moving in with Negal? If so, they were moving a little too fast, but who was she to judge?

Everyone had their own timelines for things.

"You weren't kidding about this place being swanky." She turned in a circle, taking in the professionally decorated living room portion of the cabin with its floor-to-ceiling sliding doors that overlooked a spacious balcony and the ocean beyond.

"Mine is just as nice," Edgar said from behind her.

Crap, she'd forgotten that he was there. Plastering a smile on her face, Jasmine turned toward him. "You remember Edgar, Margo, right?"

Margo offered him her hand. "Of course. How could I forget the pilot who brought me Negal?"

"It was my pleasure." Edgar shook what he was offered.

Margo pulled him into a quick one-armed embrace. "I'm glad that you two found each other." She let go of Ed and regarded him with curious eyes. "How have you been?"

"I've been good, but I'm even better now that I was allowed to venture down to the staff quarters and reunite with Jasmine." He took her hand and brought it to his lips for a kiss. "As you know, males are banned from the lower decks because of the rescued women, but Amanda convinced Kian to let me visit."

"I'm glad." Margo sat down, looking exhausted just from standing for a few minutes.

Joining her friend on the couch, Jasmine regarded her with a frown. "What's going on with you? You look like a ghost."

Margo grimaced. "It's nothing. Probably a bug I caught while on shore, or maybe the whole kidnapping ordeal is finally catching up to me. How about you? Are you okay?"

Margo was so sweet, always worrying about others.

"Honestly? The whole thing feels surreal. I keep waiting to wake up. First, it was Alberto turning out to be a scumbag, but that wasn't such a big surprise. I was starting to suspect something was off about him long before I met you, but I had no idea how bad it was going to get. Then I got kidnapped, dragging you along into the abyss, and then Edgar flew a team to our rescue." She smiled at Ed. "But ending up on this ship almost makes it all worth it."

"Really?" Margo arched a brow. "Even though you were restricted to the staff decks?"

"It wasn't all bad." Jasmine crossed her legs. "I made new friends, met interesting people, and I even got tested by a neuroscientist and a probe lady." Jasmine chuckled. "The wonders never cease." She waved her hand over the cabin. "And now this. I plan to explore the upper decks and all the luxuries they have to offer."

Frankie perched on the arm of the chair Dagor sat in. "You will need to hurry up with your explorations. The cruise is almost over, so you don't have much time left." She sighed. "I'm going to miss this ship with all its comforts, especially the dining room. I love having all my meals prepared for me."

When Negal finally emerged from the bedroom, Jasmine was reminded how incredibly handsome he was. Edgar was a good-looking guy, but next to Negal, he looked almost plain.

"Hello, Jasmine." Negal smiled at her. "I'm glad that you are finally free to visit. How are you feeling?"

"Great. I was just telling everyone how it all feels surreal."

"I bet." He turned to Edgar, who squeezed in next to Jasmine and sat down on her other side, and arched a brow. "Hello to you too, Ed."

"I'm here with Jasmine." Ed clasped her hand. "We are together."

"I see that." Something unreadable flickered through Negal's eyes. "I wish you the best of luck. Can I offer you a drink? Tea or coffee?"

"What do you have?" Ed let go of Jasmine's hand and rose to his feet.

"Let me show you," Negal said.

As the guys were joined by Dagor at the kitchen counter, Jasmine leaned toward Margo. "Things look serious between the two of you."

"They are," Margo whispered conspiratorially. "Negal is amazing."

Frankie snorted. "He's like a mother hen, fussing over Margo and not letting her move an inch. I'm glad my Dagor is not such a fusser."

Margo snorted. "Right, says the girl whose boyfriend was so anxious to see her that he couldn't wait for the boat to get to the ship, jumped into the water, and swam the rest of the way."

As Frankie's lips quirked in a half smile, Jasmine leaned back and crossed her arms over her chest. "Now, that's a story I want to hear all the details of. What was Dagor doing in a boat, and why was he so anxious about you?"

Frankie slid into the armchair that Dagor had vacated. "I got shot."

Jasmine's eyes widened. "Really? How? When? By whom?"

Frankie cast a quick look at the men before leaning forward and whispering, "I'm not supposed to talk about it, but did you wonder where the rescued women came from, and who rescued them?"

A shiver ran down Jasmine's spine. "I thought they were just given passage like I was."

"There is more to it," Frankie said. "It all started with a cursed amulet."

Jasmine laughed. "I knew you were pulling my leg, but I'm always game for a good story."

The doorbell ringing stopped Frankie from telling the rest of it, and as Dagor opened the door, Mia drove in, exchanging quick greetings with the guys before joining the girls.

"I'm so happy you are finally free." She returned Jasmine's hug. "We can now plan a get-together on the Lido deck. Did you bring a swimsuit?"

Margo chuckled. "It's not a suit. I first met Jasmine by a pool, and what she had on was a skimpy bikini that would have made even Amanda blush."

Jasmine pretended to be offended. "That's a huge exaggeration. My bikini is not scandalous at all. It's not my fault that I'm generously endowed."

Margo cast her a fond smile. "I wasn't talking about the front. I was talking about the back. I didn't even know that thong bikinis were a thing until I saw you in one. But I have to say, you look damn good in it."

44

EDGAR

A surge of possessiveness swept through Edgar as he watched Jasmine laughing with her friends. She was so damn beautiful, and it wasn't only about her physical attributes. Jasmine was vivacious, and it was the first time he had ever used that word to describe a woman because he'd never met one who fit that adjective so well. Her eyes sparkled, her smile was bright, and her laughter wrapped around his shaft as if it were her hand.

He wanted to pull her into his arms, carry her out of Margo's cabin, and lock her in his until the end of the cruise.

The problem was that she would not be on board for that. Ever since they had arrived at Margo's, Jasmine had been distant, her attention divided between him and the others, which usually wouldn't have bothered him, but he had a niggling sense he couldn't quite shake that she wasn't into him as much as he was into her.

He tried to tell himself that it was just the excitement of finally being allowed on the upper decks and getting to spend time with Margo and Frankie, but it seemed like Jasmine was doing her best to avoid his eyes, and her laughter sounded a little too loud, too forced, which led him to believe that she was nervous, but he didn't know why.

Was she intimidated by Dagor and Negal's presence?

That wasn't likely. Jasmine didn't know that they were gods, and she didn't seem like the kind of woman who got nervous around attractive men. On the contrary, that was where Jasmine was in her element.

"So, what changed Kian's mind about letting you up here?" Margo asked.

Jasmine flipped a dark lock of hair behind her shoulder. "He sent a woman named Edna to probe me. She's a hypnotist like Kevin but with a slightly different ability. She can determine people's inner motives and intents. She must have arrived at the conclusion that I was harmless, but she definitely didn't come in thinking that way. She brought a hunky guard with her, a guy named Max, who did his best to intimidate me."

Edgar felt a hot spike of jealousy pierce his gut, and it only got worse when Frankie and Margo started peppering Jasmine with questions about her interactions with the Guardian. Edgar tried to tune them out, but it was difficult to hear Jasmine gushing over Max's impressive muscles and piercing eyes.

The jealousy was irrational. Jasmine sounded like she was describing a movie star, admiring his attributes but not saying anything that would indicate that she was attracted to the guy, and Max had assured him last night that he had absolutely no interest in her.

Edgar had returned to the wedding party to catch the Guardian and have a talk with him about staying away from Jasmine. It also hadn't hurt that Max could smell her on Edgar. He might not be one of Max's buddies, but he knew the guy wouldn't go after a woman he was interested in. It was a matter of honor.

Still, males might claim to adhere to a code of honor only to throw it out the window when an attractive female caught their eye. Shamefully, he had been guilty of doing that once or twice, but then neither he nor his friends had been pursuing females for anything other than a tumble between the sheets.

In fact, that's how he should think about Jasmine instead of getting all worked up about her. He had no right to claim her or feel possessive or territorial about her.

Easier said than done after the incredible, mind-blowing night that had left him aching for more.

He'd thought that it meant something to her and that the connection he'd felt wasn't just in his imagination.

But watching her with her friends and seeing the way her eyes kept darting to the door as if she was waiting for someone else to arrive, Edgar felt a sinking sensation in his gut that Jasmine did not consider last night a preamble for more.

She probably saw him as a convenient stepping stone, a way to pass the time until someone better came along. Someone like Max, with his chiseled jaw and rippling muscles and aura of power.

Edgar clenched his fists, fighting back the urge to punch something.

He was just a civilian pilot, a glorified chauffeur in the grand scheme of things, but he was fun to be with, and he had a much better sense of humor than damn Max. Females loved Ed, as evidenced by the endless parade of beautiful women who had graced his bed.

He needed to take a step back and breathe and give Jasmine space to figure out what she wanted. If he wasn't the one for her, so be it.

The world was full of beautiful women. But beautiful women who were also Dormants were rare, and there was a slight chance that Jasmine was a Dormant.

Nevertheless, he wouldn't make a fool of himself, even if it meant watching her flirt with other men. He would grit his teeth and smile through the jealousy that clawed at his insides and pretend that he was fine with it.

That didn't mean that he wouldn't fight for her, though. Just that if he lost to someone else, he wouldn't be a sore loser.

Even if she was just a human, Jasmine was still worth fighting for, if for no other reason than to prove to those macho Guardians that charm and wit were no less important than bicep size.

When there was a slight pause in the chatter, he leaned over and put a hand over Jasmine's thigh. "Can we talk out on the balcony for a minute?"

Jasmine glanced at her friends, hesitated for a moment, but then nodded and rose to her feet. "Lead the way."

Margo and Frankie regarded him with twin puzzled expressions, but the knowing looks in Dagor and Negal's eyes told him that they understood what was going on.

When they stepped out to the balcony, he closed the sliding door behind them and pulled Jasmine into his arms. "I need to kiss you."

She giggled. "Is that what you wanted to talk about?"

"Yeah. More or less." He wrapped his palm around the back of her neck and kissed her hard, pouring all of his uncertainty and pent-up possessiveness into the kiss.

When he finally let her go up for air, she was breathless. "Wow." She brought a finger to her lips and rubbed it over them. "Whatever you wanted to talk about, that was a very convincing argument."

He chuckled. "I'm glad that we have that settled." He took her hand and turned toward the sliding door.

"Wait." She tugged on his hand. "Is that really all you wanted? To kiss me?"

He hesitated for a moment. "I wanted to remind you how good it is between us, just in case you forgot while drooling over Max's biceps."

"Oh, Ed." Jasmine laughed. "I'm not interested in Max, and he's not interested in me. I think he doesn't like me for some reason. He was borderline rude to me and kept looking at me as if I had dog poo stuck to my shoe."

Now, that made Ed angry almost as much as hearing that Max had flirted with her would have. "I'll talk to him. He has no right to regard you with anything other than respect."

"Oh, sweetie." She lifted her hand and cupped his cheek. "That's so chivalrous of you, and here I was thinking that chivalry was dead."

He felt his chest puff up even though he hadn't commanded it to do so. "I'm glad to restore your faith in my gender."

She leaned in and feathered a soft kiss over his lips. "As much as I appreciate the gesture, please don't talk with Max about me. You don't need to risk your friendship with him over a silly thing like that. Besides, I'm a big girl, and unless I've been drugged and kidnapped by a drug lord, I can take care of myself."

45

MARGO

After Jasmine and Edgar left to explore the ship, Margo leaned back on the plush couch, listening to Frankie and Mia talk about Karen.

"Gabi told me that Karen doesn't want to do the test," Mia said. "I need to have a talk with the woman and explain that it's not about making sure she has transitioned, but about tradition. All transitioned Dormants do it. It's like a rite of passage."

Frankie shrugged. "Karen strikes me as the practical sort, and she doesn't need the proof, so why go for it?"

"That's what she says." Mia let out a breath. "Karen told Gabi that the disappearance of her fine lines was proof enough that it worked."

As her friends debated the merits of Karen's decision, Margo's mind drifted to her own situation. Bridget believed that her symptoms were consistent with the transformation, and Negal was convinced of it, but part of her still doubted. What if they were all mistaken and something else was responsible for her symptoms?

Frankie's test was a simple cut on the palm of her hand that had healed in a matter of moments. The ceremony around it had been a much bigger deal than what was needed for the test.

Margo wanted the certainty that came with concrete proof that she was truly becoming immortal, and as she listened to the others talk, an idea began to form in her mind.

A brief moment of pain was worth it, to know for sure, and she didn't even need the doctor for that.

"I need to visit the bathroom." Margo put her teacup down on the coffee table.

Mia smiled at her. "I should go. I promised Toven that I wouldn't stay long. He wanted to go to the Lido deck."

"I think Dagor and I will join you," Frankie said. "Jasmine and Edgar headed there." She cast a glance at Margo. "Do you want to come? You can lie down on a lounger, and it will be like being on the couch here, just out in the fresh air. Am I right?"

"Maybe tomorrow." Margo pushed to her feet and gave Frankie a quick hug and then another to Mia. "I'm sure that by tomorrow, I'll feel well enough to go out there, but today, I'd rather take it easy."

She walked by Dagor and Negal, who were sitting on barstools in front of the tiny counter, sipping on bottles of that potent beer that the immortals liked.

She pecked Negal on the cheek. "I'm just going to the bathroom. I will be right back."

He nodded and got to his feet to open the door for Mia.

So far, so good.

Margo felt like a teenager sneaking away to smoke a cigarette where her parents wouldn't find her.

Negal would be furious if he found out what she was about to do, but she needed to know.

After locking the bathroom door behind her, Margo rummaged through the drawers but found no scissors, no clippers, and not even a razor. Negal used an electric shaver, and she had forgotten to buy a disposable blade for the few stubborn armpit hairs that no amount of laser treatments had managed to obliterate. Not that it was such a big deal. The hairs were blond and barely visible, but they annoyed the heck out of her.

She should just tweeze them away.

Well, what do you know? She could use the tweezers to make a scratch, right?

The cool metal felt slightly ominous in her hand, and she hesitated for a moment, not because she was afraid of a little pain but because she was debating the wisdom of her plan.

When Frankie was transitioning, Bridget had claimed that she had to wait to test her until Dagor's venom cleared her system because Frankie's body had been saturated with it, so the wound could have healed because of that and not the transition.

That wasn't the case with Margo. Negal had bitten her only once, so if she healed faster than normal, it would be a sign that she was transitioning.

Taking a deep breath, Margo hiked up her skirt, exposing an expanse of her thigh. She needed to make the scratch somewhere inconspicuous in case it didn't heal faster than it should, and she would be stuck with the evidence of her subterfuge.

With a shaking hand, she pressed the tip of the tweezers against her skin, wincing at the sharp sting of pain. It wasn't a deep cut like the one Bridget had given Frankie, but even a scratch would normally take days to heal on Margo's fair skin.

Transfixed, she watched as a thin line of blood welled up along the shallow wound, the deep red a stark contrast against her pale flesh. It didn't happen right away, and she was starting to despair, but then the blood flow stopped, and then the edges of the scratch started knitting together before her astonished eyes. It took long minutes until the wound vanished entirely, but it was still a miracle.

Normally, she would have never healed so fast.

A giddy laugh bubbled up from her throat. There was no more doubt. It was happening. She was truly transitioning.

Bursting out of the bathroom, she ran to the living room in a whirl of excitement and launched herself at Negal, who was sprawled on the couch. "I'm becoming immortal." She peppered his astonished face with kisses.

He let out a startled grunt, his arms coming up automatically to catch her as she clung to him like a koala. "Did you doubt it?"

She nodded.

A slow grin spread across his face as he took in her elated expression. "Of course you are, Nesha. But what has changed in the last five minutes?"

Margo's smile turned sheepish, a blush staining her cheeks. "I needed to see it for myself. I needed to know that this was really happening."

Understanding dawned in Negal's eyes, followed quickly by a flash of concern. "What did you do?" His gaze roamed over her body as he searched for injury.

Margo shook her head, pressing a reassuring kiss to his lips. "Just a little scratch to see how fast I would heal."

Negal's frown deepened, his hands tightening on her hips. "Margo, you shouldn't be doing stuff like that.

Your body is going through enough changes as it is, and it's too early for testing. You should have waited for Bridget to determine the right time."

She sighed, resting her forehead against his. "I needed to do it, Negal. I needed proof. The anxiety of the uncertainty was making me sick. I feel so much better now that I know for sure."

He softened, one hand coming up to cup her cheek. "I understand," he murmured before taking her lips in a kiss. "How much stronger do you feel?" He whispered against her ear.

"Much, much stronger." Margo pulled back to look at Negal's eyes, which were sparkling with mischief. "And I feel like celebrating."

His gaze darkened with desire, his hands sliding down to cup her backside. "And what exactly did you have in mind for your celebration, Nesha?"

Margo grinned, pressing herself against him in a way that left no doubt as to her intentions. "Oh, I can think of a few things," she purred.

Negal's answering growl sent a shiver down her spine, and then he was lifting her into his arms and carrying her toward the bedroom with single-minded purpose.

As he laid her down on the mattress, his body covering hers in a delicious weight, Margo wrapped her arms around her mate and held him to her. "I love you."

"And I love you, my soul."

He began worshipping her body with gentle hands, lips, and tongue, and as he brought her to the heights of pleasure, Margo let herself get lost in the sensations.

Later, when she lay quivering and boneless in his arms, she looked into his beautiful blue eyes. "What about you?" She reached between their bodies and took hold of his hard length through his pants.

He shook his head, removed her hand from his erection, and brought it to his lips for a kiss. "I don't think I should give you more venom while you are transitioning. In fact, I'm sure that I shouldn't. Bridget told Frankie and Dagor to abstain until Frankie was out of the woods."

She smiled sheepishly. "That doesn't preclude a hand job."

"It does because I'm too tightly wound up to refrain from following up with a bite. I can survive one more day."

"I love you." She lifted her hand to cup his cheek.

Negal smiled, his hand coming up to cover hers. "I love you too, Nesha. More than I ever thought possible to love someone." He pressed a kiss to her temple. "But now, you need to rest."

"I do." She let out a breath and nestled into his embrace, letting the steady beat of his heart lull her into a sense of peace.

46

KIAN

"Join us." Syssi wound her arms around Kian's neck. "Allegra loves playing in the pool with you, and you are supposed to be on vacation, not working all the time."

Usually he brought work with him on vacations, but this time he'd intended to do as little as possible and enjoy time with his family. Obviously, the Fates had different plans for him.

He kissed the tip of her nose. "You know that I'm not a great fan of public pools."

That's why he had a private lap pool at home for his exercise.

Kian was the leader of his community, and he had to maintain a certain distance whether he liked it or not. No one would bat an eyelash if he showed up on the Lido deck in his swim trunks, but he wasn't comfortable doing so.

Besides, he needed to talk to Turner before Yamanu's bachelor party.

"You don't have to go into the water if you don't want to." Syssi pouted. "You can just chat with my father over a drink. You know how much he enjoys talking to you."

Syssi's parents had come over earlier to take Allegra to the pool, and Syssi had stayed behind for a few moments to put her swimsuit on and gather a few things. Allegra loved her granddaddy, and Adam adored Allegra, but Kian had no doubt that his father-in-law would love some adult conversation. Regrettably, he couldn't oblige him today.

"I love chatting with your father as well, but I haven't checked with Turner about Margo's parents' place yet, and then I need to get ready for Yamanu's bachelor party."

Yamanu was one of the oldest Guardians on the force and one of its most valued members. His bachelor party was not one that Kian wished to skip.

"Fine." Syssi let go of his neck. "My dad is going to be disappointed, but he will understand. Enjoy the party, and I'll see you when you get back."

Syssi looked a little disappointed herself, but it couldn't be helped. Besides, she was meeting her parents and Andrew and his family, so she and Allegra would have plenty of company.

"I love you." He dipped his head and kissed her cheek. "Give Allegra kisses from Daddy."

"I will."

When he closed the door behind Syssi, Kian pulled out his phone and called Turner.

Turner answered after several rings. "Good afternoon, Kian."

"Good afternoon. I hope I'm not interrupting. I just wanted to know if you've heard any news from your teams in regard to Margo and her family's residences and workplaces. Did anyone come snooping around?"

"I've just got off the phone with my assistant. So far, no suspicious activity has been recorded."

Kian was glad that there was no activity but only because he didn't have Guardians in the area to take care of it.

Things were going to change once they returned home.

"Keep me posted if anything changes."

"As soon as I hear anything, I'll let you know."

"Thank you, and I'm sorry about making you work on your vacation."

Turner chuckled. "Don't be. I've realized that I don't enjoy long vacations. I get bored. I like doing what I do too much to want to be away from it for too long."

"I know what you mean, and we are both certifiable. Try to enjoy the rest of the day."

"Same goes for you," Turner said.

Ending the call, Kian sank into his chair and rubbed a hand over his face.

Unless Carlos Modana and the Doomers he was working with had decided to drop the investigation of what happened in Acapulco and what had made Julio change his stripes, they would want to have a talk with Margo and Jasmine, if only to cover their bases.

Now that Margo was transitioning, one problem was solved. She was not going back to her apartment and her old job. She was most likely going to accompany her mate on his journey to Tibet.

Her family was still a big problem that needed to be resolved, though, and naturally, it was up to him. They needed new identities and new jobs, and that was going to cost a bundle.

Perhaps he could get Toven to take care of that. After all, Margo and Frankie were on the cruise at his personal invitation.

Jasmine would be much more difficult to hide and protect.

Her customer service job was easy to replace, but she also had a modest acting career, and that made her face recognizable, so hiding her would be tougher.

Or maybe not?

She could get a new name, a new agent, and maybe, with Brandon's Hollywood connections, better parts.

That wasn't smart, though. Putting Jasmine in front of cameras was too risky. Her looks were too distinct to be forgettable, and not even plastic surgery could do much about it. Besides, the woman didn't need anything done, and she wouldn't want to change what she was given by the Fates.

He needed to find something else for her that would keep her out of the public eye, at least for a couple of years until Modana and the Doomers forgot about her.

The easiest thing would be to put her up in a hotel and ask her to stay put for a few weeks. After that, Toven could arrange a Perfect Match job for her. Given her experience in customer service, that wouldn't be a problem. Those departments always needed new people.

47

AMANDA

Amanda scanned the dining room for Jasmine and Edgar. "I don't see them." She turned to Dalhu. "Do you?"

She was wearing flats, so he had a good half a head or more over her.

"I don't. Maybe they went to the Lido deck."

Frankie had said that Ed had taken Jasmine on a tour of the ship, but the only public spaces were the dining room, the gym, and the bars on the promenade deck and the Lido deck.

Amanda cast a sidelong glance at her mate. "Do you want to grab something to eat before we go up there?"

They had eaten brunch at her mother's, but that had been an hour ago. She wasn't hungry, but Dalhu might be.

"I'm full." Dalhu adjusted Evie in his arms. "Let's go."

They only got as far as the elevator. As soon as the doors opened, Jasmine and Edgar stepped out along with several other passengers.

"Amanda!" Jasmine spread her arms and hugged her as if they were the best of friends. "Thank you. You freed me."

"You're welcome." Amanda patted her back. "Are you heading to the dining room?"

"Yes." Jasmine beamed happily. "I'm curious whether the food up here is better than the food down in the staff dining room."

"Why would it be? It's cooked in the same kitchen."

Jasmine looked surprised. "Really? I thought there was another kitchen down there adjacent to the dining room."

"There is, but most of the cooking is done in the main one." Amanda turned to her mate. "Dalhu, this is my new friend Jasmine. Jasmine, this is my husband Dalhu and our daughter Evie."

"A pleasure to meet you both." Jasmine gave Dalhu one of her flirty smiles, but by now Amanda knew that didn't mean she was actually flirting with him. It was just the way she was, and she probably couldn't help it.

Evie regarded the woman with shy curiosity and after a moment gifted her with a small smile before ducking her head and hiding her face in the crook of Dalhu's neck.

"She is adorable," Jasmine said. "And she looks like a mix of the two of you. More like you, Amanda."

Dalhu kissed the top of Evie's head. "Thank the merciful Fates for that."

"Have you eaten already?" Edgar asked.

"We did, but we will come to keep you company." Amanda threaded her arm through Jasmine's. "I want to ask you a few questions about your Wiccan practice if that's okay."

"Of course." Jasmine leaned into her. "What would you like to know?"

Amanda slanted her a smile. "I'm fascinated by the occult, and I'm an amateur practitioner, but I never had the time to study the rituals and spells. I'm also interested in the deities you honor and your guiding beliefs."

More than that, Amanda wanted to understand the woman herself and get a sense of the person behind the tarot cards and the talk of princes. She had a feeling that there was more to Jasmine than met the eye.

The woman's face lit up, her eyes sparkling with excitement. "After acting, that's my second favorite topic, but I only talk about it with people who have at least some knowledge about it and don't think it's devil worship." She grimaced. "Like my father."

Amanda had a feeling that there was a story there, but it was better reserved for another time.

They found a table, and once Dalhu had set Evie down in a highchair, he and Edgar went to the buffet to collect a sampling of the dishes.

"I've already eaten," Amanda said. "So I'm not hungry, but if you want to go get something, I'll wait."

"It's fine." Jasmine waved a dismissive hand. "I trust Edgar to get me things I like."

Amanda arched a brow. "When did he have the time to learn your culinary preferences?"

Jasmine chuckled. "He didn't, but I'm not very choosy with food. I can eat anything."

That was unusual for someone who was pursuing a career in acting, but Jasmine seemed to be unconcerned with Hollywood's unrealistic beauty ideals and was comfortable in her own skin.

Amanda put a hand on the woman's upper arm. "The more I get to know you, the more I like you."

Jasmine grinned. "Ditto."

"So, Jasmine," Amanda said, leaning forward with a conspiratorial grin. "Tell me more about your Wiccan practices."

"I'm a beginner witch myself, and I learned what I know from the internet, other practitioners on social media, and books. So far, I like that Wicca is all about honoring the cycles of nature and the interconnectedness of all things. I believe that by attuning myself to the rhythms of the universe, I can tap into a deeper wisdom and power that can guide me." She looked at Amanda from under lowered lashes. "Does that sound like a load of crap to you?"

"Not at all. That's how I feel as well."

Jasmine looked relieved and then glanced around to check who was listening to their conversation before leaning closer to Amanda. "One of my favorite rituals is the Drawing Down the Moon," she said. "It's a powerful invocation of the Goddess's energy, a way of connecting with the divine feminine and bringing her wisdom and guidance into our lives." She continued to describe a few more rituals, but her main tool of divination seemed to be tarot cards.

Amanda nodded along. "I've never paid much attention to tarot reading, but you mentioned that the cards have been pointing to a prince in your future. Can you tell me more about that?"

"It started with a simple three-card spread," Jasmine said in a near whisper. "The first card was The Six of Cups, which represents innocence, nostalgia, and the promise of a new beginning. The second was The Lovers, which speaks of a deep, soulful connection blessed by the divine. And the third was The Knight of Cups, the embodiment of romance, chivalry, and the arrival of a suitor."

She paused, letting the significance of the cards sink in before continuing, but since Amanda wasn't all that familiar with tarot, it was all pretty meaningless to her. The few times she had gone for a reading, she paid more attention to the lady interpreting the cards than to the cards themselves.

"Together, they painted a picture of a profound, fated love and a connection that would transform my life. If it was a one-time occurrence, I would have dismissed it, but the same cards continued to come up."

Jasmine's excitement was contagious, and Amanda felt a flicker of it in her own heart. "Was that it, or did you get any more clues from the cards?"

"Not yet," she admitted. "The cards are frustratingly vague on that point. But I trust that when the time is right, he will reveal himself to me. Until then, I just have to keep my heart open and my eyes peeled."

Amanda shifted her gaze to the men who were heading back with loaded plates.

"Could the prince be Edgar?" she asked quickly.

"Maybe." Jasmine shrugged. "Maybe the card meant it metaphorically." She chuckled. "Instead of the knight in shining armor arriving on a noble steed, my knight arrived in a shining helicopter and brought along two noble saviors."

As the guys put the plates down, Amanda smiled at Edgar. "Are you planning on inviting Jasmine as your date to the wedding tonight?"

Edgar's face split into a wide, boyish grin as he trained his eyes on Jasmine. "Of course. That was the main reason Jasmine wanted to be allowed on the upper decks."

The smile slid off Amanda's face as she remembered that Jasmine was not allowed full disclosure. "Just as a reminder, Jasmine will have to wait to come in until after the ceremony." She looked apologetically at the woman. "I know it's disappointing, but that's the way it has to be."

"Why is that?" Jasmine leaned forward with a quizzical frown. "If you're practicing some kind of witchy ritual, you know that I'm totally on board. I love learning about new traditions and practices."

Amanda shook her head. "We have other reasons for the secrecy that I'm not at liberty to disclose. It's nothing personal, and you are not the only one who has to wait until after the ceremony to be allowed inside. Marina and Larissa will also be waiting in the bar for their boyfriends to escort them into the dining hall, so the three of you can keep each other company."

48

YAMANU

Yamanu sprawled on a lounge chair and surveyed the group of males gathered around him with a contented smile playing on his lips. The balcony of his cabin was filled with the rich aroma of cigars, laughter, and, most importantly, camaraderie.

Looking at the faces of the males who had stood by his side through countless missions, he felt a surge of gratitude. Arwel, Bhathian, Anandur, and Brundar were like brothers to him, and Kri a sister, and it was a damn shame that she had bowed out, saying that she didn't really belong with the boys. She was the youngest Head Guardian, and he was so damn proud of her.

She should have been here.

Then there was Onegus, the chief, and Kian, the big boss. The Clan Mother's son was a good leader, fair and just, and no less importantly, the guy had an uncanny knack for business, which had them all living in style and armed with the best weaponry money could buy and William could produce.

Julian was the odd one out in the group. The young doctor wasn't a Guardian, but he had joined the force on several missions and had proven himself to be cool-headed and capable under fire, which was admirable for a civilian.

Yamanu had befriended Bridget's son when he had started volunteering at the halfway house for the survivors of trafficking, running the weekly karaoke night. Julian was charged with managing the place, and he did that remarkably well considering that he had never managed anything before. Having a mate who had been a victim of trafficking herself probably made Julian better suited for the position than most.

Yamanu had found himself looking forward to those karaoke nights. Bringing the girls joy through singing was a different path for him to make the world a slightly better place. As a Guardian, he protected his clan and saved victims of trafficking when not running missions against the clan's enemies. His singing was just something he enjoyed doing, while his powerful thralling and shrouding abilities were weapons in the clan's arsenal that he had spent centuries honing and developing through great personal sacrifice.

Celibacy had enabled him to channel all of his energy into his massive thralls and shrouds, diverting hordes of marauders away from his people and enabling countless missions that would have been impossible to pull off without it.

And yet, the Clan Mother had been willing to give up that protection just so he could find happiness in the arms of the female he loved. As it turned out, his abilities had not disappeared when he had broken his vow of celibacy, but the goddess couldn't have known that, and he would be forever grateful to her for encouraging him to mate Mey.

He had never expected to find love, had never even dared to dream of it, but the moment he'd seen Mey for the first time, Yamanu had known that she was the one, the missing piece of his soul.

His talents had not diminished after their union but had only grown stronger, as if Mey's love had unlocked some hidden reserve of power within him.

He had never been happier, and he owed it all to Mey, Annani, and the group of friends gathered on his balcony.

Smiling to himself, Yamanu pushed to his feet and lifted his whiskey glass, the amber liquid glowing in the soft light of the setting sun. "To Mey." He raised a toast. "My one and only, my mate, who became the owner of my heart and gave me a reason to live. And to all of you, whom I'm honored to call brothers, thank you for always having my back."

After they had all clinked their glasses and emptied them in one go, Arwel grabbed a bottle and refilled them. "To Yamanu." He lifted his glass. "We all owe you big time for sacrificing so much to protect our sorry hides."

Arwel had sacrificed himself plenty and was still sacrificing almost daily, but Yamanu didn't think this was the time or place to mention it. He planned on toasting his brother-in-arms at his own bachelor party, which would happen tomorrow, the last day of the cruise.

Nodding, Kian rested his cigar on the lip of an ashtray. "I don't even want to speculate about what would have befallen our clan if not for your immense shrouding and thralling abilities, Yamanu. And you did that all while keeping secret the great sacrifice you were making to be able to do so."

Yamanu felt self-conscious. "That's precisely why I kept my vow of celibacy a secret from you all. I didn't want this." He waved the hand holding the cigar. "I didn't want to be treated differently and put on a pedestal. Each one of you would have done the same given similar circumstances."

As the others averted their gazes, Yamanu laughed. "I know what you are thinking. No way would you have given up sex to grow your power, but I assure you that you would have done it if you knew that your sacrifice would save your loved ones from annihilation by our enemy or by humans. After all, what are our lives worth without those we love to live it with? Nothing."

A few moments passed as each of the males contemplated his words and tried to imagine themselves in his position.

"I agree," Kian said. "When I was still a bachelor, I would have sacrificed everything to protect my clan. But now, I'm not so sure. My wife and daughter will always come first, then the clan, and lastly, my own needs."

"I'll drink to that." Yamanu lifted his glass again. "To our mates!"

Onegus waited until they all emptied their glasses before opening another bottle of fine whiskey and refilling them. He raised his glass in a final toast. "To Yamanu and Mey and their everlasting love and commitment to each other and to the clan."

Yamanu clinked glasses with everyone before downing another shot. Fine whiskey was meant to be savored, and it was a shame to drink it like that, but it was for a good cause.

Julian raised his glass, his eyes shining with mischief. "Now that the toasts are done, it's time for a song." He bowed to Yamanu. "I believe that the one about the bonny lass in the blue dress is most appropriate for the occasion."

It was one of the favorites on karaoke nights, and the girls asked for it each time.

"That's a fine one, indeed." Bhathian wrapped his arm around Julian's shoulders. "We will join you for the chorus."

Yamanu grinned. "Aye, 'tis a fine choice." The song was more funny than romantic, but the melody was lively, and it always put everyone in a good mood.

He cleared his throat, and as he began singing, the others joined in, their strong voices blending in a harmonious chorus despite some of them slurring their words. Bhathian's deep, rumbling bass provided a solid foundation, while Julian's smooth tenor wove a melodic counterpoint. Anandur added his rich baritone, and Brundar tapped his foot to the beat, which made Yamanu stupidly happy because Brundar never actively participated in things of that sort.

The chorus swelled, and the men clapped their hands and stomped their feet in time with the tune. The sound carried on the breeze, and soon, more voices joined them from the other balconies.

As the final notes faded away, the men erupted in laughter, and applause sounded from the other balconies.

"Thank you!" Yamanu called out to his impromptu audience.

"A toast!" Onegus leaned over the railing, raising his glass high to the spectators from the other balconies. "To all the bonny lasses who've captured our hearts!"

49

SYSSI

"Sweet dreams, my precious." Syssi kissed her sleeping daughter's cheek.

After exhausting herself and her granddaddy in the pool, Allegra had fallen asleep in Syssi's arms on the way back to the cabin. The girl needed a bath, but Syssi knew better than to wake her up for that.

Allegra was a sweet child, but if anyone dared to wake her up before she was good and ready, she was cranky for the rest of the day and had a hard time falling asleep again at night.

The good news was that she would not wake up during the next two hours, so Syssi could use that time to summon a vision about Khiann and his fate, but the bad news was that Kian wasn't there, and he didn't like it when she induced a vision without him watching over her.

It wasn't necessary, and Okidu could help her if she ended up needing it, but Kian wouldn't be happy with the butler doing that, and maybe he was right. After all, Okidu had limited executive functioning, and he might not know what to do.

Tiptoeing out of the bedroom, Syssi walked over to the couch and pulled her phone out of her purse. Amanda had watched over her during a session before, and Kian had accepted her as a good substitute, but she might be busy doing something else.

After placing the call, Syssi cradled the phone against her ear and loaded the coffeemaker while waiting for Amanda to pick up.

She answered after several rings, sounding a little breathless. "Hello, my favorite sister-in-law."

Syssi chuckled. "I'm your only sister-in-law." It suddenly occurred to her that Amanda might be at Mey's bachelorette party. "Are you busy? Am I interrupting?"

"You are not interrupting anything, darling. Mey's party hasn't started yet."

Syssi frowned. "Yamanu's bachelor party has already started. How come hers hasn't?"

"Yamanu's groomsmen are going to have a break between the bachelor party and the wedding, while Mey's bridesmaids are supposed to stay with her the entire time. She wants them to get dressed in Jin's cabin and then escort her to the event hall from there. Not that I intend to do that. I'll excuse myself and join them for the ceremony."

"I can totally understand that." Syssi needed to decompress after social interactions, and going from one party to the next without a break would have exhausted her mentally and physically.

Funny how certain things hadn't changed after her transition, proving how strong the mind-body connection was.

"It's a busy day for you, so I'm hesitant to even ask, but is there a chance you can come over for half an hour to watch over me when I induce the vision I promised your mother about Khiann? Kian is at Yamanu's party, and if I attempt it without anyone here to monitor me, he will pop a vein."

Amanda snorted. "Yeah, he totally would, even though it's physically impossible for him. I'll be there in five minutes."

"Thank you," Syssi said. "You are the best."

"Oh, I know, darling," Amanda purred. "I know."

Syssi ended the call with a smile. It was the Amanda effect and one of the reasons she still worked at her lab. They weren't making much progress with the paranormal research, but they enjoyed spending time together, and being around Amanda was uplifting. There was rarely a day that Syssi came home from the lab in a bad mood, and when she did, it was because Amanda turned the radio on and listened to the news on the way back home.

Lately, the distressing stuff Syssi heard was so overwhelming that she tried to stay away from it, but then she felt like a coward for hiding her head in the sand. It was even worse now than it had been right before she met Kian. Things had gotten better for a few years, and her visions of doom had subsided, but she should have known that it wouldn't last.

Surprisingly, though, the visions hadn't returned.

Perhaps motherhood was shielding her from the darkness the world was spiraling into.

Was it Navuh's doing?

She had no doubt that he had a hand in it. The worldwide chaos had his signature all over it, and if he was indeed behind what was going on, it explained why he hadn't bothered the clan in a long while. They had assumed that he was busy breeding the next generation of smart warriors, but he hadn't been idle in the meantime. He'd been steering things via his drug and trafficking enterprises, enlisting the help of cartels and terror organizations to propagate his agenda of world domination.

Still, as evil as Navuh was, she doubted that he had a hand in child trafficking. His cohorts did that of their own accord.

Syssi let out a sigh. She wasn't helping anyone by getting depressed over the sorry state of the world, but she could help Annani, even if it was just to provide her closure.

The mystery of Khiann's fate had been weighing on her mind ever since Annani had first shared her suspicions about Ahn's possible subterfuge. If Annani's beloved mate was still alive, trapped somewhere in stasis, it would be a miracle. In a way, the unintended results of Ahn's machinations could have been the survival of his daughter and her mate.

Then again, if Ahn hadn't framed Mortdh for Khiann's murder and instead had sent a rescue team to dig out Annani's husband and the immortals who had been with him, the gods could have still been around because Mortdh would not have flown over the assembly with a deadly weapon in his small aircraft.

Well, not really.

The Eternal King's assassins would have found a way to destroy all the exiled gods and their descendants and blame it on the humans or some natural disaster.

They all needed answers, and Syssi was the only one who might be able to get them. Allegra's presence had enhanced previous visions, and since it hadn't affected her daughter in any negative way, Syssi intended to meditate in the bedroom next to her daughter's crib to give herself the best chance of getting those answers.

As the door chime pulled her from her thoughts, Syssi rose to her feet and went to greet her sister-in-law.

"Thanks for coming." She pulled Amanda into a quick, one-armed hug. "I'm sorry if I interrupted your afternoon nap."

Leaning down, Amanda kissed her cheek. "You didn't interrupt anything important." She walked over to the kitchenette and opened the fridge. "I'm making myself a drink. Do you want one before doing your thing?"

Syssi shook her head. "I don't want anything interfering with my concentration. I will do it in the bedroom and leave the door open."

"That's fine." Amanda pulled a container of orange juice out of the fridge. "I'm going to read on my phone and not make any noises to disturb you."

"Thank you."

Syssi left her sister-in-law in the living room and walked into the bedroom, where Allegra was still napping peacefully in her portable crib, her little face relaxed and serene, and her little mouth parted.

She was a vision of perfection, and Syssi felt a rush of love for her daughter wash over her. There were many types of love, but the strongest one in the universe was the love of a mother for her child.

Fighting the urge to bend over the crib's side and kiss Allegra's soft cheek, Syssi took a deep breath, sent a silent prayer to the universe, and settled herself in the armchair beside the crib.

She closed her eyes and let the world fall away as she slowly slipped into the quiet place in her mind and envisioned what she wanted to see. If Khiann was buried under the sand, she needed the location, and if he was gone, she needed to see his death.

Fates, she really didn't want to see that and then have to tell Annani that there was no hope and that Khiann was really dead.

With her concentration shot, she had to start deep breathing and clearing her mind again. She pictured Khiann as Annani had described him—tall, strong, and beautiful, with chestnut dark hair and bright blue eyes that shone with love and mirth.

For a long moment, there was nothing, only darkness and silence and the steady beat of her own heart, but then, slowly, an image began to take shape in her mind's eye, hazy at first but growing clearer with each passing second.

She saw a mountain steeped in heavy mist, its rocky slopes rising starkly against a pale, washed-out sky. And as she hovered up to the very top, she discovered that the peak was hollow. There was a gaping crater at its center, a deep, yawning hole that seemed to plunge down hundreds of feet into the earth.

The barren, rocky mountain and the gray sky above it couldn't be located in a desert.

She was being shown something else.

Her consciousness hovering over the gaping hole, Syssi peered into its dark depths, her mind straining to make out the details of what lay at the bottom. When the clouds parted for a moment, letting the sun's rays through, the light bounced back from the reflective material of a sleek object that was nestled at the bottom of the crater.

She couldn't see any details, but her mind conjured the answer to what she was looking at without having all the necessary visual data.

It was an alien pod.

If she could force her consciousness to float down into the crater, perhaps she could see more details, but the vision refused to let her move from the one spot she was hovering over.

Syssi couldn't dive down or move to the side. It revealed another clue, though. The weak sunshine managed to vaporize the mist just as four people crested the top and walked over to look down the crater.

Syssi recognized all four.

The three males were the gods Aru, Negal, and Dagor. The fourth member of their group was the most surprising one, though.

It was Jasmine, the woman who had crashed into their lives like a comet, trailing occult mysteries in her wake.

As the four gathered around the crater's edge, Syssi wondered where the gods' mates were and why Jasmine was with them. And then, as quickly as the vision had come, it faded, and Syssi's eyes flew open.

"Talk about strange," she murmured.

"Did you say something?" Amanda asked from the living room.

"Give me a moment." Syssi brushed her hair away from her face.

For some reason, the vision had decided to show her one of the missing Kra-ell pods instead of Khiann.

Poor Annani would be so disappointed.

Still, it was an amazing development, even though Syssi couldn't tell where that mountaintop was. There had been no clues about that, but it was clear that Jasmine was somehow connected to the pods.

50

AMANDA

When Syssi emerged from the bedroom looking pale and shaken, Amanda tensed. "What did you see?" she asked, even though she was afraid to hear the answer.

"I didn't see Khiann." Syssi sat next to her on the couch and let her head drop back against the cushions. "I'm not sure what I saw or why I was shown it."

Syssi's visions were often vague, and it wasn't the first time she hadn't been sure what she'd been shown or why.

Tucking one leg under her, Amanda shifted so she was facing Syssi. "Just tell me, even if it's nothing more than a stream of consciousness. We can reconstruct it together."

"I might have seen a Kra-ell pod, and Jasmine was there with the three gods. I don't know how she's connected to their mission or why she was there with the gods while their mates were not. She was standing over a crater, looking down, and pointing. I think the vision's purpose was to show me that she needs to go with them to Tibet."

The dots were connecting in Amanda's mind. "I think so, too."

On the face of things, Jasmine's obsession with the prince that her tarot were showing her had seemed like a silly fantasy, a whimsical notion born of reading too many fairy-tale romances and not enough real-world experience. But Amanda had already suspected that there was more to it even before Syssi's vision.

"It was?" Syssi turned to her. "Because it doesn't make any sense to me, and don't start with your silly theory about her tarot prince."

"It's not silly." Amanda tapped a finger over her lower lip. "Jasmine keeps seeing a prince in her tarot readings and other divinations, and it's such a recurring motif that she follows the hunch and accepts Alberto's invitation to take her out of the country even though she doesn't know him well enough to trust him. Jasmine is not stupid, and she's not reckless. She felt compelled to do so, and in a roundabout way, it was the right step for her to take to get closer to finding the prince because it got her on this ship, where she met the three males that could potentially lead her to him. She might be the key to locating the Kra-ell pods, and if her drive to find her prince is for real, it means that the twins are still alive."

"That's crazy." Syssi frowned.

"Not really." Amanda waved a hand. "Think about how improbable it was for Orion and Toven to find their way to our clan, or Geraldine for that matter. When the Fates are behind the steering wheel, anything can happen."

"True," Syssi conceded. "So what do we do with this dubious information?"

"We need to talk to Jasmine and get her to join Aru's team. It's obvious that her help is needed to find at least the one pod you saw in your vision."

Syssi shook her head. "Kian will never agree unless she is a Dormant. Jasmine's help being essential to finding the royal twins is too long of a shot."

"And he might have a point." Amanda slumped against the couch cushions. "We need to think about it a little more. Should we even assist Aru and his team in finding the twins? They might be so dangerous that it would be better to leave them where they are."

Syssi cast her an incredulous look. "Can you really do that in good conscience? Leave them buried alive when we can do something to help find and save them?"

"To protect my clan and Fates know how many humans, yes, I can. I don't like it, but sometimes the only option is to choose the lesser evil."

Syssi shook her head. "I'm glad that I'm not a leader and don't have to make those kinds of choices. I don't think I'm capable of that."

"You are still very young, Syssi." Amanda patted her arm. "That being said, I'm also thankful for being able to leave the decision to Kian."

Syssi smiled ruefully. "We are such big chickens."

"We are." Amanda shifted on the couch. "It's too early to tell whether Edgar and Jasmine are meant for each other, but he can't start inducing her without her consent, so she needs to be told about us anyway, and if we tell her that, we might as well tell her about the vision, provided that Kian agrees, of course."

Syssi grimaced. "Telling Jasmine that her Prince Charming is waiting in a pod will not go down well with Edgar, and he will probably decide to drop his pursuit of her. And if she's adamant about finding her prince, introducing her to other immortal males wouldn't be fair to them either. The two objectives are mutually exclusive."

"Not necessarily." Amanda tapped a finger on her lower lip. "Jasmine is more like me than she is like you, and she has no compunctions about having fun with other males while awaiting her prince. As long as she is honest with Edgar or other males who will volunteer their services, no one will get hurt."

"Perhaps we should talk to Edgar and Jasmine but not together," Syssi suggested. "Check how they feel about each other. What if they are in love?"

"It's too early in their relationship to know one way or another," Amanda said. "Even for fated mates, it takes more than one hookup to know."

"Really?" Syssi arched a brow. "When I first saw Kian, it was like getting hit by lightning. I knew he was my destiny. Maybe not in my mind, but in my heart."

Amanda smiled. "I know. I was there when it happened, remember?"

"How can I ever forget?" Syssi slanted her a look. "You were the one who made it happen."

"True." Amanda grinned. "Kian was such a stubborn old goat. He refused to meet you, but then the Fates forced his hand, or rather I did, and when he came to berate me at my lab, he saw you, and it was game over for him."

Syssi nodded. "Yup. He got zapped at the same moment I did. What about you and Dalhu? Did you know right away?"

Amanda scrunched her nose. "Dalhu terrified me the first time I saw him, but I felt the pull right away, which was quite telling given that he was my enemy and he was kidnapping me."

It had been confusing and exhilarating at the same time, and as much as she had fought against it at first, as much as she had tried to deny the truth of what she felt, she'd eventually come to accept that Dalhu was her one true mate.

But not everyone's journey was the same, and not every Dormant had the luxury of waiting for their fated match to come along. Some, like Eva and Eleanor, had transitioned after a random hookup and had found their mates later.

"We need to talk to Kian about this," Syssi said.

Amanda nodded. "We don't have much time. Send him a text and ask him to call you."

51

KIAN

t's not urgent, but when you have a moment, please call me, the text read.

Kian always had a moment for his wife, no matter what he was doing, but he had to find a quiet space to talk to her.

She probably hadn't waited and had induced a vision without him. Hopefully, she had called one of his sisters to monitor her in case she fainted. It wasn't only about her now. She needed to think about Allegra.

Leaving the balcony and the sounds of boisterous laughter and clinking glasses, Kian walked into the living room of the cabin, sat down on the couch, and placed the call.

"You didn't have to call right away," Syssi said. "But thanks for doing so."

"What happened? Did you induce a vision?"

"Amanda watched over me, and I didn't suffer any ill effects, but regrettably, the Fates decided not to show Khiann, and the vision was about something completely different."

"That's indeed regrettable." Kian's heart clenched with sorrow for his mother. "But the Fates must have their good reasons." He pushed to his feet. "What did they show you?"

"It was about the Kra-ell pods. Or rather one pod."

Damn. Kian hadn't expected that.

"I'm on my way. I'll be there in a few minutes." He opened the balcony door and stepped out.

"What about the party?" Syssi asked.

Kian glanced back at the group of males, some sprawled on loungers, others standing next to the railing and puffing on what little was left of their cigars. The party was winding down, with the toasts and laughter giving way to quieter conversations and contemplative sips of whiskey.

"It's almost over," he said. "I'll just say goodbye to Yamanu."

"Amanda and I are waiting."

Kian ended the call, slipped the phone back into his pocket, and walked over to Yamanu, who was standing by the railing and chatting with Arwel.

He put his hand on the Guardian's shoulder. "I had a great time, but I need to go. I'll be back in time to escort you to the altar."

A big grin spread across Yamanu's handsome features. "I'll hold you to that." He clapped Kian on the shoulder.

"Do you need me to come with you?" Anandur asked Kian.

"No. I'm just going to my cabin. Stay and enjoy the party."

It took Kian less than five minutes from the time he had ended the call with Syssi until he opened the door to his cabin. He found Syssi and Amanda seated on the couch, each holding a cup of coffee, which was a good sign. If the news were bad, Amanda would be nursing a drink.

"Hello, ladies." He leaned to kiss Amanda's cheek and then Syssi's. "You don't look like you have seen a specter, so I assume that the vision wasn't about doom and gloom."

Syssi's visions were rarely about happy events, which was the reason she dreaded them so much and tried to avoid them most of the time. The only reason she occasionally induced them was when she was trying to help someone else.

Had she used Allegra's amplifying power?

The door to the bedroom was open, and through the doorway, he could see their daughter sleeping peacefully in her crib.

Hopefully, assisting her mother just by being around wasn't detrimental to her in any way.

"What did you see?" Kian sat down on an armchair, facing her and Amanda.

Listening to Syssi describe what she had seen, Kian had to fight his natural skepticism. If those words were coming from anyone else, he would have dismissed the story as a dream or a hallucination, but his mate had a perfect track record for prophetic visions that, in one way or another, had come to pass.

"Jasmine needs to be told," Amanda said after Syssi was done. "I wish we had more time and didn't need to make rush decisions, but the cruise is almost over, and Aru and his team plan to head out as soon as they can."

"I need to think this through," Kian said. "It's not as easy as just telling Jasmine about gods and immortals and asking her to join Aru's team. We don't know what methods she uses other than the tarot cards, and whether there is any way she can actually guide the team to the location of the pod."

"She was there," Syssi said. "That means that she knows, or will know, how to get there. I don't see any other reason for the vision to show me that scene if it wasn't about to happen." Syssi leaned toward him. "We have just one more day at sea, Kian. You need to decide quickly."

He nodded. "Perhaps I need to discuss it with Turner. He usually sees clearly through the worst of messes. We also need to tell Mother." He looked at Amanda. "She will be so disappointed that Syssi didn't see what happened to Khiann. It was a long shot, but she had her hopes up."

"I can try again," Syssi said. "I gave it a lot of thought, and there is one commonality between the royal twins and Khiann. They are all in stasis. Maybe that's why I was shown the twins instead of Khiann. I was thinking about him buried deep in the earth." She sighed. "But maybe it's not the reason, and the Fates just wanted to show me the pod so I would know that Jasmine was needed to find it. This makes me think that they will not show me anything other than the Kra-ell pod until we find it. After that's done, I will try again, and maybe then I will be granted answers about Khiann."

52

ANNANI

Annani had a pretty good idea as to the reason Kian had called her to invite himself, Syssi, and Amanda over with only an hour or so remaining before the wedding ceremony was to start.

Syssi had probably induced a vision, and what she had seen was not good.

When Ojidu ushered them in, Annani scanned their faces for signs of sadness but found cautious excitement instead.

Had Syssi found anything? Perhaps she had seen a clue about Khiann's fate?

Hope surging in her heart, Annani wanted to cling to it for a little longer, so she did not ask about that. Instead, her gaze shifted to Syssi's empty arms. "Where is Allegra?"

"She's napping," Syssi said. "She was so exhausted from playing in the pool with my father that she fell asleep on the way to the cabin, and I had to put her in her crib without even giving her a bath. You know how she is if someone wakes her up before she is good and ready, so I left her with Okidu to watch over. If she wakes up before we're back, he'll bring her over."

Annani nodded, a smile tugging at her lips. Her granddaughter had a formidable will, which would make her a good leader one day, but it was not making her parents' lives easy, especially Syssi's, who was sweet and softhearted.

As her visitors sat down, Annani regarded Syssi with a calm expression, one she had honed over thousands of years of hiding her emotions. "I assume that you have news for me?"

"Not the news you hoped for, Clan Mother. The universe has chosen not to show me Khiann's fate and instead showed me clues about the Kra-ell royal twins."

Annani was indeed disappointed, but not as much as if Syssi had told her that she had seen Khiann's murder and that all hope was gone, so in a way, no news was good news.

"We should not refer to them as the Kra-ell royal twins," she said. "They are my half brother and sister, half god and half Kra-ell, so we should drop the Kra-ell part." She sighed. "I wish I knew their names."

Their mother had even hidden that from her people when she had conscripted her children to the priesthood. Kra-ell priestesses were referred to as holy mothers and, before that, as acolytes, but since there had never been male priests before the prince, Annani did not know how he should be referred to. Perhaps a holy brother? That made sense since the only reason he could have joined the priesthood was being his sister's twin.

Annani had no doubt that the Kra-ell queen had done so to further protect them and hide them from their grandfather.

She gave her daughter-in-law an encouraging smile. "Please tell me what you have seen, my dear."

As Syssi spoke of Jasmine appearing next to the pod, Annani was surprised. She had not met the human, but ever since Jasmine had been brought aboard, Annani had a feeling that there was something special about her. Still, she could have never imagined that the woman would lead them to the twins.

"I'm so sorry that I didn't bring you news of Khiann," Syssi said. "But I promise that I will try again once this vision is fulfilled. Until then, I doubt I will be shown anything else."

Annani leaned over and patted Syssi's knee. "Do not fret, my child. The Fates work in mysterious ways, and they reveal only what they want to reveal when they want to reveal it."

Syssi let out a breath. "I'm glad you see it that way."

Annani nodded to her daughter-in-law and then turned to Kian. "I am considering telling the queen about the twins when I speak with her tonight. I do not know whether she suspects that they are Ahn's. After all, his legacy lives on in them as well."

Kian frowned. "The twins didn't know who their father was, and all they have is his genetic material. You are the only one who carries on his legacy, and I don't think it is wise to confirm the queen's suspicion. She must be aware of them because the Eternal King wouldn't have needed to eliminate them if they were fully Kra-ell, and she knows that was his intention. Still, she does not know for sure, and maybe we should leave it at that. We don't know how she will react and what she will do with the information."

Annani shook her head. "It is the right thing to do. Ahn's mother deserves to know about all of his children, and that includes Areana. I mentioned that my sister had survived, but the queen did not ask about her."

"I'm not surprised that she didn't," Kian said. "She must have assumed that Areana was a mere immortal, and despite her lofty ideals, the queen will never accept a hybrid. That's also true of the twins, so she might be well aware of them being Ahn's, but she just doesn't care."

Kian might be right, but Annani refused to leave it at that. The queen was not an emotional female, and everything she did was for Anumati. She might really not care about any of Ahn's other children who were not his legitimate heirs.

Annani hoped that they were all wrong about that, and that her grandmother cared. "I told the queen that my father offered Areana to Mortdh as a substitute for me, and Ani knows that Mortdh would have never accepted an immortal. Only a full-blooded goddess could have been offered."

Kian nodded. "You are right, of course. Queen Ani is too shrewd to overlook such a detail, but her lack of interest in Areana is telling, and if she feels like that about a granddaughter who is a full-blooded goddess, just not a legit heir, I'm curious about the queen's feelings toward Ahn's half Kra-ell children. She might be conflicted about the twins and wish them ill as the king did, not because she's worried about them taking down the king, but because they might be a threat to you, the heir to the throne, the one in whom she places so much hope."

Kian was right. The queen's reaction to the news of Ahn's other children could be unpredictable. She might see them as a threat to be eliminated rather than a potential ally to be embraced, or she might simply ignore them and pretend that they did not exist.

"The queen might be right about the twins being a threat." Annani let out a breath. "I am not concerned about Areana posing a threat, and yet I am careful about what I tell her. I never reveal anything that can lead Navuh to us, and I hope that Lokan and Kalugal are just as vigilant when they talk to her. The twins are an enigma, though. If we give any credence to the Eternal King's suspicions, they are extremely powerful and, therefore, dangerous. Still, that does not mean that they mean me harm. They could become valuable allies."

"We need to prepare for both contingencies," Syssi said. "I will start summoning visions about the royal twins. We need to know if they pose a threat to the clan and if they are friend or foe."

Kian nodded, his jaw clenching, probably at the thought of Syssi summoning too many visions and draining herself. "Aru and the other two gods are physically a match for the Kra-ell. They were engineered that way. But they weren't given protection against the twins' rumored compulsion power. They will need to be equipped with the special earpieces we developed to filter out compulsion, to protect themselves in case the twins are malevolent. Whoever accompanies them on the search will need those as well."

Amanda leaned forward, her eyes shining with excitement. "They will need reinforced handcuffs and tranquilizer darts as well."

A rueful smile tugged at Kian's lips. "Aru's team did not arrive on Earth empty-handed. They have all kinds of sophisticated weapons that Aru refused to share with me. The one thing they don't have, though, is the means to protect themselves from compulsion, which is both surprising and it is not. A society as technologically advanced as the Anumatians should have developed the means to protect its soldiers from compulsion, but that would have eliminated the Eternal King's grip on them. He wants everyone susceptible to his power and under his control."

Breaking the king's grip and freeing Anumati from the chains of oppression and tyranny would be no easy feat. It might even be impossible.

"We need to discuss this with Aru before we approach Jasmine." Kian pulled out his phone. "There is no time to do so before the wedding, but we can meet tonight an hour before the scheduled meeting. Is that okay with you, Mother?"

Annani nodded.

"Can I come?" Amanda asked.

Kian turned to look at his sister. "I don't have any objection to that, but your sisters might not appreciate being left out, and I don't think Aru will appreciate having to conduct the telepathic conversation in front of a crowd. I'm surprised he can do that with just the three of us there. A fourth person might not be a big difference, but he might be uncomfortable with six people in the room, all watching him as he talks with his sister in his mind."

53

EDGAR

Taking a deep breath, Edgar tugged on the lapels of his tuxedo, raised his hand, and rapped his knuckles on Jasmine's door. Unlike the cabins on the upper decks, the staff quarters were equipped with standard insulation and sound-proofing so Jasmine would hear his knock loud and clear.

"Just a moment!" Jasmine called out, and then the door swung open, revealing a vision that stole the breath from his lungs and sent his heart racing with a surge of pure, unadulterated lust.

"Well, hello there, handsome." Jasmine gave him a once-over before ushering him in. "You look spiffy." She put a hand on the lapel of his jacket, her lush lips curving in a coquettish smile.

Her hair and makeup were done to perfection, and she was breathtakingly beautiful, but it was what she was wearing, or rather what she wasn't wearing, that made his blood run hot and his body tighten with need.

The short, silky robe clung to her curves like a second skin, the fabric so thin it was nearly translucent and left little to the imagination. She had no bra on, and the creamy swell of her breasts and the shadowed valley between them were pure temptations. Below, the hem rode high on her thighs, exposing miles of smooth, golden skin that seemed to glow in the soft light of the cabin.

Edgar swallowed, his mouth suddenly dry and his tongue feeling thick and clumsy in his mouth. He wanted to reach out and touch her, to run his hands over those lush, inviting curves and feel the heat of her skin under his fingers, but if he allowed himself to succumb to the tide of desire, they would never make it to the wedding.

"You look beautiful, but you are not ready," he stated the obvious.

"I just need a few more moments." She gave him a slight push. "Take a seat,"

Edgar nodded, his jaw clenching with the effort of restraint as he lowered himself onto the edge of the bed, his eyes fixed firmly on the floor. He could hear the swish of fabric as Jasmine moved around the tiny cabin, and he could feel the heat of her gaze on him, which made his skin prickle with awareness, but he refused to lift his gaze to her.

She chuckled. "You can look, you know. You've seen it all already."

"I did," he admitted, his voice rough with barely suppressed desire. "But if I see it again, we won't make it to the wedding."

Jasmine laughed, a throaty, sensual sound that sent shivers racing down his spine. "Well, in that case, don't look," she said in a mock-stern tone. "I really want to attend that wedding."

"Can I ask you something?" He still refused to look at her.

He heard her pause and felt her eyes on him. "Of course. What do you wish to know?"

"That prince you mentioned, the one who keeps showing up in your tarot cards. What's that all about? I mean, am I just a placeholder until you find your Prince Charming? Or am I misunderstanding the situation?"

There was a moment of silence, a pause that seemed to stretch uncomfortably long. "You could be my prince." Jasmine walked in between his spread thighs and placed her hands on his shoulders. "Divining the future is not an exact science, and the signs can be interpreted in many ways. The cards might have meant a real royal prince, or they could have meant it metaphorically, like a prince of a man." She gave him a sultry look as she rubbed herself against him. "You were definitely princely between the sheets. I don't recall ever coming so hard and so many times."

Edgar tried to stifle a wince. He was a generous and skilled lover, but Jasmine's explosive orgasms had been the product of his immortal biology, so he couldn't take credit for them. It was the venom hitting her system that had induced the string of powerful climaxes and sent her on a psychedelic trip through the clouds. He had thralled her to forget the bite, to blur the edges of the euphoria that had consumed her in the aftermath, but he'd left the memories of the pleasure intact.

That was what she remembered.

Lifting his head, he looked at her beautiful face, and as he took in the sultry gleam in her eyes and the wicked curve of her lips, he couldn't help but wonder if that was enough. Could he be satisfied with just being her lover but not her partner, not her prince?

"I'm flattered," he said. "Although not surprised. I've been told that before."

She laughed. "Now you're making me jealous." She took a step back, dropped her robe, and gave him a mouth-watering view of her ass that was covered by such a thin strip of fabric it was like it wasn't covered at all.

And it was glorious.

She pulled on a tight dress that looked like a bandage around her delicious body, stepped into a pair of stilettos, and then turned around and struck a pose. "How do I look?"

"Like a goddess," Edgar breathed. "The goddess of carnal pleasures."

Jasmine chuckled. "I'll take it. Anything that is preceded by the word goddess is music to my ears."

JASMINE

J asmine felt a flutter of excitement as Edgar led her to the bar, her eyes widening at the sight of Marina and Larissa, both decked out in beautiful evening dresses. The women were accompanied by two hunky guys, who were hovering over them like bees over honey.

"Jasmine." Marina pursed her lips. "You look absolutely stunning. Are you attending the wedding tonight?"

"I am." Jasmine grinned. "Amanda convinced her brother to let me out of the lower decks dungeon. And I have to say that you ladies look gorgeous." She slanted a glance at Edgar. "Ed, these are my friends, Marina and Larissa. Ed is my escort to the party tonight."

He wrapped his arm around her waist. "I hope that I am much more than that."

"Of course, darling." She turned to kiss the side of his face. "But you are my escort tonight because I wouldn't be attending the wedding if you didn't invite me as your date."

He cast her an amused look before turning to the men. "Peter, Jay, this is Jasmine. The lady we rescued from the drug cartel."

"Everyone on this ship knows who you are." The dark-haired one who was standing next to Marina extended his hand. "You are famous, Jasmine. I'm Peter, and it's a pleasure to make your acquaintance. I'm glad that we got to you in time."

She put her hand in his and smiled. "Not as glad as I am. If not for Margo and your security team, my life, as I know it, would have been over. I would have become the plaything of a mobster until he tired of me and got rid of me, and by getting rid, I don't mean letting me go free."

Jasmine shivered.

She didn't like to think of what would have happened to her if she hadn't befriended Margo and been rescued along with her. One thing was certain. She would never have touched a tarot deck again or lit white candles asking for true love.

"I'm Jay." The blond guy, who looked a little like David Beckham, offered her his hand. "I'm glad that you are not going to be swimming with the fishes anytime soon."

Marina gasped at his crude comment, but Jasmine laughed. "Yeah, I'm glad too."

As she sat down next to the women at the bar, Edgar joined the two men, and the six of them continued chatting. Jasmine tried to rein in her flirtatious persona, but it was so second nature to her that she didn't know how to act differently, especially around men.

It was so easy and fun to engage in playful banter, so entertaining to make even the most stoic of males melt with a simple bat of her lashes or a well-timed laugh. She knew the power of her own charm and felt helpless not to use it.

Perhaps she could channel Edna.

After all, as an actress, she should be able to assume any role she pleased, but what was the fun in acting so dry and reserved? Edna was a young woman, but she acted as if she was ancient.

Jasmine meant nothing by her lighthearted banter, and it was too enjoyable to flex her flirting powers over men to stop.

Still, her charms seemed to be lost on Peter, whose eyes never left Marina's face. The intensity of his stare sent a shiver down Jasmine's spine. There was something there, a connection that ran deep, a bond that made her a little jealous.

Did Edgar look at her this way? Like she was the most wonderful creature in the world, and he was happy to bask in her glow?

Casting him a sidelong glance, she caught him looking at her with annoyance in his eyes instead of the adoration she'd hoped for. Obviously, Ed didn't like the way she was interacting with the other men, but he should have known that her flirting was harmless.

She smiled and cupped his cheek. "Can you be a dear and get me a drink, please?"

"Of course. What would you like?"

"A classic margarita, please. With salt."

As Ed turned to the bartender and placed the order, Jay gave Jasmine a suggestive smile, his gaze roving over her figure with an appreciative gleam that made her skin prickle with awareness.

If she wanted to, she could have him wrapped around her little finger in no time, but she wouldn't, and not just because she was with Ed.

Larissa's eyes followed Jay's every move, the longing and adoration in her gaze so plain and raw that it made Jasmine's heart ache. The poor girl was clearly enamored with the handsome guy, and her feelings were written all over her face for anyone to see.

Jay, on the other hand, was either oblivious or simply not interested in anything serious with her. Curiously, though, his attention wandered to Jasmine but not to

Marina. It was probably because he considered Peter his friend and didn't wish to antagonize him.

Did it mean that Jay and Edgar were not on friendly terms?

Maybe there was some bad blood between them and that was why Jay was allowing himself to pay Jasmine so much attention even though she was with Ed?

"Here you go." Edgar handed her the margarita and then turned to the other two men. "We should go."

Jay glanced at his watch and nodded. "Fifteen minutes to show time." He leaned over and kissed Larissa's cheek. "I'll be back for you in about forty-five minutes to an hour. Don't go anywhere."

"I be here," she said in heavily accented English.

Peter leaned over Marina, but instead of kissing her cheek, he took her mouth in a passionate kiss as if he was leaving her for weeks and not less than an hour.

Ed was less inclined to make a public show of affection and just pecked Jasmine's cheek. "Be good," he murmured against her ear.

She laughed. "The term good can refer to a lot of things."

He didn't look amused.

As Edgar and the other men excused themselves, leaving Jasmine alone with Marina and Larissa, she lifted the glass to her lips and took a grateful sip.

"So, now that I'm finally allowed to attend a wedding, can you tell me who is getting married?"

Marina and Larissa exchanged looks, and then Marina shook her head. "I'm sorry. We can't tell you."

"Can you at least tell me if it's anyone famous?"

Marina hesitated and then shook her head. "Not that I know of, but I'm new to this country, and I don't know all the famous people here."

Jasmine was impressed. She'd thought that Marina had been in the US for many years. "Your English is very good. Where did you learn to speak it so well?"

"I started back in Russia, and I kept practicing for long hours after we got here."

Jasmine knew better than to ask again how they had found their way to the US and got work on the cruise ship. When she'd asked her poker buddies, she'd been told that it was confidential.

Even after being allowed on the upper decks, Jasmine still had a nagging sense that something wasn't quite right, and that she had no idea what was really going on. When she asked questions and tried to probe for information, she once again found herself running up against a wall of secrecy and evasion.

Looking nervous, Larissa said something in Russian to Marina while her fingers were plucking at the fabric of her dress, the same one she had worn the night before.

Marina laughed and clapped her friend on her back. "Larissa is not happy about wearing the same dress two nights in a row," she translated for Jasmine. "I told her that Jay doesn't mind."

Larissa mumbled something under her breath and blushed profusely.

"What did she say?" Jasmine asked.

"That Jay only cares about taking the dress off her."

As the three of them laughed, Marina turned to her. "So, how did you and the handsome Edgar meet?"

"He's the helicopter pilot who flew Kevin over to the mobster yacht. We talked a little on the way to the ship, but then I didn't see him until yesterday when he suddenly came down to see me and brought me delicious food from the wedding party."

Marina regarded her with a wicked gleam in her eye. "I've heard that he left your cabin early this morning."

"You've heard right."

"Good for you." Marina let out a whoop of laughter, her hand coming up for a high five that Jasmine met with a grin. "Life is too short to wait for pleasure."

"I'll drink to that." Jasmine lifted her margarita glass.

As they giggled and gossiped like schoolgirls, with Marina translating for Larissa, who was too tipsy to concentrate on finding the right words, Jasmine still couldn't shake off the nagging sense of unease.

There was something different about Marina and Larissa. Jasmine was no stranger to girl talk, and women usually had much more to say about their lovers, their friends, and their life in general than those two were sharing.

Maybe it was the difference in cultures.

She tried to probe deeper, to ask about their pasts, their families, the places they had come from. But each time, she was met with vague, evasive answers, a polite but firm deflection that left her feeling even more frustrated and confused.

"We're from a remote region of Russia that is near Finland," Marina finally said after being asked for the umpteenth time where they were from. "You've probably never heard of it."

Jasmine decided to let it go.

It was just no use.

And then there was the matter of the nondisclosure agreement that, for some reason, no one had mentioned to her.

Margo had told her that everyone on the ship was supposedly required to sign one and that she wouldn't be allowed to mingle with the guests without it.

And yet, Jasmine hadn't been asked to sign anything.

Heck, no one had even told her what she could and couldn't say about her time on board.

Things didn't add up, and the more Jasmine thought about it, the more worried she became. There were too many secrets and too many unanswered questions.

Thankfully, it wouldn't be long before the ship docked back in Los Angeles, and she would be back on solid ground and in control of her own life.

But what if the cartel was looking for her?

Julio Modana had been made to forget about her, but what about Carlos? Kevin hadn't hypnotized the other brother, who was supposed to be even more evil than Julio. What if he decided to come after her?

Jasmine shivered, her hand coming up to rub at her arm as a sudden chill raced down her spine. She needed to talk to Kian and find out what he knew. He seemed to be the only one with any real answers.

55

MEY

Mey's heart was full to bursting as she walked toward the altar. Yamanu was waiting for her with a huge grin on his handsome face and eyes that shone with love and adoration.

Keeping her senses heightened so she wouldn't miss even the most minute of details and commit everything to memory, she was acutely aware of the gentle sway of her gown, the soft rhythm of her steps, and the radiant smiles on her bridesmaids' faces.

She was about to wed Yamanu, her fated mate, the male who had captured her heart and soul with his big smiles, his enormous capacity for love, and his boundless kindness.

Just like his unparalleled thralling and shrouding ability, her mate did everything on a grand scale, and that included his love for her.

And yet, even as happiness swelled within her, Mey couldn't help but feel a twinge of regret that her and Jin's adoptive parents couldn't be there to witness this momentous occasion. They had been the best parents any girl could hope for, raising her and Jin to be resourceful, independent, powerful women and doing so with gentle words, lots of hugs and kisses, and endless love and patience.

They were the best people she knew, and given that she was surrounded by a clan of wonderful people, that was saying something. It was so unfair that they couldn't be here now to share in the joy and celebrate their adopted daughters' weddings.

Mey silently vowed to make it up to them with proper human ceremonies. Jin wanted that as well, and Yamanu and Arwel would do whatever it took to make their mates happy, including traveling across the globe and attending a traditional wedding.

But even as she made that promise, Mey couldn't help but wonder, for what felt like the thousandth time, about her and Jin's birth parents. Who were they? What had happened to them? Were they still out there some-where, thinking of the daughters they had lost or given away?

The mystery had haunted Mey for as long as she could remember, lingering in the back of her mind like a persistent itch that she needed to scratch and didn't know how. Even though she was the older sister, she had no memories of her birth family and no clues as to their fate. The only things she knew about her biological parents came from her and Jin's genetic makeup. Their mother must have been a Dormant, and their father a hybrid Kra-ell.

Returning her focus to Yamanu, Mey felt all those thoughts evaporate like mist beneath the sun, or rather her mate's broad grin, which was warmer than sunshine and overflowing with love and joy because tonight they were being officially joined with nearly the entire clan witnessing the ceremony.

Yamanu would never admit it, but he loved the attention. He was a showman who hadn't gotten to perform much during his long centuries of celibacy when he had been forced to drink a muting potion and meditate daily to maintain his vow and continue honing his incredible powers.

The potion had muted more than his libido, though, and he had often kept to himself. But those days were over now that he had broken the vow with the Clan Mother's blessing.

Shifting her gaze to the petite goddess, Mey dipped her head in silent thanks. She would be forever grateful to Annani for being willing to lose one of the clan's most valuable assets and releasing Yamanu from his vow so he could be happy.

Nothing was more sacred to the goddess than the connection forged by destiny itself. Annani believed that to stand in the way of such a bond was to court the wrath of the Fates.

Thankfully, mating Mey had not diminished Yamanu's incredible ability to manipulate the minds and perceptions of others. His power remained unparalleled, and the clan hadn't lost the protection that had saved countless lives and turned the tide of battles time and again over the centuries.

Taking her place beside Yamanu at the altar, Mey slipped her hand into his, and as a sense of rightness settled over her, she gave his hand a light squeeze.

The Clan Mother smiled at them both, her eyes shining with love and joy, and then shifted her gaze to the gathered crowd. "My dearly beloved. We are gathered here today to celebrate the union of two beautiful souls. Yamanu and Mey's love story is so exciting and unconventional that it could be made into a movie." She chuckled. "I think it is the first time that international espionage was used by the Fates to weave the common thread in the destiny of two people who were meant for each other."

Mey smiled at Yamanu through the haze of happy tears. The Clan Mother had a way of turning the mundane into spectacular, and giving significance and meaning to events that were at the time far from glamorous.

"Yamanu." The goddess turned her gaze to him. "You have been a true hero to our people, a Guardian and protector who has always put the needs of others before your own. You have saved countless lives and turned the tide of battles, and for that you have our gratitude."

Yamanu bowed his head. "It's my duty, Clan Mother, and I'm honored and grateful to the Fates for giving me the tools to protect my people."

Mey couldn't be prouder of Yamanu. He had never been one to seek glory or acclaim, never been driven by ego or ambition. Everything he did, every sacrifice he made, was for the greater good, for the safety and well-being of his clan.

"You have acted above and beyond the call of duty, Yamanu," the goddess said. "But your greatest act of heroism was your willingness to give up your immense powers for love." The Clan Mother smiled at him fondly. "When the Fates brought you and Mey together, you were prepared to risk everything to be with your truelove mate."

Mey squeezed Yamanu's hand, her heart overflowing. She knew how much his powers meant to him. To be willing to give that up, to put their love above all else, was a sacrifice beyond measure.

"And Mey," Annani said, turning her warm gaze to her. "You are such a wonderful addition to our clan, and not just because you make Yamanu happy, or because you possess a talent none of us has. You exemplify strength, courage, and unshakable loyalty, you also embody grace, elegance, and entrepreneurial spirit. You and your sister make me, your mates, your clan, and your adoptive parents proud."

Mey felt a lump form in her throat, and tears threatened to spill down her cheeks. Hearing the goddess's words, she felt the love and acceptance of her clan enveloping her in a warm embrace.

"Yamanu and Mey," the Clan Mother continued. "Your love is a testament to the unbreakable bond between fated mates. You have faced countless challenges and obstacles on your path to this moment, but through it all, your love has only grown stronger.

"And so," the goddess said, "it is my great honor and privilege to bless this union, to stand as witness to the joining of two hearts, two souls, two lives. Yamanu and Mey, you have proven yourselves worthy of the great gift of fated love, and it is my deepest wish that your bond will only continue to grow and flourish in the years to come."

Mey felt Yamanu's hand tighten around hers.

The Clan Mother smiled at them. "And now, it is time for you to exchange your vows. Yamanu, Mey, please turn to face each other and join hands."

Mey turned to face her mate, her heart racing with anticipation. This was the moment they would pledge their lives and their love to each other in front of their entire community.

YAMANU

As Mey turned to face Yamanu, her eyes shimmering with unshed tears of joy, his heart swelled with love. He had never seen her look more beautiful than she did at that moment, and it had nothing to do with the expertly done makeup and hair or the exquisite wedding gown. It was the radiance of her spirit and the love that shone through her eyes.

Mey took a deep breath and squeezed his hands lightly. "Yamanu, my love. When I first met you, I knew that my life would never be the same. You were like a bolt of lightning, a force of nature that swept me off my feet and showed me what true love was all about."

Yamanu's throat tightened with emotion as he listened to her words.

"You have been my anchor and my staunchest support-er," Mey continued, her voice growing stronger with each word. "You have loved me unconditionally and believed in me even when I doubted myself. You have always put me first, even when it meant sacrificing your own needs and desires."

Yamanu swallowed hard, his heart so full that he thought it might burst. It was true that he had always put Mey first, but he had never seen it as a sacrifice or felt like he was giving up anything. Loving her and being loved by her in return was the greatest gift the Fates could have ever given him.

"I promise to love you, to cherish you, and to stand by your side through thick and thin," Mey said, her eyes locked on his. "I promise to be your best friend, your lover, and your soulmate. I promise never to take you for granted and to always remember how lucky I am to have you in my life. And I promise to spend every day showing you just how much you mean to me and how deeply and completely I love you."

Mey let go of his hand and reached to her sister, who handed her a ring.

"With this ring, I bind my life to yours." She slipped it over his finger.

Overwhelmed with emotion, Yamanu lifted Mey's hand and kissed the back of it while collecting his thoughts. He had written a dozen different vows, but after listening to so many others, he'd decided to keep it simple.

"From the moment I first saw you, my love, I knew that you were the one. You walked out of that room in the modeling agency, and I felt like I was zapped by high voltage. I was burning, and you were the only one who could save me." He smiled. "Luckily for me, you didn't shy away from the wreck that I was and embraced me, faults, warts, and all, with open arms and a wide open heart."

Yamanu lifted his hand and cupped her face, his thumbs brushing away the tears that had started to fall.

"I promise to love you, to cherish you, to stand by your side through the ups and the downs and everything in between. I promise to be your best friend, your lover, your greatest cheerleader, and your rock. I promise to always put you and your happiness first. And I promise to spend every day of forever showing you just how much you mean to me, just how deeply and completely I love you."

As he finished his vows, Yamanu leaned in and pressed his forehead against Mey's, their breath mingling in the space between them.

Reaching into his pocket, he pulled out a ring and slipped it on her finger. "We don't need rings to bind us to each other, so think of it as a symbol of my ever-lasting love and devotion."

The Clan Mother stepped forward and placed her hands on their joined ones. "Yamanu and Mey. By the power vested in me by the Fates, I now pronounce you bonded mates. Two souls united for all eternity."

She smiled. "You may now kiss."

Yamanu needed no further encouragement. He pulled Mey into his arms and kissed her with all the love and passion he felt for her, pouring his heart and soul into that most important kiss that served to seal their vows to each other.

As they broke apart and turned toward the cheering crowd of their friends and family, the love, happiness, and support that surrounded them led Yamanu to feel as if the Fates themselves were celebrating with them at that very moment.

JASMINE

As Jasmine stepped into the transformed dining room of the luxury ship, she was struck by its grandeur. She'd seen the place when it had been set up for lunch, but she'd been so overwhelmed by her newfound freedom and talking to Amanda that she hadn't noticed the details.

Above her, multiple crystal chandeliers hung from an intricately designed ceiling. The dining area stretched around a large dance floor, where several couples were already dancing.

The tables were draped in white linens and topped with fine china, sparkling silverware, and polished crystal glassware. Rich wood paneling lined the walls, contrasting beautifully with the soft, opulent decor, and one side was all glass, overlooking a large terrace and the ocean beyond.

A buzz of conversation filled the place, accompanied by the clinking of cutlery, while soft music was playing on the hidden loudspeakers.

"Would you like to dance?" Edgar asked. "Or do you prefer to sit down first and munch on some appetizers?"

She was hungry, having only eaten a snack in the staff lounge, but the dance floor offered her a great opportunity to look around and search for celebrity faces in the crowd of guests.

"Let's dance first." She smiled up at him. "Are you a good dancer?"

He leaned to nuzzle her neck. "I'm an excellent dancer."

As they walked by the tables, Jasmine smiled and made eye contact, but although everyone was incredibly good-looking, she hadn't spotted any celebrities yet.

In fact, most of the people she'd seen so far had features so striking and perfect that they seemed almost unreal like they had stepped straight out of a movie screen or a magazine cover.

Her eyes roved over the flawless skin, the chiseled jawlines, and the luminous eyes. It was like being surrounded by a sea of supermodels, each one more gorgeous than the last, and for the first time in her life, Jasmine felt inadequate.

Who were these people, and why were they all so damn perfect?

Suddenly, a thought struck her. What if Perfect Match wasn't really a virtual experience? What if the avatars that users interacted with in the so-called virtual experience weren't computer-generated at all, but real people, flesh and blood actors hired to bring the customer's fantasies to life?

The virtual experience promised to be indistinguishable from real life, and it wasn't because of the revolutionary technology but because it was a huge scheme. The clients were probably drugged and put in studios where their fantasies were enacted with a host of attractive actors.

It seemed implausible because the cost of producing the fantasies would be prohibitive, but perhaps the math worked somehow. With prices per person starting at thirty-five hundred dollars for a three-hour session and seven thousand for a couple, it could be possible to pull it off even if they had to pay actors to pretend to be the avatars for three hours.

Did she want in?

Could she act out someone else's fantasies?

Nah, that was too freaky even for her.

It would certainly explain the need for such strict nondisclosure agreements and the air of secrecy surrounding the entire operation. If word got out that Perfect Match was essentially pimping out its employees, the scandal would be explosive and the fallout immeasurable.

Jasmine shook her head. It was a crazy idea, a conspiracy theory that belonged in the pages of a tabloid magazine, not in the real world. And yet, as she looked around at the impossibly beautiful people that surrounded her, she couldn't help but wonder.

On the dance floor, Edgar pulled her closer, his hand resting on the small of her back as they swayed to the music. "Is everything alright? You seem distracted."

Jasmine forced a smile, trying to push down the unease churning in her gut. "I'm fine. It's just strange how everyone here is so incredibly beautiful that they look like animated mannequins."

Edgar nodded, his gaze sweeping over the crowd with a knowing smile. "A lot can be done with makeup and clothing. Even plain-looking people can be made to look exceptional."

She arched a brow. "Makeup and clothing can go a long way, but they cannot perform miracles. This place looks like a supermodel convention."

He laughed. "You're right, they are all incredibly good-looking. Perfect Match only hires the best of the best, the most talented and attractive people they can find. It's part of what makes the experience so immersive, so believable."

Was Edgar admitting that they were using real people in their so-called virtual adventures?

Jasmine hesitated, biting her lip as she tried to find the right words. "Don't you think it's a little strange?" she asked, her voice dropping to a whisper. "It's like they're all playing a role in some kind of elaborate fantasy."

Edgar's brow furrowed, a flicker of confusion passing over his face. "I'm not sure I follow. What do you mean by playing a role?"

He seemed genuinely perplexed, so perhaps she was wrong, and there was some other explanation for why they were all beautiful and seemed to be of the same age group.

Come to think of it, she should have been suspicious when Amanda and Syssi had come to visit her, and then Kian. Heck, even Edna and Max. The last two were not as gorgeous as Amanda and her brother, but they were still very good-looking, and they all seemed to be about the same age.

Jasmine sighed. "Ignore what I said. I'm being silly. I guess I'm just overwhelmed by all the grandeur. I feel like I've stepped into another world where everything is just too perfect to be real."

Edgar smiled, his hand tightening around hers. "We are in the business of fulfilling fantasies. Only the most beautiful, most talented people make the cut. It's like a club within a club, an exclusive inner circle that only a lucky few get to be a part of. It's a very rigorous screening process."

Jasmine frowned as she tried to reconcile what Edgar was saying with the wild theory that had taken root in her mind. It made sense, in a way. Perfect Match was a luxury service, catering to the wealthiest and most discerning clients. Of course they would want to hire only the best and the brightest, the most stunning and charismatic people they could find.

"I also noticed there aren't any children around," she said, giving voice to the other thing that bothered her about the crowd. "Is this an adults-only cruise? I mean, besides the obvious reasons for privacy and discretion."

Edgar chuckled, shaking his head. "There are children on board," he said. "Just not many, and during the nightly festivities, they mostly stay in the cabins with their babysitters. These parties start and end too late for children to be present."

Jasmine nodded, feeling a little foolish. "Oh, that's right. I remember now that I saw Amanda's little girl with her, and she showed me a picture of Kian's daughter when I first met him."

Of course, there were children on board. Not everyone who worked for Perfect Match would be single or childless. Some of them probably had families, spouses, and kids waiting for them back home. And it made perfect sense that the ones who were on board would not be present for a late-night event.

She had let her imagination run wild with crazy theories and baseless suspicions instead of focusing on what she could gain from being here. This was the opportunity of a lifetime, a chance to be a part of something truly extraordinary, and she needed to get her head in the game and mingle like there was no tomorrow.

EDGAR

E dgar wasn't surprised that Jasmine was suspicious. Any normal person would be. The guests were almost all immortals, and they were all exceedingly beautiful by human standards. They also seemed to be the same age more or less, and the lack of elders and dearth of children was another clue. Still, all the oddities could be explained away by the Perfect Match cover story, which made it a stroke of genius.

He wondered who had originally come up with it.

It had probably been Toven's mate. When Mia had invited her best friends Frankie and Margo on the cruise with the promise of jobs as beta testers for the service's virtual adventures, she must have told them that they were joining a Perfect Match company ten-day cruise.

For now, he had to perpetuate the lie, but at some point he would have to tell Jasmine the truth about himself and his clan and ask for her consent to be induced into immortality.

If she agreed but didn't want to leave her life behind and immediately join him in the village, he would have to make her forget what he had told her and keep seeing her until she either transitioned or proved not to be a Dormant.

Naturally, he hoped she possessed the necessary godly genes, and his hope was not unfounded.

Jasmine had a modicum of paranormal ability that marked her as a potential Dormant, and in addition, she had a way of drawing people to her, which indicated affinity.

But as much as he wanted to believe that she was meant for him and that the Fates had brought them together for a reason, Edgar couldn't ignore the nagging doubts that whispered in the back of his mind. If Jasmine was truly his fated mate, his one and only, then why did her eyes wander so freely around the room?

Why did her smile light up for every male who made eye contact with her?

It bothered him more than he wanted to admit and more than he had a right to. He wasn't in love with Jasmine, but it wasn't only about lust either. At the moment, she was a potential that he wanted to explore, a female he was still examining his feelings for.

Still, he couldn't help the annoyance that flared in his chest every time her gaze lingered on another guy and every time her lips curved in a seductive smile that wasn't aimed at him. It wasn't jealousy, or at least he didn't think it was, but it was insulting. While Jasmine was with him, she should turn off her flirtatiousness because showing interest in other males while dancing in his arms was disrespectful.

How would she feel if his eyes kept wandering to other females?

So yeah, most of those present were either his relatives or mated to them, but Marina and Larissa weren't related to him, and although they were accompanied by Peter and Jay, he still had eyes and noticed that they were both attractive women. Not that he would have flirted with either. He knew better than to infringe on what the two Guardians considered their turf, even temporarily.

While Jasmine was with him, he wanted her eyes on him and her smile directed at him and him alone, the same way his attention was focused on her.

When the song ended, Jasmine looked at him with a tired smile on her face. "Can we sit this one out? My feet are killing me, and I need to take a break."

"Of course." He took her hand and led her to the table.

It was easy to forget that she wasn't immortal and that she couldn't keep up. She looked the part so well, and for a human, she was also surprisingly strong and resilient.

Frankie and Dagor were already seated at the table, their heads bent together, no doubt whispering sweet nothings in each other's ears. Aru and Gabi were still on the dance floor, and Margo and Negal were not attending for obvious reasons.

Edgar pulled out Jasmine's chair for her, the chivalrous gesture earning him a warm smile and a murmured thanks. As he took his own seat beside her, her eyes drifted to the empty chairs surrounding their table. "I hope Margo is okay. I thought she would be here tonight."

Frankie turned to look at her. "She's still a little under the weather. Dagor and I are going to bring them to-go plates later."

"What's wrong with her?" Jasmine frowned. "Is it serious? I mean, she seemed fine this afternoon, a little tired maybe, but nothing that would keep her from attending the wedding. Did the doctor check up on her?"

Frankie winced. "Yeah, she did. But you know how doctors are. She told Margo to rest, drink plenty of fluids, and call her if she didn't feel better in the morning."

Jasmine nodded. "I know exactly what you mean. If you are under thirty years old, they treat you dismissively. A friend of mine suffered for years from stomach pains, and her doctor told her that it was all because of stress and recommended therapy. Turned out she had irritable bowel syndrome."

"How did she find out?" Frankie asked. "Did she go to another doctor?"

As the two continued talking about human maladies and the various treatments available for them, Edgar exchanged a knowing look with Dagor.

Having a human mate or one that used to be human was a different experience, and he hoped Jasmine wouldn't direct any health questions at him. He really didn't want to add more lies to those he'd had to tell her so far, and besides, he didn't know enough about human ailments to lie convincingly.

"I feel bad for Margo." Jasmine sighed. "This is such a beautiful event."

Edgar draped his arm over the back of her chair. "Oh, I have no doubt that Margo and Negal are finding ways to entertain themselves."

Provided that her transition symptoms had not worsened since he had last seen her, Margo seemed well enough to partake in some one-on-one fun.

"I bet." Jasmine laughed, her eyes sparkling with mirth as she leaned into him, her shoulder brushing against his. "In fact, they might be having more fun than we are."

He leaned closer and brushed his lips over hers. "The night is not over yet, beautiful. I promise that there is much more fun in store for you."

59

PETER

Peter's eyes drifted between Marina and the newlyweds on the dance floor. On his other side, Jay was engaged in a lively conversation with Larissa, their voices rising and falling in a loud mix of Russian and English and their hands gesturing the things they didn't know how to say to each other. Marina interjected from time to time, helping to bridge the language gap between them.

He was still amazed at the speed she had taught herself English. Jay, an immortal with a natural aptitude for languages, was still struggling with basic Russian after spending hours in an online course. For a human, Marina's achievement was extraordinary. Peter would have been inclined to assert that her aptitude for languages was a paranormal talent and, therefore, an indicator of godly genes, but the absence of the most obvious indicators overruled that possibility.

Given how many times they'd had sex and how many times he had bitten her, she would have started transitioning already if she was a Dormant.

A crushing sadness overtook him as he thought of her short lifespan. It was a blink of an eye in comparison to his, and by staying with her instead of cutting off the relationship, he was only delaying the inevitable heartache by a few decades yet amplifying it immeasurably.

He was so damn selfish. He couldn't give her children because they would be mortal like her. The smart thing to do would be to let her go so she could find happiness with a human male who could give her what she needed.

A home and a family to call her own.

But the ship had sailed on that. He was in love with Marina, and in his selfishness, he couldn't let her go.

Even the thought of her returning to Safe Haven without him for a short while was intolerable to him. Peter had never imagined that he could feel this way about a human, that he could form a bond so deep and so unbreakable with someone who wasn't even a Dormant.

How was it possible that he felt like he had found a missing piece of himself in her?

How could the Fates be so cruel and merciful at the same time?

Except, if someone asked him whether he would have preferred never to have met Marina, he would have replied that it's better to have loved and lost than never to have loved at all.

Peter wasn't angry at the Fates for bringing her into his life. He just wondered what they had been thinking.

What was the Fates' grand plan for him and Marina?

As an eternal optimist, he hoped that there was a solution down the line, and in the meantime his concern was how to ensure the minimal separation possible between them.

He didn't want to wait weeks for her transfer request to go through the proper channels.

Perhaps he could convince Kian that Marina was needed in the village because of her translation skills? Many of the village's new residents still struggled with English, and the Kra-ell knew Marina and would be comfortable with her helping them with the language barrier.

On the other hand, his approaching Kian directly could backfire.

Kian would approve Marina's transfer request if he believed she wanted to move to be close to the other former occupants of Igor's compound or for a different sort of work than what she was tasked with in Safe Haven. He might not approve of her transferring to be with Peter.

Immortals were discouraged from having long-term relationships with humans, and the term discouraged was putting it mildly. It was more like prohibited.

It would be better to tell Eleanor and Emmett about Marina's translation ability and have them add it to the transfer request. The problem with that was that it wouldn't be immediate, and if he tried to expedite it, he would show his hand.

He needed to pretend that his interest in Marina was no different than any he had before with human females. Perhaps Kian wouldn't care that Peter was planning to keep Marina with him and would think nothing of it, but Peter couldn't take the chance that Kian would have an issue with that and not approve her request.

In the meantime, he could take a few days off and join her at Safe Haven, or even better, he could ask Onegus to transfer him there for a couple of weeks. After all, Guardians were rotated between Safe Haven, the keep, and the village, so it wouldn't be anything unusual for him to request a particular post.

Leaning over, he hooked a finger under Marina's chin and planted a soft kiss on her lips. "I love you," he murmured against her mouth before leaning away. "But don't tell anyone," he added with a wink.

She frowned. "Why not?"

"Because it needs to remain our secret," he said in a teasing manner, so if Jay heard him, he would think nothing of it.

"If you say so." Marina looked deflated.

"Hey." He leaned closer. "No need to pout. Do you want to dance?"

He had to explain why he was acting this way and also to tell her his plan.

60

MARINA

As Peter led Marina onto the dance floor, she was once again assaulted by fear and doubts. She thought about the borrowed dress she was wearing and the immortal female to whom it belonged. Was she watching her and telling her friends about her charitable gesture?

Were they pitying the poor human who was trying to be one of them?

But then Peter put his hand on the small of her back and pressed his body close to hers, and she forgot about everyone else around them and focused on the way he made her feel.

She had no doubt that he loved her, but she was disappointed that he wanted to keep his love for her a secret, even though she could understand his motives. His family wouldn't approve of her as his mate, but if he pretended that she was just a passing interest, just another body to warm his bed, perhaps they wouldn't mind.

They swayed together to the music, their bodies molded together as if they had been made for each other, and as Marina let herself get lost in the moment and the feel of Peter's arms around her, she couldn't help but steal a glance at the other couples on the dance floor and the way they moved with such effortless grace and fluidity.

Especially the females.

Their bodies were lithe and supple, and their movements were fluid and seamless. They seemed to glide across the floor with their feet barely touching the ground as if they were floating on air.

Compared to them, Marina felt clumsy and uncoordinated, her own movements stiff and awkward next to theirs, but when she looked up at Peter and saw the way he regarded her, his eyes expressing so much love and adoration, Marina felt all her doubts and insecurities melt away.

She didn't deserve to be loved like that, and the intensity of his feelings terrified her, because she knew how badly it was going to hurt him just by being by her side as her life span would be over in the blink of an eye, while he would go on forever, young and strong and beautiful.

How could she let him love her, knowing that she would cause him so much anguish in the end? How could she be so selfish, so cruel, as to let him tie himself to her?

But even as those thoughts swirled in her mind, the guilt and shame threatening to overwhelm her, Marina knew that she couldn't let Peter go by pushing him away.

She loved him too fiercely, too selfishly.

Maybe that made her weak, and perhaps it meant that she didn't love him enough or wasn't strong enough to do what was best for him, but she couldn't bring herself to set him free to find someone who could give him the forever he deserved.

Letting out a breath, she clung to him, her arms wrapped even tighter around his neck and her face buried in the crook of his shoulder.

"I want to explain," he whispered in her ear. "Why I want my love for you to remain a secret."

"It's okay," she murmured into his neck. "I understand. Your family will not approve of you having deep feelings for me, but they might be okay with you having fun with the human for a little while."

"Yes, but I wouldn't have given a fuck about what they think if changing their perception wouldn't have jeopardized your transfer to the village. For now, I want them to believe that what we have is casual, so no one will think of putting roadblocks on your transfer."

A weight lifting off her chest, she kissed the spot on his neck that her mouth was pressed to. "Thank you for telling me this. It means a lot to me."

He tightened his arms around her. "There is nothing casual about my feelings for you, and to prove it, I'm coming with you to Safe Haven." He brushed his lips against the shell of her ear. "I'll ask to be stationed with the team of Guardians on duty there and stay with you until your transfer is approved. That way, we don't have to be apart for more than a day."

Marina pulled back to look at him. "I love you so much that it hurts."

He frowned. "Why does it hurt?"

She averted her eyes. "You know why. But I'm too selfish to let you go, so I'll take everything you are willing to offer and enjoy it as long as it lasts."

Lifting a hand, he cupped her cheek, his thumb wiping away a tear she hadn't realized she'd shed. "Let's not think about the future. Let's just focus on the here and now."

Marina nodded, her throat tight with emotion. Peter was right. There was no point in worrying about the future when the present was so wonderful and perfect.

ARU

Aru glanced at his watch, his heart quickening as he saw the hands ticking closer to midnight. He had seen Kian and Syssi rise from their seats a few moments earlier, making their way over to the newlyweds to offer their congratulations and farewells.

Now that Kian's sisters were in on the secret, they could cover for him and make his early departure seem less conspicuous. In a way, it was a relief to have more people in the know and not have to carry the weight of this burden alone, but it was also the main cause for the churning in his gut.

It was illogical to feel that way about people who couldn't reveal his and Aria's secret even if they wanted to, but it was so ingrained in Aru's psyche to guard the telepathic connection with his sister that he couldn't help but feel exposed and incredibly vulnerable despite the safety precautions the princess had provided by compelling her children and their mates to keep the information from leaking out of their small group.

"Go." Gabi patted his arm. "You don't want to be late."

Aru hated leaving her alone. "Are you staying or going to call it a night?"

Gabi smiled. "I'm staying. I'm going to spend some time with Karen, Gilbert and the rest of the family. Everyone is fussing over Karen, and I need to do my share of fussing as well. It's my duty as her sister-in-law."

Aru leaned in to press a soft kiss to her cheek, breathing in the sweet, familiar scent of her perfume. "Enjoy yourself." He brushed his lips against her soft skin. "And if anyone asks where I am, tell them that I had something I needed to take care of, but I didn't tell you what it was."

Gabi chuckled, her eyes sparkling with mischief. "I'll tell them that you are sick of attending weddings."

Aru shook his head. "Only if you make it sound like a joke," he warned.

She laughed. "Of course."

The truth was that he had attended enough weddings to last him a century. The princess's speeches were great, full of warmth and wisdom and heartfelt emotion, but even though she had tried to make them individual for each couple, there was only so much variety she could introduce and only so many ways to say the same things over and over again.

With a final squeeze of Gabi's hand and a murmured goodbye, Aru slipped away from the table and made his way out of the dining hall.

Thankfully, he didn't encounter anyone in the elevator, and as he entered the corridor leading to the heir's cabin, he glanced at his watch and saw that he had exactly two minutes left to get there on time.

Hurrying his step, he got to her door and was about to ring the bell, when he heard a cabin door open behind him, and as he turned around, he saw Kian and Syssi stepping out of their cabin, which was located on the other end of the long hallway.

Unlike the previous nights, they were still dressed in their evening clothes, most likely because they hadn't had time to change out of them.

Aru waited for them to catch up.

He had no idea what Kian wanted to talk to him about before the telepathic meeting took place, and he hoped that it wasn't about revealing his and Aria's secret communication method to even more people.

Kian looked aggravated, and as the couple reached Aru, he tugged on his tux lapels and pressed the doorbell. "Saying goodnight to all these people cost us valuable time. We only had enough left to grab Syssi's notepad and had to rush over."

The door opened, and the princess's Odu bowed. "Good evening, Mistress Syssi, Master Kian, Master Aru. Please come in."

"Thank you," Kian said before ushering his wife in.

Avoiding eye contact with the cyborg, Aru walked in behind them.

His aversion to the Odus was another illogical thing that he couldn't help, and he wondered whether it had been encoded in his genetics.

"Good evening, Clan Mother." He bowed to the princess.

She smiled and inclined her head. "Please call me Annani, Aru. If you do not, I will correct you every time you use my title until you get used to using my given name."

"As you wish."

He was not going to address the heir to the Anumati throne so casually. He would just have to perform verbal gymnastics to avoid addressing her directly.

They sat down, Syssi next to the princess and Aru and Kian each taking an armchair, more pleasantries were exchanged, and then the Odu served tea and coffee.

When each of them held a cup in hand, Aru turned to Kian. "So, why are we here early?"

"Syssi had a vision about the pods," Kian said without preamble and turned to his wife. "Would you like to tell it, or do you want me to do it?"

Aru was grateful on two counts. The first that Kian was not asking to let more people in on the secret, and second, that he wasn't wasting time.

"I'll do it." Syssi put her teacup down. "Bear in mind that visions usually should not be taken literally, and sometimes their purpose is just to hint at things. Also, I didn't ask to be shown where the pod with the royal twins was buried. I asked for something else entirely and was shown this instead." She continued to tell him what she had seen and what she and Amanda thought about Jasmine's role in the vision.

As Aru listened, he found it hard to believe that two intelligent females like Syssi and Amanda had put so much faith in tarot cards and Jasmine's ramblings about her promised prince. Not only that, but it also seemed that they had managed to rope Kian and his mother into supporting that questionable narrative.

Aru didn't want to offend Syssi, but he couldn't contain his incredulity. "Are you seriously suggesting that a human who bases her life decisions on tarot cards and crystal balls can help us locate the pod with the royal twins?"

Syssi smiled indulgently as if he were the one whose logic was skewed. "Tarot cards, crystal balls, and other instruments of divination are just conduits for the energy that is inside the individual. On their own, they are just inanimate objects with no innate power.

Jasmine has something, a spark of potential that we can all feel. And besides, my visions are never wrong."

She had just told him that her visions shouldn't be taken literally, and now she was telling him that they were never wrong.

"So, let me understand what you are suggesting." Aru took a deep breath. "You want us to take Jasmine with us and have her direct our search for the pods?"

Syssi nodded. "What harm could that do? One more person on your team is not going to make much of a difference, but she might be able to point you in the right direction when you have no other clues."

"Jasmine is human," Aru said. "She will slow us down."

Syssi smiled again. "Yes, she will, but on the other hand, she might save you a lot of time by pointing you in the right direction."

He couldn't argue with that, but there was one more point he could raise. "What if we determine that she's useless?"

"She won't be," Kian said. "I have full faith in Syssi's visions. But if you decide that Jasmine is not helpful to your search, you can send her back home. We will cover the bill."

"Sounds reasonable," Aru agreed. "Did you speak with her about it? Maybe she doesn't want to go?"

"We've told her nothing so far," Kian said. "I wanted to check with you first. There are also a few other concerns that we need to address."

"Like what?" Aru asked almost defensively.

Kian lifted the teacup to his lips and took a small sip. "The twins are rumored to be powerful compellers, and your team will need the specialty earpieces William developed that block the sound waves carrying compulsion."

Aru shifted in the armchair and crossed his legs. "That would be much appreciated. Thank you."

Kian regarded him for a long moment. "Does the queen know that her son fathered the twins with the Kra-ell princess?"

"I believe so, but you need to understand that my interaction with the queen has been minimal, and my sister serves the oracle, not the queen. We provide information, but we don't get much back, and we can only speculate on what the queen knows and thinks. There were rumors that claimed a dalliance between her son and the Kra-ell princess, who later became the queen, but I don't think the Anumati queen believed them at the time. She probably thought it was more of the Eternal King's negative propaganda aimed at discrediting his son and painting him as a deviant. The Kra-ell queen was very good at concealing the twins from the public eye and shrouding the identity of their father, and even the Eternal King, with all his spies, wasn't sure that the twins were his grandchildren. It's common for the Kra-ell queens to hide the identity of their children's fathers, especially those who father the daughters that will rule one day, so no one thought much of it. On the other hand, the twins became acolytes at a very young age, so they must have raised a lot of brows at the time. That was very uncommon."

Kian nodded. "I keep forgetting that this is ancient history to you. We've only learned all of this recently, and the Kra-ell, who told us about the twins being in stasis for thousands of years, said it was recent history for them as well. The question is whether my mother should inform the queen of Anumati about this new thread that might lead to them."

Aru leveled his gaze at Kian. "There is nothing I keep from the queen. I don't share every thought and speculation I have, and I don't bother her with every unimportant detail, so I can refrain from telling her about this new line of inquiry until it is proven to be relevant, but if it is, then I need to inform her." He dipped his head toward the heir. "My apologies, but my first loyalty is to my queen."

Annani nodded. "I understand, and I appreciate your loyalty to my grandmother and your honest reply, but I have no intention of keeping this from her."

62

ANNANI

Annani suspected that Aru had communicated to his sister every important tidbit of information he had learned about her and the clan.

She would not have been concerned, but there was always the possibility that the queen's part in the resistance would be discovered, and she would be tortured for information.

There was not much she could do about it at this point, though. Her resemblance to her grandmother had given her away, and the moment Aru had informed the queen about her, the cat was out of the bag, so to speak, and there was no way to put it back in.

If the Eternal King discovered Annani's existence, he would not hesitate to destroy Earth just to get rid of her, and since there was no communication with Anumati, and no one was officially allowed anywhere near it, the king could annihilate the entire planet without worrying about his reputation.

Annani sighed.

It was not easy to live with a tangible and ever-present existential threat, but it was nothing new for her. Annani's life had prepared her well to not only handle and cope but to thrive under adverse situations. She would find a way to weather this storm as well.

"The queen is ready to begin," Aru said.

Annani nodded. "So am I."

Beside her, Syssi reached for the yellow notepad and pen and got ready to transcribe the conversation.

Once the initial greetings and pleasantries were out of the way, Annani humbly requested to take the first turn and tell the queen about her family.

"But of course," Aru said for the queen. "I am very curious to hear about you and your family."

"I would like to begin with my half-sister Areana." It would be a good way to ease the queen into a conversation about the royal twins. "I mentioned her before. She was the one who volunteered to take my place as Mortdh's bride, and that was how she was spared. Areana was on her way to Mortdh's stronghold when the assembly was bombed, but I did not know that she had survived until very recently. To my great surprise, Areana had mated Mortdh's son Navuh, and he has been keeping her hidden in his harem for thousands of years."

Aru looked at her with shock in his eyes. "He kept a goddess in a harem with human females?"

Annani nodded. "Immortal females mostly, and some human, but it is a sham. As shocking as it seems, Navuh and Areana are fated mates, and he does not grace the beds of any of the others. He is devoted to Areana. But since he does not want his army of goons to know that his mate is a goddess who outranks him in status, he keeps her locked in his harem, and none of them know that he has a goddess in there."

Aru's eyes looked like they were about to pop out of their sockets. "Why does she allow it?"

Annani sighed. "She loves him. Areana is a sweet and gentle soul, but she is a weak goddess. Navuh might be only an immortal, but he is more powerful than she is, and with his strong compulsion ability, he is also more powerful than many of the gods on Anumati." She smiled. "After all, he is the Eternal King's descendant."

So was Areana, but somehow, she had not inherited any of their grandfather's power. Her mother's genes must be dominant in her genetic composition.

Aru shook his head. "It will take me a few minutes to explain all of this to my sister."

"Take your time." Annani lifted her teacup for Ojidu to refill.

The queen's response came several moments later. "It is a disgrace that a daughter of Ahn, even one who is the product of an unofficial relationship, is kept as a sex slave by the hybrid son of Ahn's nephew. I find this appalling."

Annani winced. "Something must have been lost in translation. Areana is not a sex slave. She lives in a harem, but she is surrounded by luxury and treated with love and respect by her mate. I cringe at saying anything positive about Navuh, but that is the truth. I do not wish to go into a lengthy explanation, but we were able to plant a spy in the harem and establish a mode of communication with my sister. The spy confirmed what my sister had told me. Areana is the undisputed queen of that harem."

Aru dipped his head. "My apologies, Clan Mother. There is no word in Anumatian for a harem, so my translation was inaccurate."

"I see." Annani tried to think of a way to explain it better. "What do the Kra-ell females call the males in their extended family unit?"

"It is a word that is similar to a tribe," Aru said.

"You can tell your sister that Areana is part of such a tribe, but instead of one female with several males, this tribe consists of one male and several females. She is Navuh's favorite, and he does not engage with any of the other females. He lets others impregnate them and claims their children as his own."

Aru looked like he had bitten on a lemon, but he nodded. "I will try my best to convey this to the queen."

Annani waited patiently for the response, sipping on her tea and thinking of how she was going to move to the subject of the twins.

"The queen says that Areana is unimportant in the grand scheme of things," Aru said. "She is a weak goddess, the result of a dalliance, and she is not in the line of succession. Queen Ani wants to know more about Navuh."

Annani felt a flare of anger at the queen's casual disregard for Areana, at the way she seemed to brush her aside simply because she did not fit into the neat, tidy line of royal succession. But then, as quickly as it had come, the anger faded, replaced by a flicker of understanding.

The queen seemed to assume that Areana was the daughter of a concubine whom Ahn had kept in addition to his official wife, and Ani might have felt disappointed that her son conducted himself in the same shameless way as his father did.

"Areana was born long before Ahn met Nei, my mother," Annani explained. "Since the moment my father met my mother, he did not look at another female."

Aru took a moment to convey the queen's words. "The queen is still not interested in Areana. She wants to hear more about Mortdh's son."

The queen was right. Areana was important to Annani because she loved her and appreciated her, but regrettably, her role in history was not nearly as important as her despicable mate's.

"Navuh is my sworn enemy, and he seeks to destroy me, my clan, and all that I stand for. While my clan and I strive to improve human society to promote progress, peace, and prosperity, Navuh wants to enslave humans and control them. I do not wish to go into a lengthy explanation, but Navuh managed to create an immortal army that is many thousands strong. They are brainwashed and compelled daily to hate, destroy, and kill indiscriminately. Human lives mean nothing to them. They are barbarians who thrive on cruelty as a way to intimidate and control, and there is absolutely no chance of peaceful coexistence with them or even some sort of compromise. It is either us or them." She sighed. "It pains me to even say that. I do not wish to destroy what is left of our people, but the longer this conflict lasts, the more I realize that there is no other option."

Come to think of it, the queen probably did not hold human lives in high regard either. If she did not deem her own granddaughter important only because she was a weak goddess and not in the line of succession, she certainly did not deem humans as having any value whatsoever.

"Navuh is a threat to your safety," the queen replied through Aru. "How are you protecting yourself?"

As Annani had expected, the queen had not reacted to Navuh's disregard for human lives, but at least she was concerned with Annani and her clan's safety. On second thought, she was only concerned with Annani, the heir to the throne.

"I assure you that I am more than capable of handling Navuh and his forces. I have done so for thousands of years. He may have a large army of immortal warriors at his command, but we have always been several steps ahead of him thanks to our superior technology and knowledge."

Annani went on to explain the role of Ekin's tablet that she had 'borrowed,' a treasure trove of knowledge that had allowed her clan to stay ahead of Navuh's powerful immortal army and the humans under his poisonous control.

"We did not decipher all of the science that is contained in that tablet, and I understand only a small fraction of it," Annani admitted. "One of my great-grandchildren, who is much cleverer than I, was far more adept at deciphering the complex equations and formulas that Ekin had inscribed upon its surface."

A long moment passed until Aru relayed the queen's answer. "Did your father or Ekin find the Odus I sent to Earth with the information of how to build more of them? They were meant to arrive before the Kra-ell settler ship and its cargo of assassins so Ekin could build an army of them to protect Ahn and the others."

Annani glanced at Kian. "We have guessed correctly. The queen was the one who sent them." She was sure that Aru had told Aria about the Odus, so the queen knew that they had found them. Her grandmother's question was about the blueprints that she had hidden inside their brains and whether they had found them.

Annani was not sure that she wanted to reveal that highly confidential information in front of Aru.

After the Odus had been used for warfare, the technology for building robotic servants was banned on Anumati. Aru was a rebel, so he did not care about the ban, but he was not fond of Odus. He had grown up on horror stories that the official propaganda had spread about the Odus so people would be terrified of them, and no one would dare to build them again.

"You might as well tell her," Kian said.

"We found them," Annani told Aru. "But the information about how to build them was only recently discovered following an accidental reboot of one of the Odus. We are still trying to figure out what he wrote down. The biotechnology on Earth is not anywhere near as advanced as what you had on Anumati all those thousands of years ago, and we will probably be able to develop only a much less life-like product."

"The queen says that it is a shame the Odus were not as useful as she hoped," Aru said. "She took a great risk by sending these seven to Earth. But now that you and your clan finally have access to the information stored in them, you can build your own army and protect yourself from Navuh's immortals. The queen wants to hear more about the conflict and why Navuh is so determined to destroy you."

Annani explained the long and bitter history of the conflict between her clan and Navuh's forces. She spoke of the way they had fought by proxy, using their influence and their knowledge to shape the course of human history, to guide and protect the mortals who looked to them for guidance and support.

"Navuh helps the humans he controls and uses them against the people we are assisting with our technological and ideological knowhow. And we do the same, using the humans we helped to elevate and advance to counter his moves."

It was a never-ending game played out across the millennia, and through it all, Annani and her clan had endured. But now, the royal twins might affect the balance of power and change the game.

The question was how.

63

QUEEN ANI

When Annani had spoken about her sister, Ani had listened to her words with a sense of detachment. She didn't really care about Areana, who had mated the enemy of her sister. She must be weak of character in addition to being weak in power to mate a despicable male like this.

But then Ani was mated to a no less despicable male who was not even her fated mate, and she was still married to him because it was a position of power that allowed her to mitigate El's schemes to some degree and slow down his plans.

She found it hard to believe that, at one time, she had convinced herself that she loved El. He had not always been a monster, had not always been the cruel and tyrannical ruler he had become. Once, a long time ago, he had been a visionary, a leader who had united their people and brought peace and prosperity to a fractured and war-torn world. But power had corrupted him, twisting his mind and his soul until there was nothing left but greed, paranoia, and an insatiable hunger for control. And now, after millennia of his iron-fisted rule, there was no hope of redemption or change.

Ani despised him with every fiber of her being but continued playing the role of the dutiful wife and queen, all the while working in secret to undermine him and to build a resistance that would one day overthrow him and restore freedom and justice to their world.

It was not all that different from what Annani was doing on Earth; except Annani did not have to pretend to care for Navuh.

As her granddaughter shifted the narrative to the Kraell royal twins, though, Ani's interest was suddenly piqued.

She had heard the rumors about Ahn's supposed affair with the Kra-ell princess, his counterpart in the rebellion, but she had never believed them.

To her, the Kra-ell were barbarians, only one degree above the animals they hunted for blood, and to copulate with one was just disgusting. Still, it was possible that El believed that Ahn had fathered the twins because he had despised his son and his progressive ideas.

The royal twins had always been a mystery, consecrated to the priesthood and shrouded in secrecy.

Their faces had been hidden behind veils their entire lives, and there had been rumors of deformity and abnormality, but Ani had never been one to put much stock in rumors.

Now, however, she was forced to confront the possibility that there might have been some truth to those rumors after all. If the twins were indeed the product of a forbidden union between a god and a Kra-ell, not necessarily Ahn but some other god, then it was no wonder that their mother had kept them hidden and their features obscured.

Perhaps Ekin had been the father?

He had shared Ahn's ideology, and he had always been sexually adventurous. If anyone was capable of coupling with a Kra-ell savage female, it was him.

Ekin was not her son, and Ani abhorred El's hordes of concubines, including Ekin's mother, but she had always been fond of Ekin despite his unconventional beliefs that had been even more radical than Ahn's.

Ahn had always been more reserved than Ekin, more refined, and she found it hard to believe that he had violated the taboo on copulating with lesser species and fathered children with the Kra-ell princess, who had later become the queen.

When Aria was done relaying Annani's story, Ani chose her response carefully. "I always assumed that the rumors about the twins were baseless—malicious propaganda spread by the Eternal King. But if what you say is true, if they are indeed the children of Ahn and the Kra-ell queen, then they might be just as dangerous as the Eternal King thinks they are, and they should be approached with extreme caution."

"I am not sure that they are dangerous," Aria gave voice to Annani's response. "I think that the Kra-ell queen sent them to Earth not to undermine Ahn and take over. I think she sent them to their father because she feared for their lives. If anyone had discovered that they were half god, half Kra-ell, they would not have lasted more than a day. Their own people would have slaughtered them along with the queen who had committed the greatest transgression. The only place they could be safe was on Earth among the rebels who believed in equality and were led by their father. If they were as powerful as the king believed them to be, their mother wouldn't have been so worried for their safety."

It was a smart observation, and the queen was proud of her granddaughter's deductive ability, but it was very possible that Annani was wrong. She was a little soft-hearted, and she believed in people's good intentions.

It was naive.

"The twins are a wild card," Ani said. "And depending on the power they can actually wield, they can be a variable that could tip the balance of power in either direction. You must ensure that it tips in your favor." Ani paused for a moment, thinking about the role of the human Syssi had seen in her vision assisting the team of gods. "The human needs to be watched carefully. The Fates work in mysterious ways, and the role they gave that woman might not be as straightforward as your daughter-in-law's vision suggests."

64

JASMINE

Edgar leaned back in his chair and rubbed his stomach. "I'm stuffed." He looked at the half-eaten cake on his plate. "This is delicious, but I can't take another bite."

Jasmine chuckled. "We've danced off the calories, so it's not so bad."

She wasn't sure that the net effect was zero, but she'd made a valiant effort to make it so. She had danced until her feet ached, sampled every delicacy the buffet had to offer, and got Edgar to introduce her to a bunch of people. Regrettably, none of them specified their positions in Perfect Match, so she still didn't know who she needed to impress to get a job at the company.

Kian had promised to talk to the owners on her behalf, but she hadn't heard from him yet. Besides, he might have meant to ask about some entry-level job for her to replace the customer service one she was probably going to lose.

She'd told him that she dreamt about being a spokes-woman in the Perfect Match commercials, but she'd also told him that any other job would be great, and that was probably what he'd remembered from their talk if he remembered her quest for a job at the company at all.

Edgar draped a lazy arm over the back of her chair. "Ready to go?"

Jasmine looked at the dwindling crowd on the dance floor and the partially empty dining tables and sighed. "I enjoyed this evening tremendously, and I don't want it to end." She turned to him and smiled. "I feel like Cinderella at the ball. The clock has already struck a few times, and I'm anxious about it striking twelve."

He leaned over and brushed his lips over her cheek. "It's way past midnight, beautiful, and the fun doesn't have to end just yet." He trailed his lips down her neck, eliciting a delicious shiver. "I'm not tired. Are you?"

Jasmine chuckled. "My answer would be my place or yours, but since your place is probably much nicer than mine, it has to be yours."

The lascivious smile he sent her made her tingle in all the right places. "Let's go." He rose to his feet and offered her a hand up.

Guiding her to the newlyweds through the throng of well-wishers and lingering guests, he stopped to congratulate them and then paused to say goodbye to Marina and Larissa and their dates.

As they made their way towards the exit, Jasmine's gaze landed on Max, his tall, imposing figure cutting a striking silhouette against the wall he was standing next to. Almost without thinking, she smiled and raised a hand in a small wave, immediately regretting the gesture.

After the way Max had treated her, he didn't deserve to be acknowledged by her.

When Edgar's arm tightened around her waist, pulling her close against his side in a possessive display, Jasmine bit back a smirk. Let the stuck-up Max see that she was desired and appreciated by a good man who deemed her more than worthy of his attentions.

As they stepped out into the corridor and Edgar pressed the button to call the elevator, Jasmine smiled and leaned into his embrace. "I bet your bed is bigger and more comfortable than mine."

He looked at her with a slight frown. "Your cabin is private, though, and mine isn't. I have a roommate. Charlie has his own bedroom, but it's not like he wouldn't know that you spent the night with me. Knowing him, he's probably sitting in the living room and watching a movie even though he has a television in his bedroom."

"I don't mind," she said, her fingers playing with the lapel of his jacket. "If you haven't noticed yet, I'm not shy. But if you are, I can be quiet." A wicked grin spread across her face as she leaned in closer, her lips brushing against his ear. "Or I can try. I can't promise that I'll succeed."

She wasn't an exhibitionist, but she got a certain thrill from making public displays of affection.

Edgar's answering chuckle was low and deep, sending shivers racing down her spine. "You can be as loud as you want," he assured her, his hand splaying across the small of her back. "The upper deck cabins have excellent soundproofing. The moment I close the door, Charlie won't hear a thing."

"Awesome. I hope your ears aren't overly sensitive," she whispered in his ear.

The woman who was waiting for the elevator next to them smirked as if she'd heard what Jasmine had whispered in Ed's ear, but it was unlikely.

The doors to the dining room were open, and the music spilling from the inside was still quite loud.

As the elevator arrived, a thrill of anticipation coursed through Jasmine, but since they weren't alone in the cab, holding hands was all they could do, and when they stepped out on Ed's deck, the same woman got out as well.

By the time they reached Edgar's cabin, Jasmine's skin was practically humming with need.

EDGAR

E dgar pushed open the door, ready to make the introductions, and sure enough, Charlie was on the couch just like he had known he would be, with a beer in one hand, the remote in the other, and his feet propped up on the coffee table.

Seeing Jasmine, Charlie's eyes widened, and he scrambled to his feet, hastily buttoning his shirt and smoothing down his hair.

"Hello, Charlie," Ed said. "This is Jasmine. Jasmine, this is Charlie, my roommate and a fellow pilot, only he flies planes and I fly helicopters."

"Hi." She gave Charlie a little wave. "It's nice to meet you. I wish I could say that I've heard a lot about you, but Ed only mentioned you when we were on the way up here."

"I'm not surprised." Charlie flashed her a smile. "He only remembers that I exist when he needs something from me."

Edgar shot his friend a warning look, but Jasmine just laughed. "That's what friends are for, right?"

Shrugging, Charlie pushed his feet into his slippers. "Yeah, he didn't bother to introduce me to you at the wedding." He cast Ed a baleful look.

Ed lifted his hands in the air. "If you wanted an introduction, you should have approached us."

Charlie shifted his gaze to Jasmine and smiled. "You seemed busy, making the rounds and charming your crowd. Everyone was watching you."

"Oh, thank you." She put a hand over her chest. "That's so sweet of you to say, but with all the beautiful women in attendance tonight, I doubt many people noticed me. I plan to rectify that at tomorrow's wedding, though. If the couple is agreeable, I will sing for them. I have a decent singing voice, and since I'm not an invited guest, I need to pay my way, right?"

Charlie didn't know what to say, and neither did Ed. It was a nice idea, but Jin and Arwel might object.

Jasmine didn't wait for either of them to approve or disapprove of her idea and continued, "If the big bosses like my voice, perhaps they will offer me a job. I would love to be part of the Perfect Match family and get free access to their adventures."

"Perfect Match?" Charlie's brow furrowed in confusion, his gaze darting to Edgar. "What does that have to do with anything?"

Ed's mind raced to come up with a plausible explanation. "Charlie has nothing to do with hiring for our company," he told Jasmine. "His job in Perfect Match Virtual Studios is with flight simulations; just like mine, only he simulates flying jets instead of helicopters." He slipped his arm around her waist. "He's helping the company develop flight simulators that are on par with the studios' other virtual adventures."

Understanding finally dawned in Charlie's eyes, and he nodded, a sly smile playing at the corners of his mouth. "The new simulators are top secret for now. It's very hush-hush because of the lucrative government contracts that are in the works, so don't tell anyone."

Who knew that Charlie was such a storyteller? He'd just run with the idea, making it more believable.

Jasmine's posture relaxed as she leaned into Edgar. "Your secret's safe with me."

"Well, it was very nice meeting you in person, Jasmine, but I think I should hit the hay. Goodnight." With a wink and a grin, Charlie ducked into his bedroom and closed the door behind him with a soft click.

Edgar turned to Jasmine with an apologetic smile. "Well, that was awkward. Can I get you a drink?"

Before he could finish his sentence, Jasmine pounced, her arms twining around his neck and her legs wrapping around his hips as she claimed his mouth in a searing kiss.

Bracing her weight with his hands on her ass, he carried her to his bedroom and kicked the door closed behind him.

The room was dark, with only a sliver of moonlight shining through the seam in the closed curtains, but Edgar had no doubt that his eyes would start glowing soon, and the additional illumination would be impossible to hide.

Jasmine had taken him by surprise, and even though he had good control over his fangs and the glow in his eyes, he could only maintain it for so long. Still kissing her, he delved into her mind and thralled her not to see oddities or rather to ignore them. He had done it so many times before, with so many women, that it required no longer than a few seconds, and once he was done, he tumbled onto the mattress with Jasmine on top of him.

She laughed, and he immediately started on her dress, eager to get to her skin and her lush curves.

"Careful," Jasmine hissed when he pulled down the zipper at the back of her dress. "My hair got caught in it."

"Sorry." He lifted her and turned her around so her back was to his front and freed the trapped strand from the zipper while trailing kisses down her back.

When they were both naked, skin to skin, Jasmine moaned and undulated her hips as he worshipped her, his hands and mouth mapping every inch of her exquisite flesh.

Impatient to be inside of her, Edgar got between her spread thighs, remembering at the last moment that he needed to protect her. He didn't want to induce her without her consent, and now wasn't the time for lengthy explanations.

The problem was, he hadn't thought that they would end up in his cabin tonight and hadn't prepared a condom.

With a groan, he dropped his forehead to hers. "I don't have protection."

Caressing his back, Jasmine chuckled. "It's in my purse."

He lifted his head and smiled even though his fangs were on full display by now. Jasmine was blind to them as if they didn't exist. "Thank the merciful Fates one of us was thinking." He slid off her and darted his gaze around the room in search of her purse.

"On the floor. Right there." She pointed.

He didn't follow her finger. Instead, he drank in the beauty sprawled on his bed. "You are a goddess, Jasmine. The goddess of love and lust and carnal desire."

She grinned. "Ooh, I love it, but you know what I'd love even more?"

"What?"

"For you to get the condom, put it on, and give me what I need." She reached with her hand to the juncture of her thighs and cupped herself.

Edgar nearly climaxed just from that, and when she lifted her other hand to her breast and started tweaking her nipple, he leaped off the bed, upended her purse, and found the packet among all the items that had tumbled out.

He was sheathed in two seconds flat and entered her with one swift thrust.

Jasmine cried out his name, but he knew it wasn't because he'd hurt her. She clung to him, her nails digging into his buttocks, urging him to move, and as he did, she wrapped her legs around his torso and let him dictate the rhythm.

With their moans and groans echoing off the walls of the cabin in a symphony of bliss, Edgar went deeper, harder, until her pleasure crested, and she threw her head back with a scream that even the cabin's impressive soundproofing couldn't contain. And when he erupted and bit her at the same time, she screamed and climaxed again and again until her voice gave out, and all that came out was a croak, and then she fell silent.

Edgar licked the puncture wounds closed, tenderly kissed the spot, and lifted his head to look at Jasmine's blissed-out expression.

She would be hoarse tomorrow, but hopefully, his venom would heal her injured throat enough so she could sing at the wedding.

66

KIAN

Kian leaned back in his chair, savoring the rich, bold flavor of the coffee Syssi had made for him. She might have only chosen the right pod to pop in the simple machine they had on board, but it still tasted fantastic because he was enjoying it with her.

The morning sun was casting a warm glow on her multicolored hair, making it look like gold, polished copper, and even a few strands that were so pale they looked like silver or platinum.

Allegra was spending the morning with her grandparents, so it was a rare pocket of time where they could simply be together as a couple and breathe. For once, Kian allowed himself to relax and bask in the simple joy of his mate's company.

"My parents are spoiling Allegra rotten," Syssi murmured, her fingers curled around her own steaming mug. "She's going to miss them so much when the cruise ends and they go back home." She sighed. "As amazing as the cruise has been, adventures and all, I'm ready to go home too."

Smiling, Kian reached for her hand. "Me too. I should have stuck to my original plan of making the cruise only a week long. Ten days is too much. Besides, I bet your main impetus for going home is the fancy cappuccino machine that you can't wait to get back to."

"Guilty as charged," Syssi admitted. "For the next cruise, I'm ordering one for the ship. I'm so spoiled that I can't live without it."

Kian raised an eyebrow, his expression skeptical. "You do realize that every bar on this ship is equipped with a state-of-the-art La Marzocco machine, right? You chose them."

Syssi shook her head. "It's not the same as having one to myself. There's just something about being able to fiddle with the settings, to tweak and adjust them until I get the perfect cup. It's an art, really."

Kian held up his hands in surrender. "Far be it from me to argue with the master barista," he teased. "I will admit, though, your cappuccinos are the best I've ever tasted."

"Thank you." Syssi's eyes sparkled with pleasure. But after a moment, her expression turned serious. "Do you want me to be there when you talk with Jasmine?"

"Of course. I'm going to ask her to come here." He pulled out his phone. "And after we talk to her and she agrees to help look for the prince, I will ask Aru to join us as well. I would have asked him to come over now, but I don't want to overwhelm her."

Syssi chuckled. "I don't think that Jasmine gets easily overwhelmed. I think she dissociates, but I'm not an authority on the subject. David could probably assess her better."

"What do you mean by that?" Kian knew it was a psychological term, but he didn't know what it described.

Syssi shrugged. "Jasmine always smiles like she is perpetually in a good mood. Some people are naturally upbeat, so that's not enough of a reason to suspect dissociation. But add to the equation her being lied to, manipulated, and betrayed by her boyfriend, the trauma of being drugged and kidnapped, and Edna's comment about old childhood pain, and you have a prescription for dissociation. After all that Jasmine has been through, she needed a coping mechanism, but I doubt she developed it recently. She was probably well practiced in that before her ordeal."

Kian let Syssi's words sink in for a moment and then nodded. "Do you think she's acting out a persona? That who she is underneath is different from what she shows the world?"

"She might be, but I'm not an expert, and what I know comes from a few articles I read a long time ago. David would know much more about it, but he will need to talk to Jasmine at length before he can give you his opinion."

"So what are you suggesting I do? Should I ask David to analyze her first? We have an expert on post-traumatic disorders at our disposal, so why not?"

Syssi shook her head. "It won't change the outcome. We still need her to help Aru find the pods. It was just an observation."

Kian nodded. "As long as she's not going to fall apart because of whatever psychological issues she is coping with, we don't need to fix her, right? I wouldn't even feel comfortable suggesting it unless it was pertinent to the mission." He opened his phone and started scrolling through his contacts. "It's so inconvenient that Jasmine doesn't have a phone. The only way I can find out where to locate her is by calling security."

The call was answered right away. "How can I help you, boss?"

"I need Jasmine's current location. One of the two humans we saved from the cartel boss."

The Guardian chuckled. "We have only one Jasmine on board, and we know who she is. Right now, she is in Edgar's cabin. She walked in with him last night after the wedding and hasn't emerged yet."

"Thank you. That will be all."

Next to Kian, Syssi smiled. "Jasmine is a fast operator."

"Good for her." Kian scrolled for Edgar's number. "Makes things easier for me. I can just call Edgar and have him bring Jasmine here."

Syssi arched a brow. "Do you want Edgar to hear everything we tell her?"

That was a good point. Ed had a high-security clearance, and the two were a couple. If things were serious between them, he would probably have to accompany her on the mission anyway.

"Edgar's security clearance is as high as the Guardians. I have no problem with him being here. And if there's a chance that Jasmine is his fated mate, then he will want to accompany her wherever she's going."

Syssi's eyes widened. "Do we have another helicopter pilot?"

Kian chuckled. "Eric can fly helicopters, and so can I, but I wouldn't want to be my own pilot."

"Why not?"

"I learned how to fly on a simulator. It's better than nothing, but I would rather have a pilot with real-life experience."

Kian pressed send, and a moment later, Edgar answered.

"Good morning, Kian. Do you need me to fly you somewhere?"

Naturally, Ed assumed that was why Kian was calling. "Actually, I'm not calling for you. I'm calling for Jasmine. I need her to come to my cabin. You know where it is, right?"

There was a short pause. "I do. Is she in trouble?"

"Not at all. I just need to discuss something with her, and it cannot wait. How soon can you get here?"

Edgar cleared his throat. "Is twenty minutes okay?"

"That's fine. I will see you both here." Kian ended the call and scrolled for Aru's number.

"Amanda should be here as well," Syssi said. "I know she's not essential, but she will be annoyed if we don't include her in this talk."

"You're right. Can you please call her?"

"Sure thing." Syssi rose to her feet and removed her phone from the charger. "I'll call Amanda from the bedroom so you can talk with Aru without distractions."

67

JASMINE

"What was that about?" Jasmine yawned and turned on her side to face Edgar. "Where do we need to be in twenty minutes and why?"

They had just made love again, and she didn't want to be anywhere other than under the covers with him. She certainly didn't want to rush to be somewhere in twenty minutes.

"Kian wants to see you, and he didn't say why. We should get out of bed right now," Ed said but didn't move a muscle.

"Can you call him back and tell him that I fell asleep or something? I don't want to get out of bed."

Ed's lips tilted up in a smile. "Do you really want to get on the boss's bad side?"

She grimaced. "No, I don't."

It couldn't be anything bad because she hadn't done anything to violate the rules. No one had told her that she couldn't stay the night on the upper decks, and why would they? It wasn't like there were any secrets hiding in Edgar and Charlie's cabin.

Then, a thought occurred to her. Charlie looked surprised when Ed showed up with her at their cabin. Maybe he was the prudish type and didn't approve?

"Could Charlie have complained about me staying the night?"

Edgar laughed. "No way." He let his arms fall away from her body. "We are down to fifteen minutes. I suggest you get dressed."

Oh, crap. She hadn't brought a change of clothes with her, and there was no way she was showing up at Kian's place in the dress she'd worn to the wedding. It didn't matter that he knew she had spent the night with Edgar. Appearances mattered.

"I have to go back to my cabin to change. I can't show up there in the dress I wore yesterday. "

"If we do that, you will need to do it super-fast." Edgar's lips twitched. "The other option is wearing something of mine. I can lend you a T-shirt and a pair of gym shorts."

She cast him an incredulous look. "Not happening."

Sliding out of bed, Jasmine rushed into the bathroom, took care of business, brushed her teeth with a finger, and tried to use Ed's comb on her hair, but it was no match for her thick tresses.

When she got out, Edgar was already dressed in a pair of jeans and a t-shirt, and he traded places with her in the bathroom without copping a feel on the way, which was a little insulting.

Well, they were in a rush, but still.

By the time she'd put on her panties and bra, he was already out of the bathroom and helped her zip up the dress.

She pushed her feet into her high heels, wincing at the pinch of the too-tight shoes, but there was no time to worry about comfort or fashion, not when Kian was waiting, his summons hanging over her head like a dark, ominous cloud.

"I would really love a cup of coffee." She pouted as they rushed out the door. "Maybe you can get me a cup from the staff lounge room while I get changed?"

"Of course." Edgar pulled her in for a quick kiss as they waited for the elevator.

"You don't need to come with me," she said as they rushed out of the elevator on the staff deck. "I can handle Kian on my own."

Edgar shook his head. "Kian expects me to be there, but even if he didn't, I wouldn't have left you to face this alone, whatever it is."

Something warm unfurled in Jasmine's chest. It was nice to have someone in her corner, someone who had her back. She'd never had that, not since she left home and not even before that. Her father had often been distant, and her stepmother just hadn't cared about her.

When the elevator door opened, they ran out. Ed was rushing into the staff lounge to get her coffee, and Jasmine headed toward her cabin.

Bursting through the door, she fumbled with the zipper of her dress as she kicked off her shoes. She stripped off the gown, tossed it on the bed, and reached into the closet for a simple, pull-on sundress.

She quickly ran a brush through her hair, wincing at the tangles and snarls that snagged on the bristles, but there was no time to untangle it gently and style it or to reapply makeup. Instead, she grabbed a makeup removal wipe, hastily scrubbing at her face until her skin was clean and bare.

When she got out, Ed was waiting for her with a cup of coffee. "I didn't know whether you wanted cream and sugar, so I put in both." He handed her the paper cup.

"Thank you." She took a grateful sip even though it was too sweet. "I needed that."

Edgar regarded her with a smile. "You're even more gorgeous without makeup." He lifted his hand and cupped her cheek.

Jasmine leaned into his touch, her eyes fluttering closed as she savored his reassuring presence for a moment.

"We need to hustle." She took his hand and broke into a light jog toward the elevators.

By the time they got to Kian's deck, Jasmine's palms were damp with sweat, and the churning in her stomach was making her nauseous.

Edgar rang the doorbell, and a moment later, the door swung open, revealing a stocky butler in a three-piece suit and a mannequin smile on his face.

Wow, talk about stereotypes. He was perfectly cast for the role of a British butler in an aristocratic house.

"Good morning, Master Edgar, Mistress Jasmine. Please, come in."

Jasmine was impressed that Kian had told his butler to greet her by name. Did it mean that she was a valued guest?

She certainly hoped so.

Kian was sitting in an armchair while Syssi and Amanda were on the couch. Both women smiled warmly, making her feel more at ease, and Syssi got to her feet, but Kian remained seated and looked even more imposing and unapproachable than the last time she'd seen him, which was at the wedding.

Jasmine swallowed hard, her mouth suddenly dry as sandpaper. But she forced herself to meet Kian's gaze and smile. "Good morning."

Syssi walked over to her and gave her a quick hug. "Can I offer you some coffee?"

"Yes, please. I would love some."

She had discarded the cup Edgar had made her in a trashcan by the elevators because it had been so sweet that it was undrinkable, and she desperately needed something to wet her throat.

"How about you, Edgar?" Syssi asked. "Would you like some coffee as well?"

"Thank you," he said. "If it's not too much trouble."

"It's not. Okidu will gladly make it. The simple pod machine we have here does not require any finesse."

That was kind of insulting to the poor butler. It was as if Syssi was implying that he was a simpleton and couldn't handle a more sophisticated coffeemaker.

Not that the guy seemed to care. With a wide grin and a bow to his mistress, he hurried into the tiny kitchen and got busy making coffee.

And what was the deal with him addressing everyone as master and mistress? What was this, the eighteenth century?

"Please, sit down next to me." Amanda waved Jasmine over.

Jaz cast a quick look at Edgar, who gave her a reassuring smile and headed toward the armchair next to Kian's.

When Jasmine sat down next to Amanda, Syssi sat on her other side. "I can't start my day without a good strong cup of coffee either, so I know how you feel." She smiled. "I'm sorry for the early wake-up call."

Jasmine didn't blush often, but she felt her cheeks heat up. "That's okay. Edgar and I just overslept. We stayed up very late last night at the wedding."

Amanda chuckled. "And I bet you didn't go to sleep right away."

"We didn't," Jasmine admitted with ease. She had nothing to hide or be embarrassed about.

When the butler returned with coffees for her and Edgar, the familiar aroma of the fresh brew and the ritual of stirring in the cream and sugar helped to ease some of the tension that was coiling in Jasmine's gut.

But the reprieve was short-lived.

"Amanda." Kian turned to his sister. "Do you want to do the honors? Out of the four of us, you are the best suited for the task."

Jasmine's heart stuttered in her chest, a creeping sense of dread washing over her. "What task?" she asked.

Amanda just smiled, her eyes sparkling with a strange inner light. "You are about to fall down the mother of all rabbit holes, so brace yourself." She snorted. "Except in your case, you won't find a queen, but you might discover a prince."

68

AMANDA

manda moved from the couch to a nearby armchair and settled in so she could fix her eyes on Jasmine's face as the other woman sat perched on the edge of the sofa, anxious and a little frightened.

She felt a smidgen of sympathy for her, but not more than that. Jasmine was about to be given a precious gift —access to the best-guarded secret on Earth, a chance of gaining immortality, and maybe even a prince. The truths Amanda was about to reveal would shake the very foundation of Jasmine's world and challenge everything she thought she knew about herself and her place in the grand tapestry of the Fates.

Jasmine was incredibly lucky. She just didn't know that yet.

Crossing her legs and steepling her fingers, Amanda assumed her teacher's voice. "What I'm about to tell you is going to sound incredible, but I need you to keep an open mind. Listen to what I have to say and try to keep your questions until after I'm done."

Edgar cleared his throat. "Excuse my interruption, but if what you are about to reveal is what I think it is, then isn't that the job of the partner to tell it to the Dormant?"

Amanda shook her head. "Not this time. I'm sorry to rob you of the privilege, but Jasmine's case is more complicated than the usual potential Dormant's. That's why I have to do it."

"What's a Dormant?" Jasmine asked.

Amanda lifted a hand. "I'll get to that in a few minutes. First, you need some background. The history of the world you are familiar with is not only inaccurate, but it is intentionally misleading."

She paused, letting her words sink in for a moment before continuing. "Have you ever noticed how similar the mythological pantheons of gods are across different cultures? How do the same twelve main gods seem to appear time and again, just under different names?"

Jasmine frowned, her brow furrowing in thought. "I guess so. I've always assumed that ancient civilizations just copied from one another, borrowed and adapted each other's deities to fit their own needs and beliefs."

Amanda smiled. "That's what most people think, and there is truth to it, but it's not the entire truth, and as you know, half-truths are often worse than lies, but I digress."

She leaned back. "The truth is that the gods were real people, and the impact they left on humanity was so great that stories about them were told all over the ancient world. They were a small group of exiles from a place light years away from Earth who called themselves gods, which in their language meant creators."

In her mind, Amanda had adapted the old, familiar story about their ancestors to include the new information that they had recently learned from Jade, Aru, and what her mother had told her about what she'd learned from the queen of Anumati.

"The gods were physically perfect, and their bodies were immune to disease and healed so fast that they were nearly impossible to kill. They also possessed incredible mind control powers over humans."

It had been done by genetic design so humans would be easy to control, but that was beyond the scope of what Jasmine needed to know at the moment.

Jasmine's eyes widened, but she remained silent, her gaze fixed on Amanda's face as she hung on every word.

"I got a little ahead of the story." Amanda lifted her coffee cup and took a sip to wet her throat. "I need to backpedal a little. These powerful aliens called themselves gods because they were masters of genetic manipulation, and they created numerous new species on the planets throughout the galaxy that they colonized with the intent of these species to serve them. On Earth, they used their own genetic material and combined it with that of an early hominid species, creating a new hybrid that would come to be known as Adam, the first human. At first, the new class of servants they created was made one at a time, but since it was inefficient, they were given the ability to procreate. What the gods didn't anticipate was just how fertile this new species would be and how quickly it would multiply."

"Is that the origin of the Adam and Eve story?" Jasmine asked. "The Bible talks about them being created by God or gods, and given the ability to procreate and fill the world with their offspring."

Jasmine should have waited with her questions until after Amanda was done, but it was a good question, so Amanda nodded. "Bingo. The story of Adam and Eve is a retelling of that original act of creation, a metaphor for the gods granting humans the ability to reproduce and thrive. But as their numbers grew and they evolved, the gods began to realize the potential threat that their creation posed and decided to cull the human population."

"The flood?" Jasmine asked.

"The flood came after they exhausted other methods. They used their mind control to create incredible myths and stories to make themselves appear even more fantastic than they were. And they used theology to shape human beliefs and behaviors and bring them closer to the state of the enlightened civilization they envisioned."

Jasmine snorted. "That must have been a big failure. Humans are still not civilized or enlightened. Well, most are not."

Amanda was surprised that Jasmine was not trying to refute what she was being told. There was none of the usual disbelief that most Dormants exhibited when first told the truth about their origins.

"I agree." Amanda sighed. "Too many are still barbarians, and regrettably, they have greater ability than ever to cause pain and destruction in their need to intimidate and dominate. But that's a discussion for another time. We are still in the distant past. Once contact with their home world was severed, the exiled gods realized that their limited numbers were not sufficient for genetic diversity and thus not viable for the continuation of their species, not to mention their urgent need to boost their numbers so they were less threatened by the exploding human populace." She leaned forward, her voice dropping to a conspiratorial whisper. "And that's another story that the Bible copied. The gods took human lovers and procreated with the very beings they had created to give rise to a new breed—the immortals."

Jasmine frowned. "The Bible said that those unions resulted in giants, not immortals."

Amanda was impressed. "You must have been raised religious to know those stories so well."

Jasmine shrugged. "Not more religious than most. I just liked the stories."

"You've probably read the English version, and as it happens all too often, things get lost in translation. In the original Hebrew version, the plural word used to describe the progeny of gods and humans was Anakim, and the singular was Anak. Do you know what other very famous ancient word sounds almost identical to Anak?"

Jasmine's brow furrowed. "No clue."

"Ankh," Amanda said. "The Ankh is one of the most important ancient Egyptian symbols, representing life, vitality, and immortality, and it is often depicted in the hands of gods and goddesses, symbolizing their ability to grant eternal life. Coincidence? I think not."

"Oh, wow." Jasmine's eyes widened. "That's so cool. So Anakim meant immortals?"

"Indeed. The children born of unions between gods and humans were immortal and gifted with incredible abilities like enhanced strength, accelerated healing, and also the ability to manipulate human minds. But when the immortal descendants of the gods took human mates, their children were born mortal. As it turned out, the children born to female immortals with human males carried the dormant godly genes that could be activated, but the children born to immortal males and human females did not. From then on, those genes were passed on from a mother to her children, and from her daughters to their children, and so on."

Amanda paused to take another sip of her coffee and give Jasmine a few moments to process what she had learned so far.

Since she was not freaking out or trying to refute what she was being told, Amanda didn't mind her asking questions during the telling.

Jasmine frowned. "So technically, there could be many humans who carry those godly genes."

Amanda nodded.

"What happened to the gods?" Jasmine asked.

"Their fate wasn't good." Amanda put her coffee cup down. "There was a dispute, and one god found a way to kill the others with a weapon that originated in their home world. Almost all died, including the assassin."

"Almost all?" Jasmine asked. "Meaning that there are still gods living among us?"

Syssi chuckled. "You are taking this incredibly well. When I first heard this story, I couldn't believe it."

Jasmine's gaze swept over Edgar, Kian, Amanda, and then landed on Syssi. "I'm a practicing Wiccan. I have no problem with believing in gods and immortals' magic and mind manipulation. And I'm also starting to understand what is going on here. Kevin didn't use hypnosis on Modana and his men. He used mind control."

"Bravo." Kian clapped. "I'm impressed."

"Thank you." Jasmine dipped her head. "So Kevin is an immortal, and so are the four of you?" She leveled her gaze at Edgar.

He nodded. "Guilty as charged."

Letting out a breath, Jasmine closed her eyes. "So, that's why everyone looks young and gorgeous. This ship is full of immortals, and you have a staff of humans serving you who are mind-controlled to keep your identities a secret." She opened her eyes. "Talk about mind blown. This would make one hell of a block-buster movie."

"That will never happen," Kian said sternly. "It is essential that humans don't know about us."

"Then why are you telling me?"

Amanda smiled. "Because, my darling, we think that you are a carrier of godly genes that can be activated. There is a chance that you can become an immortal. And there is also the issue of your obsession with meeting a prince."

Jasmine shook her head. "Now you've lost me. Why do you think I have these genes, and what does my obsession have to do with anything?"

"Do you remember the testing I did?"

Jasmine winced. "I didn't do so well."

Amanda laughed. "On purpose. I know. I found a way to test you without your knowledge, and you definitely have paranormal abilities. Telepathy for sure, and maybe also precognition. Paranormal abilities are one of the strongest indicators of godly genes. The second one is affinity." Amanda leaned toward her. "That's a little more difficult to quantify, but let me ask you this, did you always feel like you were different and didn't belong?"

Jasmine nodded.

"And when you met Margo, did you immediately feel like the two of you could be best friends?"

Jasmine nodded again.

"Then you met Frankie and Mia, Syssi and me. Did you feel more comfortable with us than you did with anyone before?"

"That's affinity?"

Amanda nodded. "Like recognizes like. Dormants and immortals are drawn to each other, and so are Dormants and other Dormants."

"I'll be damned." Jasmine slumped against the couch cushions. "I can turn immortal? How, though? Is there a blood transfusion involved, gene therapy?"

"Venom and seed," Amanda said. "And Edgar can supply both, but he needs your permission to do so first. We try not to induce anyone without getting their informed consent. Sometimes it happens by chance, but we try to do it the right way when we can."

Jasmine shifted her gaze to Edgar. "You have my consent. Whatever it takes, I'm game. I want to be immortal, and I want to be part of this world." She shook her head again. "This is so much bigger than getting a job at Perfect Match."

Kian chuckled. "I would say. But we are not there yet. We need to talk to you about the prince."

Jasmine once again glanced at Edgar before shifting her gaze back to Kian. "What about it?"

"We are looking for a lost prince," Amanda said. "We think that you can help us find him." She turned to Syssi. "Do you want to take over from here?"

Syssi nodded, and as Jasmine turned to look at her, she smiled. "I get visions sometimes. They are mostly vague and often unpleasant, but in one way or another, they always come true. I had a vision about you helping us find the prince or, rather, the royal twins. A brother and sister landed on Earth in an escape pod when their ship exploded. The pod is lost somewhere, but the people inside might still be alive. They have a type of life support that we call stasis, and they can stay in that state for a very long time."

"How long ago did the escape pod land?" Jasmine asked.

"More than a hundred years ago," Kian said. "But the life support can go on indefinitely, or as long as the pod is not too damaged."

"Poor people." Jasmine swallowed. "Naturally, I'm willing to assist in any way I can to locate them, but I'm not sure how."

"I'm not sure either," Syssi said. "But you have a connection to the prince, and in my vision, I saw you standing over a crater and looking down at a pod, and you were not alone. You were with Negal, Dagor, and Aru. Did Margo tell you about her plans after the cruise?"

Jasmine shook her head. "How is she connected to this? And what have I to do with her and Frankie's boyfriends?"

Amanda was once again impressed with Jasmine's levelheaded response. "Margo is mated to Negal, who along with Dagor and Aru are on a quest to find the royal twins and other escape pods from the destroyed ship."

Edgar emitted a low growl. "The hell Jasmine is going after some Kra-ell prince," he snarled, his eyes glowing. "Those twins are rumored to be extremely powerful, and no one knows anything about them. They might be evil, twisted beings."

Kian shot him a warning glare. "Let Jasmine absorb what she's learned so far and come to terms with the truth of who she is and what she's capable of. We will discuss safety precautions later."

Syssi leaned over and put a hand on Jasmine's knee. "Your prince is not necessarily your romantic partner. Sometimes, the most important relationships in our lives are the ones we least expect. The prince could be your mentor or your spiritual leader. It could also be that you need to find him not for your personal benefit but for altruistic reasons. The universe works in mysterious ways and uses different methods of delivering its messages. The same way I'm used as a conduit for some things, you might be used as a conduit for others."

Across from them, Edgar relaxed, his aggressive energy subsiding.

Jasmine let out a breath. "I'm ashamed to admit that I've never considered the possibility that I was shown the prince for altruistic reasons. At first, I was focused on finding my dream guy, and when the cards kept showing me the prince, I was convinced that I was destined to meet one." She looked at Edgar. "But then I met you, and I tried to give it a different spin. I reasoned that the prince was a metaphor for a good man and that you might be the one I was supposed to find. My prince."

Ed chuckled. "I'm afraid that I will always remain a frog, but I don't mind if you keep kissing me in the hopes of turning me into a prince."

69

ARU

"Good morning, Master Aru," Kian's servant bowed. "Please, come in."

Aru forced a smile, not for the Odu's sake but for its owner. Kian was very fond of his servant, and so was the princess of hers, so Aru was doing his best to get over his aversion to them, but it wasn't easy.

Being wary of them had been hardwired into his psyche.

"Thank you for coming." Kian motioned for him to sit down on the armchair next to his.

Aru glanced at Jasmine and Edgar, who were huddled together on the couch. The woman looked pale but not as shell-shocked as he had expected to find her. Perhaps it was the pilot's reassuring arm around her shoulders and the way he looked at her that was easing her into her new reality.

She must feel like the ground had been yanked out from under her, and everything she thought she knew about the world had been turned on its head. Edgar's presence was probably the only solid thing she could tether herself to.

Given how Jasmine was clinging to the guy, Aru had a feeling that they would need to include the pilot in their expedition, and he hoped that Kian would be willing to spare him. Perhaps they could even use Edgar's services on the trail. Renting a helicopter or buying one in Tibet would eat up a large chunk of the team's remaining budget, but it might shorten the duration of the search.

Well, that was provided that the tip they had gotten about strange energy signatures in Tibet was true, and they weren't going on a wild goose chase. The equipment they had at their disposal couldn't verify the claim from across the globe or even from several miles away. They couldn't be much farther than a mile from the pod for the energy to register on their equipment.

If the pod was still sustaining life after thousands of years, its energy readouts would likely be minimal and possibly critically so.

The truth was that he was basing the expedition to Tibet on a source as unreliable as Jasmine's tarot cards or crystal readings or whatever else she was using for her divinations. What Syssi had seen in her vision was the best clue he had gotten so far, but the mountaintop she'd seen could have been located anywhere, not just in Tibet.

Aru turned to Kian. "I still think that basing the search on tarot cards is questionable, but I know better than to doubt a seer. Besides, it could be that the vision and the tarot were not just about Jasmine but about Edgar as well. Perhaps the success of the mission depends on us having a helicopter and a pilot at our disposal."

Edgar grinned. "That's right. It could be all about me."

Amanda rolled her eyes. "Males. They always think that the world revolves around them."

Kian chuckled. "The smart ones know the truth."

"I was just joking," Edgar said. "I would love to accompany the team to Tibet. Never been there."

Aru was glad that the pilot was willing to join them, but he still needed to convince Kian to approve it and perhaps help with the cost of acquiring a helicopter. "Edgar flying us from one point to another would be extremely beneficial, especially now that we will need to accommodate Jasmine, who won't be able to keep up. We will need to get organized better, perhaps hire locals with pack animals so as not to exhaust her. Margo and Frankie are also not at full capacity yet while they are recuperating from their transitions, so they would need frequent rests as well."

"Their what?" Jasmine untangled herself from Edgar's arm. "What are you talking about?"

Had no one told her that her friends had transitioned into immortality?

Come to think of it, she probably didn't know that Aru was more than an immortal either.

Amanda leaned closer to Jasmine. "Remember what I told you about Dormants and that there is a way to activate their dormant genes?"

Jasmine nodded.

"Frankie and Margo were both activated. Margo doesn't have the flu. She is transitioning. And Frankie did the same thing a couple of days before her."

Jasmine slumped, her back resting on Edgar's chest. "That explains so much. What about Mia?"

"She did that a while ago," Syssi said. "But since she's re-growing her legs, she is still wheelchair-bound. Not for long, though. She's almost done."

"Unbelievable." Jasmine pinched her arm. "Ouch. That hurt, so I'm not dreaming."

Amanda laughed. "That's not a conclusive test. You could be dreaming about pinching yourself and experiencing pain."

"But I'm not dreaming, right?"

Amanda's eyes gleamed with amusement. "If I say that you aren't, does it mean that you are not?"

Kian lifted his hand. "Please, ladies. This can go on forever, and we have things that we need to settle." He turned to Aru. "You were saying?"

"I was saying that we can use a helicopter and a pilot, and Edgar here is perfect for the job. The problem is resources." Aru scratched his head. "Perhaps we can buy a helicopter and then sell it after the mission is done. The delta between the purchase and subsequent sale price of the craft shouldn't be too prohibitive."

"Don't worry about the money," Kian said. "The clan can help, and so can Toven. He would do anything for Mia, who wants her friends back as soon as possible, and in every meaningful way, Toven commands unlimited resources, some of which he will gladly extend to acquire means of faster travel."

Aru had hoped that would be Kian's answer. "Thank you." He glanced back at Jasmine, surprised to see the confident woman suddenly looking as if she was starting to fall apart.

Everyone had their breaking point, and evidently, Jasmine had reached hers.

Following his gaze, Amanda looked at her and frowned. "What's the matter, darling? What got you upset?"

"I'm just overwhelmed." She lifted a trembling hand to her lips. "It started like a pleasant drizzle and then turned into a deluge that's threatening to drown me."

Amanda smiled. "It's understandable. You've been incredibly open-minded about all of this, but it's a lot to take in, and we dumped all of it on you in one go. The best way to tackle something so big is to break it down into smaller, more manageable chunks."

70

JASMINE

More manageable chunks. That was good advice. Jasmine didn't need to absorb and understand everything all at once. She should address one problem, or rather one issue at a time.

"So, let me get it straight." She looked at Kian. "You want me to travel with a team of immortals to Tibet to help them find a life pod that contains two aliens who are royal twins because you think that one of them is the prince my divining keeps pointing to."

Kian grimaced. "When put like that, it sounds ridiculous, but I've learned to trust Syssi's visions. So yeah. That's what we want you to do, and we will pay you for your trouble, but it is up to you. We are not forcing you to do anything you don't want."

That was what Jasmine had thought. It seemed that Kian was implying they wouldn't activate her dormant godly genes unless she cooperated with them.

"So, my payment is the chance at immortality?"

Kian looked like she had slapped him and offended his mother. "Of course not. One has nothing to do with the other. In fact, you shouldn't attempt transition until after the mission because you don't want to become incapacitated while trekking through unpopulated areas. I was talking about monetary compensation. I'll double whatever you are paid at your current job."

He sounded truthful, and since Jasmine hadn't gotten the impression that he was a good actor or even a decent one, she was inclined to believe him.

"How is the transition induced?" she asked.

"I will tell you later." Edgar pulled her closer to him. "In private."

She turned to him. "Does it hurt?"

He shook his head. "Getting there is the most pleasant experience, but the transition itself is not easy. It can even be dangerous. That's why it is not advisable to attempt it away from our experienced medical staff and a well-equipped clinic."

Given how husky Edgar sounded and that he didn't want to explain how it was done in front of the others, the induction had something to do with sex.

"So?" Kian asked. "Is it a yes?"

"Say yes," Edgar said next to her ear. "It's going to be one hell of an adventure. Besides, you can't go back home or to your job until we are sure that the cartel is not looking for you. Instead of spending weeks in some hotel or a safe house, you could be touring Tibet."

Jasmine smiled. "When you put it like that, I have to say yes."

"Welcome aboard," Aru said. "The way I expect it to work is for Edgar to drop us off at the designated location, and while we continue on foot, he will head to the next refueling station. You'll be able to see each other probably every night but not throughout the whole day."

That was disappointing but not a deal breaker.

Jasmine turned to look at Edgar. "Is that okay with you?"

"I figured that's how it would have to work."

Aru leaned forward, his nearly black eyes fixed on Jasmine with a piercing, penetrating intensity. "I'm not clear on all the details yet, but we also might leave the other ladies with Edgar to watch over them while you, my teammates, and I trek through the mountains. To cover ground quickly and efficiently, we can't be weighed down by excess baggage, and hauling supplies for four is much easier than for seven."

Jasmine let out a breath. "Contrary to the impression I give, I'm not a spoiled brat. I don't need a suitcase full of clothes and makeup. But I'm not a fan of camping, meaning sleeping on the ground where all kinds of creepy-crawlies can get into my sleeping bag."

Aru smiled. "By the end of each day, we will try to reach a spot where Edgar can land and collect us. So, most of the time, we sleep in hotels and inns. But occasionally, we will have to sleep on the ground. We will get a small, fully enclosed tent for you so no bugs can get into your sleeping bag."

"Thank you." She dipped her head. "That also covers my next concern which was keeping clean. I can go without a shower for a couple of days, but more than that, I feel gross."

Syssi laughed softly. "If I were you, I would be concerned with wild animals and bandits, not bugs and showers, although those are not negligible concerns either."

Jasmine grimaced. "Thanks for pointing that out to me."

"You have nothing to worry about in that regard," Aru promised. "My teammates and I can take care of any danger we are faced with."

"Right." Jasmine smiled at him. "The mind control. You can get into the minds of humans and other beasts."

He nodded, but given the spark in his dark eyes, she had a feeling that mind control wasn't the only tool at his disposal.

"I still don't get how I'm supposed to help you," Jasmine said. "Will I be required to consult my tarots and my crystals on a daily basis?"

Aru's expression turned speculative. "I don't expect your divination to work like a scrying stick, but I will probably ask you to consult your divining tools to give us a general sense of where we need to go."

Jasmine pursed her lips. "Actually, a scrying stick is not a bad idea. My divining tools are just conduits for the energy that's already inside of me, and if I channel my energy into a scrying stick and ask the goddess to help me, it might point us in the right direction." She sat up straighter. "I can even make one myself and infuse it with my energy and intention."

Excitement thrumming through her, Jasmine was ready for this new adventure. Deep in her bones and in her very soul, she'd always known that her mundane life was just a prelude for something much greater. But unlike what she'd believed before shooting down this incredible rabbit hole, that something wasn't a Broadway stage or a Hollywood movie set.

She was a descendant of gods, and she was destined for greatness.

COMING UP NEXT
The Children of the Gods Book 84
DARK WITCH: TWIN DESTINIES

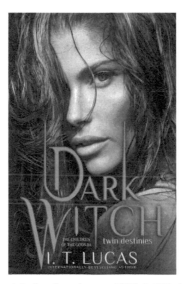

To read the first three chapters, JOIN the VIP club at
ITLUCAS.COM. To find out what's included in your
free membership, flip to the last page.

As Jasmine embarks on a thrilling quest to the remote mountains of Tibet, she must learn to trust her intuition and harness her untamed abilities to locate the long-lost Kra-ell royal twins.

Coming up next in the
PERFECT MATCH SERIES

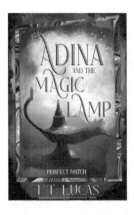

ADINA AND THE MAGIC LAMP

In this post-apocalyptic virtual reimagining of Aladdin, James, the enigmatic prince, and Adina, the fearless thief, navigate the treacherous streets of Londabad, a city that echoes London and Ahmedabad and fuses magic and technology. In the face of danger, the chemistry between them ignites, and the lines between prince and thief, royalty and commoner blur.

JOIN THE VIP CLUB
To find out what's included in your free membership,
flip to the last page.

NOTE

Dear reader,

I hope my stories have added a little joy to your day. If you have a moment to add some to mine, you can help spread the word about the Children Of The Gods series by telling your friends and penning a review. Your recommendations are the most powerful way to inspire new readers to explore the series.

Thank you,

Isabell

Also by I. T. Lucas

439

70: DARK ALLIANCE PERFECT STORM

DARK HEALING
71: DARK HEALING BLIND JUSTICE
72: DARK HEALING BLIND TRUST
73: DARK HEALING BLIND CURVE

DARK ENCOUNTERS
74: DARK ENCOUNTERS OF THE CLOSE KIND
75: DARK ENCOUNTERS OF THE UNEXPECTED KIND
76: DARK ENCOUNTERS OF THE FATED KIND

DARK VOYAGE
77: DARK VOYAGE MATTERS OF THE HEART
78: DARK VOYAGE MATTERS OF THE MIND
79: DARK VOYAGE MATTERS OF THE SOUL

DARK HORIZON
80: DARK HORIZON NEW DAWN
81: DARK HORIZON ECLIPSE OF THE HEART
82: DARK HORIZON THE WITCHING HOUR

DARK WITCH
83: DARK WITCH: ENTANGLED FATES
84: DARK WITCH: TWIN DESTINIES

PERFECT MATCH

VAMPIRE'S CONSORT
KING'S CHOSEN

LOS HIJOS DE LOS DIOSES

EL OSCURO DESCONOCIDO
1: EL OSCURO DESCONOCIDO EL
SUEÑO
2: EL OSCURO DESCONOCIDO
REVELADO
3: EL OSCURO DESCONOCIDO
INMORTAL
EL OSCURO ENEMIGO
4- EL OSCURO ENEMIGO CAPTURADO
5 - EL OSCURO ENEMIGO CAUTIVO
6- EL OSCURO ENEMIGO REDIMIDO

LES ENFANTS DES DIEUX
DARK STRANGER
1- DARK STRANGER LE RÊVE
2- DARK STRANGER LA RÉVÉLATION
3- DARK STRANGER L'IMMORTELLE

THE CHILDREN OF THE GODS SERIES SETS

BOOKS 1-3: DARK STRANGER TRILOGY—INCLUDES A
BONUS SHORT STORY: THE FATES TAKE A VACATION

BOOKS 4-6: DARK ENEMY TRILOGY —INCLUDES A
BONUS SHORT STORY—THE FATES' POST-WEDDING
CELEBRATION

BOOKS 7-10: DARK WARRIOR TETRALOGY
BOOKS 11-13: DARK GUARDIAN TRILOGY
BOOKS 14-16: DARK ANGEL TRILOGY
BOOKS 17-19: DARK OPERATIVE TRILOGY
BOOKS 20-22: DARK SURVIVOR TRILOGY
BOOKS 23-25: DARK WIDOW TRILOGY
BOOKS 26-28: DARK DREAM TRILOGY
BOOKS 29-31: DARK PRINCE TRILOGY
BOOKS 32-34: DARK QUEEN TRILOGY
BOOKS 35-37: DARK SPY TRILOGY
BOOKS 38-40: DARK OVERLORD TRILOGY
BOOKS 41-43: DARK CHOICES TRILOGY
BOOKS 44-46: DARK SECRETS TRILOGY
BOOKS 47-49: DARK HAVEN TRILOGY
BOOKS 50-52: DARK POWER TRILOGY
BOOKS 53-55: DARK MEMORIES TRILOGY
BOOKS 56-58: DARK HUNTER TRILOGY
BOOKS 59-61: DARK GOD TRILOGY
BOOKS 62-64: DARK WHISPERS TRILOGY
BOOKS 65-67: DARK GAMBIT TRILOGY
BOOKS 68-70: DARK ALLIANCE TRILOGY
BOOKS 71-73: DARK HEALING TRILOGY
BOOKS 74-76: DARK ENCOUNTERS TRILOGY
BOOKS 77-79: DARK VOYAGE TRILOGY

MEGA SETS
THE CHILDREN OF THE GODS: BOOKS 1-6
INCLUDES CHARACTER LISTS
THE CHILDREN OF THE GODS: BOOKS 6.5-10

FOR EXCLUSIVE PEEKS AT UPCOMING RELEASES & A FREE I. T. LUCAS COMPANION BOOK

IMPORTANT UPDATES. TO FIX THAT, ADD isabell@itlu cas.com TO YOUR EMAIL CONTACTS OR YOUR EMAIL VIP LIST.

Check out the specials at
https://www.itlucas.com/specials

Made in United States
Troutdale, OR
07/06/2024

21051047R00256